# SINK OR CAPTURE!

## ALAN EVANS

## Hodder & Stoughton
### LONDON SYDNEY AUCKLAND

This book is a work of fiction and the characters in it are fictitious except for the obvious exceptions of people who have gone down in history. The words and actions I have attributed to Lieutenant-Commander Roope VC are my paraphrasing and as near reality as I could ascertain.

British Library Cataloguing in Publication Data
Evans, Alan
  Sink or Capture.
  I. Title
  823.914 [F]

ISBN 0-340-55667-6

Published by Hodder and Stoughton,
a division of Hodder and Stoughton Ltd,
Mill Road, Dunton Green, Sevenoaks, Kent TN13 2YA
Editorial Office: 47 Bedford Square, London WC1B 3DP

Typeset by Hewer Text Composition Services, Edinburgh
Printed and bound in Great Britain by
Biddles Ltd, Guildford and King's Lynn

My thanks go to Francis Herbert of the Royal Geographical Society, Rick Salmon of the Bank of England and to the staff of Walton-on-Thames Library for their help when I researched this book.

Also to Dr R. Littlewood and the surgeons and staff of St George's Hospital, London, and St Peter's, Chertsey, who helped me to finish it.

But, as always, any mistakes are mine!

*"Proceed to Narvik and sink or capture enemy ship . . ."*

Signal from Admiralty to Captain Warburton-Lee,
9 April 1940

# Part One

# *Altmark*

# 1

## 7th February 1940 North Atlantic

Smith had loved her and wanted her from the moment he first saw her in Montevideo. But would he lose her soon? There were other, younger men eager to take her. He was not a young man. He had fought in the First World War twenty years before and the fair hair that showed under his cap was greying at the temples. There were wrinkles at the corners of the pale, ice-blue eyes. He had not commanded a ship in those twenty years and he was lonely in this command. But he was used to loneliness.

*"Ship bearing Red Two Oh! Could be Brandenburg!"* That shout came from Lieutenant Ben Kelso and it brought Smith running from his sea cabin at the back of the bridge, breakfast left on the table. He ran up against the bridge-screen by his high chair and set his binoculars to his eyes. He studied the distant ship off the port bow for a second or two. She was too far away for him to identify but not out of gun range.

He rapped out, "Sound 'General Quarters'!"

The fire-bell clanging of the alarm 'rattlers', triggered at his order, exploded the ship into boiling life around him. As his crew raced to their action stations Captain David Cochrane Smith still found time to run a swift glance over his ship, his love, *Cassandra*. He took in the slender grey length of her from knife-edged bow cleaving the North Atlantic swell to her stern tucked down on the foaming wake that trailed her. He leaned on the bridge-screen, looped the strap of the binoculars around his neck so they hung on his chest, then lifted them to his eyes once more. He looked again for the enemy. Because this was February 1940, this was a time of war and *Cassandra* was a light cruiser, a warship. Now all her five 6-inch guns were training around, "A" gun on the fo'c'sle forward of the bridge and the other four aft of it, spaced along her hull. Each gun was housed in a shield, the back of it open, not in a turret.

And that other was a warship – but was she an enemy? He stared at the toy ship on the far horizon, rendered colourless by the distance that also blurred the silhouette. The light was not good, the early morning sun still low behind him and peeping weakly through cloud cover. They were only minutes into the forenoon watch. Ben Kelso had that watch but this was also his station in action. Now he said again, "I think it could be *Brandenburg*." He had shouted that on first sighting her and now, as then, it was said tongue in cheek and Smith knew it. As he knew the rest of the bridge staff were watching him, whether they faced him or had their backs to him: Lieutenant Harry Vincent, the navigator, young Midshipman Appleby, the signal yeoman and his signalman, the bridge messengers and lookouts.

*Brandenburg* was a German cruiser and had sailed in company with the battlecruiser *Graf Spee*. Both ships had acted as commerce raiders, sinking a string of merchantmen from the outbreak of war in September 1939 until mid-December. The *Altmark*, a large, fast supply ship, had acted as tender for both of them. But then Commodore Harwood with his squadron of three cruisers had caught *Graf Spee* off Montevideo on 13th December. After a savage battle she was forced to seek shelter in that port and her captain had scuttled her four days later.

*Brandenburg* and *Altmark* had not been with *Graf Spee* and despite extensive searching they had not been found

4

– except for one sighting of *Brandenburg* in the South Atlantic by a British cruiser, *Calliope*, and that had ended in tragedy. Many thought *Altmark* had slipped through the net by now and was safely in a German port, while *Brandenburg*, with another tender taking the place of *Altmark*, was still lurking in the South Atlantic, a thousand miles from *Cassandra*. Ben Kelso was one who believed that. Smith was not. He was certain that if *Altmark* had returned to Germany then Hitler would have trumpeted the news to the world. He believed *Altmark* was still at sea and *Brandenburg* was also on her way home by now. Her captain had told him she would be – but Smith could not tell Kelso that. So it was possible the distant warship might have been *Brandenburg*. That was why he had sent his crew to their action stations. But now?

The two ships had been closing at their combined speeds for several minutes and now Smith could make out details of the other. He lowered the glasses and said, "No."

Kelso was broad and stocky, full-bearded. Still studying the other ship, his back to Smith, he objected, "It could be, sir." That was said ostensibly doubting, actually provoking. "We can't see much of her yet."

Smith could see Harry Vincent hiding a grin. He rasped, "I can see enough, Ben." He called his officers by their first names. It was an accepted, but in this ship a hollow, informality, a false comradeship that cloaked hostility. He thought Kelso would not have been so cool if he believed the other ship was *Brandenburg*, and that Ben was the worst of the lot, or the most open of his officers: hinting that Smith had spent too long ashore, doubting his professional competence, questioning his ability to command. It was all done subtly, indirectly. But they meant it and he and they knew it.

Were they right?

He said, "It isn't *Brandenburg*." Smith knew her as he knew her captain, too well to be mistaken, but that was from a secret chapter of his life. He could not explain that to Kelso, either. Instead he said, "This ship has two turrets forrard and one aft. I think she's probably American, one of the Minneapolis class or the Augustas. *Brandenburg* has one turret forrard and two aft."

Kelso turned and opened his mouth to argue but Smith looked him in the eye and Ben found he could only mumble, "As you say, sir."

Smith smiled at him coldly, "Yes." He watched Kelso turn away, subdued by that icy gaze – for now. And beyond Kelso's wide shoulders he saw Lieutenant-Commander John Galloway, *Cassandra*'s Executive Officer, spring lightly up the ladder and onto the bridge.

He was one of the young men eager to command *Cassandra* and despite knowing her faults. Like her new-found reputation for being an unlucky ship. She had only earned that on this cruise. She had been ordered to Montevideo to reinforce Harwood's squadron but arrived too late because her engines had broken down. Then her main wireless office was gutted by a fire that killed the wireless staff on duty. They were buried at sea. The smoke-blackened door of the main office was still locked and all wireless traffic passed through the second office. Then to cap it all her captain, ailing for months, died just before she docked at Montevideo. Smith's first duty after assuming command was to inter his predecessor in the graveyard of the English church. So now she was called an unlucky ship.

Galloway said, "False alarm, sir?"

Smith wondered if Galloway thought *Cassandra* was unlucky for him, her Executive Officer? He was a tall, darkly handsome man, liked by his fellow officers and respected by the lower deck. He came of a naval family, numbering more than one admiral among his ancestors and no doubt he would reach flag rank. He was a good officer, highly efficient, and had effectively commanded *Cassandra* these last months of her captain's illness. Did

6

he think that in any other ship he would have been captain now?

He would have made a good captain for her. That was Smith's opinion but not his alone. Within hours of coming aboard he had overheard a snatch of conversation between two of his officers: "Galloway should have got *Cassandra*, not a dug-out like Smith. This is his first ship after twenty years on the beach, for God's sake!"

Now they were close enough to make out the Stars and Stripes flown by the other ship and Smith nodded at Galloway, "She's American. Not *Brandenburg*."

Kelso muttered, "Just as well, after what she did to *Calliope* a few weeks ago. Merry flaming Christmas present, that was!" It was *Calliope*, sister ship of *Cassandra*, that had made that last tragic sighting of *Brandenburg*.

This time it was Galloway's glare that shut up Kelso and he followed it up, defending his Service with, "*Brandenburg* ran for it!"

Kelso nodded agreement now, "That's true. *Calliope* did bloody well."

Smith thought "bloody" was the right word. His voice cut between his two officers, "Not quite true. *Brandenburg* was faster and her guns outranged *Calliope*'s. So she stood off and shot the hell out of her." *Calliope* had been pounded to a near wreck in her vain attempts to come to grips with the bigger cruiser. She had lost a lot of men. And that had been in the South Atlantic on Christmas Day, just eight days after *Graf Spee* was scuttled.

Galloway had been startled by Smith's cutting in and now repeated stubbornly, "But *Brandenburg* ran."

"Not exactly." Smith had met her captain and fought him, did not think Gustav Moehle was one to run. But again, he could not tell Galloway that. "Another ship appeared, just the smoke of her on the horizon but I think *Brandenburg*'s captain suspected she might be reinforcements called up by *Calliope*. So he broke off the action. And I think that was in obedience to his orders, that he was sent out to sink merchantmen and told not to pick a fight where his ship might sustain damage." Smith lifted his glasses again, signalling that he had delivered his judgment and the argument was finished.

The Signal Yeoman reported, "She's dipping her ensign, sir."

Smith answered, "Return the compliment." *Cassandra*'s ensign dipped and rose again. Smith ordered, "Resume normal working." He made a last inspection of the other ship now passed abeam. Suppose it had been *Brandenburg*? He winced at the thought. Kelso had been right there and *Cassandra* would have gone the way of *Calliope*. Smith could only have tried to keep *Brandenburg* in sight and screamed for help but the end would have been the same. Smith loved *Cassandra* but . . .

She was a twin-funnelled light cruiser and had been built for that earlier war. She was vulnerable in her thin armour, slower and weaker than the modern German cruisers that outgunned her. She rode the seas proudly but she was an ageing, fragile beauty. Other men had loved her but used her hardly because they had to, so she was shabby in her pride. And Smith knew he was just such a man, would also be ruthless with her if he had to be. But he had commanded a ship like her in that other war. And she was his.

But for how long? He lowered the glasses and glanced at Galloway, deep in conversation with the barrel-chested, thick-legged Kelso. Galloway stood a head taller, had a commanding presence and *looked* like a captain. Would he get *Cassandra* after all? Had Smith only been given her briefly as a sop, a pat on the head in acknowledgment of his faithful but clandestine service? Was he only to take her home for a refit or conversion to an anti-aircraft cruiser like many of her class? He did not know what fate was intended for her – or himself – when she berthed in

Scapa Flow. He shifted uneasily in the chair. He was sure he had been given *Cassandra* because the other officers in Montevideo who might have qualified for her were too experienced in their posts, while he was new.

The two officers had discussed his career some weeks before in London as they marched briskly through St James's Park on a winter afternoon. The Rear-Admiral grumbled, "Smith! His trouble was always women. He was divorced years ago and now I hear he's living with some American woman in Montevideo."

His colleague said patiently, "He's not the only officer to be divorced, though I admit that's only part of it. He was involved in some scandals before that. But his wife left him not because of any infidelity but because she could not stand the long separations the Service – his particular kind of Service – forced on him. She didn't know where he was, what he was doing, when he would return to her, when leave her again. And he couldn't tell her."

"All right, that's got nothing to do with giving him a ship. But he hasn't been to sea for twenty years."

A shrug: "Because we wanted him in Intelligence for those twenty years and we were right; he was very good. But now that we have a shooting war again, well, his record in the last one was impressive."

The Rear-Admiral slashed bad-temperedly at a fallen branch with his walking stick. "He was insubordinate and rebellious! Lucky not to have been court martialled! He only got away with it time and again because he was successful!"

The other smiled to himself but let that go. He said, remembering and reminding his superior: "After his last Intelligence operation he asked for the command we had always promised him. Instead we sent him to Montevideo to join the staff of the Naval Attaché in Uruguay. On the way there as a passenger in a freighter he was captured by

9

*Brandenburg* but first took the helm of the freighter and succeeded in ramming the cruiser, damaging her bow. She hid in a Brazilian river to carry out repairs so as to be able to go to the aid of the *Graf Spee*, bottled up in Montevideo by Harwood's cruisers. God knows how Harwood would have got on if he'd had to handle both of them. But Smith escaped from *Brandenburg* and delayed her repairs by one attack after another. He was acting almost single-handedly but *Brandenburg* was too late to save *Graf Spee* and her captain scuttled her."*

"I know all about that," the Rear-Admiral growled, "and Smith was bloody lucky."

"And successful. Again. Now he is in Montevideo, so is *Cassandra* and she's needing a captain. Maybe it's the hand of Providence at work."

The Rear-Admiral scowled suspiciously, "Are you trying to be funny? It's more likely the Devil looking after his own. But we'll give him *Cassandra*." And he conceded, "He's earned her, and more. Bad-tempered, bloody-minded, bed-hopping, he's all of those – but he delivers the goods. We just have to hope his luck doesn't run out."


"Ship bearing Red Two Oh!" Now it was close to noon on that same 7th February and the Lookout was reporting from *Cassandra*'s masthead.

Smith lifted his glasses as did Galloway and Kelso. They peered out along the bearing and then Galloway said, "She's a merchantman." Not a warship nor a U-boat on the surface. The brief moment of tension passed but still they studied the distant ship.

Kelso muttered, "There's smoke but just a trace of it. She doesn't look to be under way."

Lieutenant Harry Vincent, tall, thin and stooping, the

* See *Orphans of the Storm*.

10

navigator and a good one, appeared from the chart-room to join them. Smith lowered the glasses to rest his eyes for a moment and told Ben Kelso, "We'll close her."

Kelso ordered, "Port ten." He stayed bent over the voice-pipe, beard brushing it, passing helm orders until *Cassandra*'s bow swung then steadied on the smudge lifting above the horizon.

They waited as the distance shrank and the ship grew before their eyes. Harry Vincent murmured to Kelso but his voice carried deliberately across the bridge, sarcasm aimed at Smith, "Suppose it might be *Altmark*."

Galloway's whisper cracked savagely, "*Shut up!*" He was too good an officer to allow that kind of talk. Harry Vincent reddened but shrugged, not put down though he held his tongue.

Smith had heard the exchange but said nothing, watched the ship through his glasses. It was not *Altmark*; that tender was to outward appearances a typical big motor tanker of the time. This ship was a three-island freighter, the three "islands" of forecastle, superstructure and poop standing high above the decks between.

Galloway said, "She looks to be derelict. And she's been fired on!"

She lay dead on the surface of the sea, rolling sluggishly. Her boats were gone and the falls that had lowered them to the sea hung slack from the empty davits, lines and blocks swinging against the side of the ship as she rolled. She was low in the water and listing to starboard so Smith could see over the bulwarks to the hatch covers. Her decks were empty of life. There was a shell-hole in her side and several more torn in the square superstructure amidships that held the bridge and cabins.

She was horribly familiar.

Smith told himself she could not be the same ship. That one had left Montevideo only a few hours before *Cassandra* sailed from that port and she had been bound to call at New York before sailing for Liverpool. So she

11

should be trailing *Cassandra* by hours if not days. But then he recalled that she was a fast ship and had not been sailing in convoy, while *Cassandra* had spent some days patrolling before turning north and setting a course for home. So it could be . . .

Harry Vincent read her name from her bow: "*Orion*." But Smith knew that already.

He told Kelso, "Stop alongside her and call away the sea-boat." And to Galloway, "I'm going over to her." His voice sounded strange in his ears but Galloway stared at him for a different reason.

"You're going yourself, sir?" It was odd, to say the least, for a commanding officer to lead a boarding-party.

"Yes." Smith did not explain, shoved out of his chair and dropped down the ladders to the upper deck. He strode rapidly aft to where the sea-boat's crew waited in the whaler and there he met Leading Seaman Buckley.

The big man said worriedly, "I thought you might be goin' over, sir. It's – "

Smith cut him off, harshly, "I know what ship it is!" Buckley had been with him when he had watched *Orion* sail.

He had served with Smith in that other war and the years showed in the wire-wool grizzling in the close-cropped black hair. But though he was thicker in the waist, he was still surprisingly agile and flat-bellied for a man of his size and weight. Now he knew that look on Smith's face, fell back and climbed into the boat.

Smith followed, the whaler was lowered and made its rocking-horse way over the swell from *Cassandra* with Buckley at the helm. As they closed the merchantman he hailed her, "*Orion!*" But no figure showed on the freighter's deck, no voice called in answer. The whaler slid in alongside the rust-streaked hull. Two of the hands grabbed at a Jacob's ladder that dangled beside loose falls while others held the whaler off from crashing against the steel side. The ship's list meant that the ladder hung out from the side at an angle. Buckley held on to the bottom of it while Smith swung himself onto the rungs. He did not have to climb far, only a few feet, because *Orion* lay so low in the sea. Buckley warned, "I don't think she's going to stay afloat much longer, sir."

He got a growl in reply and Smith lifted his legs over the bulwark and stood on the deck below the freighter's superstructure, just aft of the bridge. He shouted down to the whaler, "I want a search party up here!" He saw Buckley already on the ladder and climbing. Smith turned and mounted the ladder to the bridge.

A shell had cleared it. The doors at either side were smashed to matchwood, wheel and compass binnacle were twisted wreckage and the glass had gone from the screens. Smith looked out through the empty frames and saw the deck forward to the fo'c'sle littered with papers, books, items of clothing. The crew had dropped them as they ran to the boats. But not all of them had been able to run.

Buckley said quietly, "Right mess in here, sir."

Smith looked down at the blood staining the deck beneath his feet and in two other places on the bridge. He thought, That's where the helmsman stood and that second patch came from the man on the engine-room telegraph. The third was probably the officer on watch. The blood marked where they had fallen. There were no bodies. He said, "Yes."

Buckley followed him as he left the bridge and found the wireless office aft of it. That, too, had been hit so that he could stare out through the shattered bulkhead and across to where *Cassandra* lay. The wireless was smashed and there was more blood on the deck. A flimsy sheet of paper fluttered one corner on the wind that came in through the shell-hole but was held to the deck by the blood that glued it there. Smith stooped and carefully peeled it free.

Buckley sucked in his breath and swore softly. "A six-inch armament did this, sir."

13

Smith nodded agreement, head bent and reading. The flimsy was the hastily scrawled draft of a signal. If it had been sent then no one had reported receiving it. It read: *"RRR Gunned by raider. ALTMARK . . ."* It went on to give the ship's position at the time of the attack but no date nor time. Smith showed the signal to Buckley, who sucked in a breath and said, "There's rumours *Altmark* carries two six-inch guns, hidden away."

Smith had heard that. The guns could be concealed inside the ship's superstructure, like the old Q-ships. He folded the signal carefully and put it in his pocket. Then he took a breath, led the way out of the wireless office and went to search the cabins in the superstructure.

There were the remnants of a meal on the long table in the saloon where the officers and the passengers had eaten. Broken crockery littered the deck; the blast from the shelling of the bridge had done that. A water jug rolled back and forth as the hulk rocked sluggishly on the swell. The cabins all showed the signs of hasty packing, clothing strewn untidily. Their doors, open, swung creaking and slamming back and forth as *Orion* rolled heavily in the swell.

A member of the search party found them there and reported to Smith, "We've been right through her and there's not a soul aboard, sir. All of 'em left in a hurry. She must be holed below the water-line but we've had some of the hatch-covers off and looked in her holds. She's loaded with timber. Probably that's why she's still afloat, but she's nearly awash."

Smith nodded, "Thank you." They were in the last cabin. The others had all held items of uniform, a cap or jacket, showing them as belonging to officers of the ship. There was a scarf on the bunk of this one, a square of silk. Smith picked it up.

*Orion* lurched and the deck under their feet tilted to a sharper angle. Buckley said anxiously, "I reckon she's going, sir."

Smith said. "Yes." He turned and left the cabin, the scarf balled inside his clenched fist.

They could almost have stepped down into the whaler now where it rose and fell on the swell just below the level of the deck. *Orion* did not have long. The whaler's crew bent to the oars and drove it pitching back across the heaving sea. Smith sat in the sternsheets of the boat with his head turned on his shoulder and watched the freighter lurch again and settle, the sea washing over her deck between fo'c'sle and superstructure. When he stood again on *Cassandra*'s bridge he was just in time to see *Orion*'s bow go under and her stern lift. Then she dived with a sudden, swift smoothness. There was a rumbling as that steep diving angle tore her engines loose from the bed-plates inside her, and a roar of escaping steam. Then she was gone.

Smith held out the stained flimsy to Kelso and Galloway. "It seems she was shelled by *Altmark*. Her boarding-party took away everyone aboard, including the wounded and the dead. The living will have added to her cargo."

Galloway looked up from the signal. "How many prisoners do you think she has, sir?"

"*Graf Spee* sank half a dozen ships and only had a few prisoners aboard when she berthed in Montevideo. The rest must be on *Altmark*. I think probably close on three hundred of them."

Galloway swore under his breath. Kelso was reading the signal again, lips moving, as if he did not want to believe this evidence that he had been wrong about *Altmark* and Smith right. Galloway asked, "We're going after her, sir?"

"Yes. I'll send a signal to Admiralty but we'll start now. I think *Altmark* has a lead of around twenty-four hours." And any delay would lengthen that time. But which way had she gone? She was headed for Germany, that was obvious, but not directly. No, she would be on a course that would take her northabout and away from North

15

Sea patrols. It would take her to Norway and she could then run down the coast of that country. That decided, there were still two ways she could go, north of Iceland through the Denmark Strait, or south of it by the Faroes Passage.

Galloway, Kelso, Harry Vincent, all of them were waiting for his decision, and if it was wrong it could mean that *Altmark* would escape with her cargo of British prisoners – and the ignominious end of Smith's career.

But he had already decided. *Altmark* had been six months at sea, would not spin it out any longer than was necessary.

He said, "Pilot! A course for the Faroes Passage!"

*Cassandra* was already under way and now the group waiting on the bridge broke up. Harry Vincent hurried back to his charts, an abashed Kelso scowled out over the screen at *Cassandra*'s bow throwing back the green spray. Smith sat in his tall chair and was slowly aware of Galloway glancing curiously at him. He realised he still clutched the scarf in his fist, a foot of the coloured silk trailing from between his fingers.

He crammed it into his pocket. He had given the scarf to his twenty-year-old daughter Sarah on the day he had learned of his appointment to *Cassandra*. That was just before she had taken passage in *Orion* from Montevideo to Liverpool. Now she was a prisoner aboard *Altmark*. If she lived.

16

# 2

"She could lose us in this! If she came this way!" The voice came complaining and bad-tempered out of the night. That was Lieutenant George Chivers, long, thin and horse-faced, who had the watch. He stood forward, hunched behind the bridge-screen, and had bawled the words at young Midshipman Appleby at his side. Smith caught them, whipped back to him on the wind as he fought his way against it, coming up from his sea cabin and heading for his tall chair at the front of the bridge.

The storm had worked up all through the previous day with the clouds hanging leaden-bellied and never a sight of the sun. Now the night was pitch dark, the wind screaming and hurling sheets of rain that rattled on the oilskins of the men on the bridge, stung and then numbed their faces.

Smith saw the big seas washing green over *Cassandra*'s bow and sweeping aft past the gun forward of the bridge. Ships of her class were notorious for shipping the seas forward in any bad weather. But he thought she was riding them well, like a lady. He had made demands on her since she had steamed away from *Orion* but she had met them all and was meeting this latest. Chivers had already asked once in this watch if he could reduce speed because of the weather and Smith had refused his request. They could not slacken now.

He brought up against the chair, climbed into it and shouted, "Morning, Mr Chivers!"

17

"Morning, sir!" Chivers' long face was gloomy but that was his natural cast of countenance. Smith knew he was a dependable officer. He had wanted to reduce speed because he thought *Cassandra* could not stand it. Smith knew she could.

Thirty-six hours had passed since the sinking of *Orion*. Twelve of those had been lost while *Cassandra* was diverted by a signal from Admiralty to investigate a reported sighting of *Altmark* that proved to be a neutral tanker. But now *Cassandra* was passing between Iceland and the Faroes.

Smith thought that *Altmark* could be close – if he had anticipated correctly. Chivers had expressed doubt, but not of the possibility of *Altmark* being in these waters rather than a German port. Smith's officers now knew he had been right about that – and were they regarding him differently? He shrugged. As to whether they were close to *Altmark* now – he had taken a gamble, anyway, or a calculated risk. And, again as Chivers said, they could still miss her in this appalling visibility.

Smith had slept fitfully, fully clothed, and had awoken early – the change of watch was not due for another ten minutes – the worry dragging him from his bunk. He reached for his oilskins.

Was Sarah alive? Was she aboard *Altmark*?

While a part of his mind wrestled with those questions, thoughts of his daughter triggered others. He recalled again that overheard snatch of conversation: "Twenty years on the beach!" But there had been more: "Rumours are that he was always a success with the girls, too much for his career. He was shacked up with some American floozie in Montevideo!"

That had annoyed Smith because he did not believe it was true; he was not a ladies' man. The word "floozie" had enraged him. Hannah Fitzsimmons was a journalist and war correspondent for whom he had gratitude, affection, respect – and lust, he admitted that.

18

What had happened between himself and Hannah had just – happened. He did not regret that. He had left her in Montevideo but she planned soon to return to the States and then Europe. She had said huskily, straddling him in the bed, his hands on her breasts, "Then I'll look you up."

Smith was divorced in 1922 and had not seen his daughter Sarah for seventeen years. She had lived with her mother and German stepfather in Berlin but had to flee from the Nazis in the summer of 1939. She went to Warsaw seeking Smith who had gone there on an Intelligence mission but missed him by hours. Then the *Wehrmacht* had invaded Poland.

Hannah Fitzsimmons, who was in Warsaw on an assignment, befriended Sarah and got her out of Poland. Hannah knew Smith, who had earlier saved her from a firing-squad in Spain, and she wanted to see him again. So much so that she went with the girl to the Admiralty in London, where Sarah produced her passport and birth certificate and established that she was Smith's daughter. They learned he was in the office of the Naval Attaché in Montevideo – and followed him there. He had little time to get to know Sarah before she sailed in *Orion* and *Cassandra* claimed him.

He pulled his mind away from thoughts of Hannah's slim body and long legs, stared out into the murk of driving spray and rain and saw nothing. He glanced sideways at the other figures hunched miserably on the bridge. The seaman who was the messenger, the signalman and the lookouts . . . Young Appleby's oilskins, a sight too big for him, hung almost to the bridge gratings. Smith shouted against the wind, "Anyone know who Cassandra was?"

Chivers peered at him, incredulous at the question at this time. He did not answer. But after a moment Appleby ventured, "I think she was a goddess, sir, and Apollo gave her the gift of prophecy in return for her favours. But when she didn't come through he ruled that her prophecies would never be believed."

Smith grinned at him, "Good enough." He recalled that Appleby had not applied for a transfer out of the ship when Smith became her captain, when every other officer had done so. Smith thought wrily, He's young. Give him time to get up his courage. And grinned again.

So he and *Cassandra* were a pair: dug-outs, relics from a time past. And his prophecies weren't believed. He had told his officers that *Altmark* would still be at sea because Hitler would have claimed a propaganda victory if she had succeeded in getting back to Germany. Kelso and the others had been doubtful, barely polite or subtly sarcastic. Had that changed now? Or did they still regard him as a dug-out who had been right for once?

The watch would change soon. The dawn was near though there was no lightening of the darkness, the wind howled its fury and the rain drove in. Chivers stamped back and forth across the bridge to try to warm himself and Appleby moved out to the wing. Smith was left alone with his thoughts and his daughter was foremost among them.

They had met in Montevideo as strangers but after an initial shyness there was a mutual liking. They had learned a lot about each other in the few days they had together but an element of that strangeness remained, for Smith at any rate – a lone man. Then she had told him, "You have a job to do here but I haven't." So she booked her berth in *Orion*, returning to Britain. "I'll join the Wrens or drive an ambulance. Anything. We've got to win this war and I'm not helping by lazing around out here."

He knew her well enough already not to argue when she took that kind of stand. But now he wondered again, tormented, was Sarah alive?

\*　　\*　　\*

20

Appleby was young and looked younger, short and pink-cheeked. Now he was cold, wet around the neck where the spray had soaked the towel wrapped around and tucked into the top of his oilskins, but he did not complain. That had been drummed into him. Like Galloway, he came from an old naval family, his ancestors for several generations being captains. None of them had shown brilliance but had fought their way up the ladder by dint of hard work and courage. Appleby was determined to imitate them but he had heard the stories of their courage and in his heart he knew he was not one of them, would never be more than a copy. But most of the time he could forget this.

He had heard of Smith before he came to command *Cassandra*. His father and uncles had talked of him, argued about him:

". . . irresponsible, undisciplined, lucky not to have been court martialled." Or: "plenty of guts, fine seaman, ready to turn a blind eye and chance his arm." Then there were the other officers aboard *Cassandra*. She was Appleby's first ship and they were as gods to him. Every one of them was hostile to Smith and had applied for a transfer out of the ship. Surely they couldn't all be wrong?

Out on the wing of the bridge was the port side lookout, Ordinary Seaman Nisbet. He came of a family of itinerant labourers. Unemployed he had joined the Navy out of hunger. He complained bitterly at every opportunity and now grumbled at Appleby: ". . . every soddin' watch I stand in this flaming ship it pisses down. And the bloody old cow shouldn't be at sea this weather with an open bridge. Should be glassed in . . ." He clung with one arm locked around a stanchion to hold him steady as he swept the sea from bow to stern with the big binoculars and his voice droned on, whining monotonously.

Until it wore down Appleby's patience and nervousness and he snapped, "Oh, shut up, man!"

Nisbet was silent as Appleby staggered away across the bridge, then started to mutter under his breath again.

Buckley appeared at Smith's elbow. "Coffee, sir."

"Thank you." Smith took the thick china mug and cradled it in his cupped hands, feeling the heat. Buckley moved around the bridge, collecting from the shelf under the screen the other, empty mugs that had accumulated during the night.

"Ship on the port bow!" Nisbet yelled it from the wing of the bridge, one hand holding the big binoculars to his eyes, the other outstretched and pointing. Smith lifted his own glasses and looked out along the bearing, saw the ship just a shadow out there in the night. His hand fumbled for the button under the screen and thumbed it so the alarms sounded throughout the ship, calling the crew to their action stations.

Smith ordered, "Port ten! Challenge!" And as *Cassandra*'s bow swung, turning towards the stranger, the signalman on the searchlight worked the clacking shutter, blinking out the question: "What ship is that?"

Smith had to challenge because the other ship might well be friendly. At the same time he was grimly aware that if she was an enemy she could assume that any other ship out here was British. And *Altmark* was rumoured to mount a pair of 6-inch guns. Buckley appeared at his side, thrusting the steel helmet at Smith. He put it on in exchange for his cap and thrust that at Buckley.

Chivers said, "D'ye think it's – "

Smith broke in, "Can't see in this visibility, but if it is *Altmark* we'll be ready for her." He was aware of running figures on the deck below him and aft, saw the first men struggling towards the forward 6-inch gun on the fo'c'sle, clinging to the lifelines and up to their waists in water as a wave swept in over the bow.

\*    \*    \*

22

Ordinary Seaman Dobson was eighteen years old and still half asleep. He had rolled his lanky, bony body out of his hammock as the alarms sounded, for a second or two thinking that this was just the usual call to Dawn Action Stations but then he realised this was not routine. *Cassandra* was preparing to fight. He ran aft, heading for where the damage control party mustered, his station in action. He still could not believe the call was true. He had been just four months at sea, seen no fighting in that time and had loudly bemoaned the fact.

*Cassandra* bucked and rolled as the men ran, staggered and sometimes crawled to their stations. Dobson fell once but took no account of it in his excitement. But he fell again at the head of the ladder leading down from the upper deck, twisted awkwardly as *Cassandra* pitched and so plunged headlong to the deck below. He was cursing shrilly, frightened, as he fell but then he crashed to the deck and lost consciousness.

Kelso bounced breathlessly onto the bridge and took over from Chivers. Smith heard the reports coming in, from Sandy Faulknor, the Gunnery Officer in the director control tower high above the bridge, and from all through the ship until Galloway's clipped accent came from far aft with damage control. Sandy was thick-set and cool, sandy-haired – and freckled if the sun shone. The director control did just that: controlled the guns by directing their fire. The telescopic sight and rangefinder in the top were laid on the enemy and passed a common range and bearing to all guns. Then, when all that would bear on the target were ready, Sandy pressed the button and fired them together.

*Cassandra* was closing the other ship, which showed no light, made no reply to the demand being flashed again from the searchlight. But now Smith was closer and able to see her in the night. She was the right size and shape, with her superstructure standing forward and her funnel right aft. . . . *Altmark*?

But then Nisbet shouted, "'*Nother ship port quarter!*"

Smith swung his glasses, picked up this second ship almost dead astern and saw the flames prickle aboard her. He knew she had seen *Cassandra* because of the signalling searchlight and she was firing on them now. He snatched at the telephone and shouted to Sandy Faulknor, "Guns! Ship Red One-Six-Oh! Open fire!"

He heard that acknowledged by Sandy in the control top and then ordered, "Port twenty!" Because he had to turn to face this new threat, or rather to bring it onto the beam so all *Cassandra*'s 6-inch guns would bear. At the moment only those aft could fire at this new threat. But then the enemy shells screamed in to burst just ahead of *Cassandra*. They hurled up huge towers of dirty water that fell on the bridge like rain as they steamed through it. The hanging spray stank of explosive.

Smith spat it out, peered through the rain and saw *Altmark* – big as a house now and he was sure it was her – right on the bow and sliding around to starboard as *Cassandra* continued to turn. The 6-inch guns aft fired, tongues of flame leaping out yellow in the night. He turned and watched the other ship out there astern, did not see any hits, but briefly he saw her clearly through a break in the curtain of rain and spray. She was firing again, that red rash winking along the length of her. And he knew her.

Then a squall tore between and he lost sight of the enemy altogether. A second later her shells screamed in and this time he heard the hammer-blow as *Cassandra* was hit. He felt the shudder through the slender frame of her as if she winced under the blow. Another shell burst close alongside hurling water and shrapnel inboard. Splinters ripped into the canvas-covered protective padding around the bridge-screen and sliced through signal halyards so they fell across the back of the bridge. The guns aft fired

24

again and he thought, Sandy up in the control top must still be able to see her. And: We'll soon have turned far enough to fire broadsides.

He demanded, "Get me a report on that hit!"

He could not see Appleby but a bridge messenger shouted, "Aye, aye, sir!" And Smith saw him at the telephone.

Then Sandy Faulknor's voice came through the speaker on the bridge, "Can't see the enemy any longer, sir."

Smith twisted in the chair again, glasses to his eyes, and found he could see neither the ship astern nor *Altmark*, both of them lost in the darkness made impenetrable by the rain that drove in near-solid clouds on the wind. He would have to search for them. He swore and went to the compass, peered into the dim-lit binnacle. He ordered, "Steer Oh-Two-Oh!"

Taggart, the Cox'n, at the wheel now, acknowledged, "Steer Oh-Two-Oh, sir!"

And when he found them? *Altmark* had not fired a shot so probably those rumours about her carrying concealed 6-inch guns were no more than just rumours. And the signal found aboard *Orion* had been incomplete. *Altmark* had been there but so had *Brandenburg* and she had shelled *Orion*.

Now Kelso asked, "What ship do you think it was that came up astern of us, sir?"

"That was *Brandenburg*." And what could he do about her if he found her? *Calliope* had –

Kelso's expression could not be read in the darkness but his voice was dubious and he objected, "She was reported in the South Atlantic." By *Calliope*. On Christmas Day.

Smith fought down his irritation at being doubted still. He said with certainty, "Well, she's here now." He had sailed aboard her as a prisoner, studied her when she lay in that Brazilian river trying to make her repairs while he tried to baulk all the attempts of her crew. That, again, was the secret episode he could not divulge to Kelso or

25

anyone else. Because he and *Brandenburg* had fought their own private war in that empty heart of Brazil, a neutral country, in contravention of international law. But he knew *Brandenburg* was out there in the night now. Smith climbed back into his chair and left Kelso to ponder that. He would find no comfort in it. If he believed it. They had barely glimpsed that ship astern so probably Kelso still did not believe that she was *Brandenburg*. Smith thought grimly, We'll see.

The bridge messenger reported, "The hit was on the wireless office, sir. There was a small fire but that's out. The office is a total loss, though, and most of the staff. Mister Galloway says he'll let you have a full report soon." That was the second office. The main office was still a burnt-out shell, awaiting refitting in a dockyard. Now *Cassandra* had no wireless at all.

"Very good." Smith saw young Appleby was again at the front of the bridge, looking composed and seemingly not shaken by the recent action. He made a mental note then took up his glasses as *Cassandra* started to search.

Appleby thought that Nisbet had not run. When the firing started Appleby had backed away from the screen, his feet seeming to move of their own volition. Then the shell hit *Cassandra* and the splinters from the near-miss scythed across the bridge. Appleby had recoiled, fallen back into a corner and huddled there with his head buried in his arms. He only emerged when the firing ceased and made his way to the front of the bridge. No one seemed to have noticed his absence. Nisbet turned as he passed, for once forgetting to complain, and grinned at him, "Bit of excitement, eh, sir?" He sounded breathless. But he hadn't run and hid.

All through his training as a cadet, Appleby had tried harder than the others. He knew the instructors thought him too frail to last the course. But he had listened to the experience of generations as his family talked and knew what to expect, what he had to do. So from the start he

26

set out to lead, shouldered the loads, took the risks and the rough with the smooth, so in the end the instructors said of him. "Not much muscle but plenty of energy and guts."

It was an act. Part of the related experiences he had listened to with churning stomach had been the casual description of the horrors of wounding and death in action. His father, grandfather, uncles, all of them seemed to take these as a matter of course, the bloody wreckage wrought by shell, mine or fire. He had known he was different yet accepted that he had to play the part expected of him. Besides, when he joined the Navy his country was at peace. Then when the war started he was buoyed up by one comment: "A lot of chaps went through the last war and never saw a shot fired in anger." True, but . . .

But now his bluff had been called. Or would be, that was certain. He had got away with it this time but they would be in action again before long, he was sure of that, and sooner or later they would find him out. Then he would have to face them, and his family.

And Nisbet, the workshy whiner and grouser, who had not hidden.


*Cassandra* searched, quartering back and forth across the tract of ocean from where the action was fought. Smith knew now that *Brandenburg* and *Altmark* were sailing in company and both were bound for Norway. That narrowed down the cone of search but the storm reduced the area of visibility during the hours of darkness to a circle less than a mile across with *Cassandra* soaring and plunging at its centre. Smith cold-bloodedly told himself the odds were a thousand to one against his finding the enemy.

He sat in his tall chair, at first with hands thrust deep in the pockets of his bridge-coat to hide their shaking. But that passed and it had been normal, a reaction that had always followed action when he had last commanded a ship. In this one brief exchange of fire with *Brandenburg* he had forgotten those twenty years "on the beach" and acted as if they had never been. He felt lonely no longer, his self-doubt was washed away. At that moment he was light-hearted, despite his cares. He *was* captain of *Cassandra*.

So he grinned, startling Galloway as he came staggering to the bridge and reported, "The wireless office is wrecked and burnt out, sir. The shell hit us just when the watch was changing. The men going off duty and those coming on were all there." He paused and finished heavily, "Three wounded and six dead. That last figure includes all the wireless staff." Since the main wireless office burned out with the loss of the staff on duty those that were left had worked in two watches.

That ended Smith's short minutes of euphoria. He had not been long in *Cassandra* but he could match every man's name and record to his face. He knew them. He had letters to write to widows and mothers, trying to offer some sympathy and comfort.

Galloway saw his bleak stare and was silent a moment, then asked, "I heard the ship that fired on us was *Brandenburg*, sir?" It was a question as much as a statement. Galloway, like Kelso and probably the other officers, was still doubting.

Smith answered, "It was."

Galloway nodded, "I got a glimpse of her but I couldn't be certain. Difficult to be sure of anything you see in this weather."

Smith grinned wrily at Galloway and the delicate suggestion. "I'm sure. That was *Brandenburg*."

Galloway swallowed that and said, "It looks as though we might have our hands full, then." And went away.

The sky slowly lightened to a dirty grey that became a day of lowering black clouds over a heaving sea that tilted *Cassandra* first on her stern and then her bow. The green, foam-flecked wastes were empty. Smith ordered a return to his original course because he had lost the two ships and they were somewhere ahead of him now and steaming for Norway. He feared, believed, his daughter was aboard one of them. What if he came up with them? He had no illusions as to how *Cassandra* compared with *Brandenburg*, that would be an unequal contest to say the least.

And worse: he had found *Altmark* but then lost her. And without wireless he could not even report her last position to Admiralty. Nor could he cry for help. He and *Cassandra* were on their own.

# 3

*Oberleutnant-zur-See* Kurt Larsen looked out on that same wild scene of mountainous seas and clouds pendulous with rain or snow. He stood tall on the bridge of *Brandenburg*, one long arm wrapped over the screen to hold him against the wild pitching and rolling. His captain, Gustav Moehle, strode back and forth across the bridge, shoulders hunched and stepping wide-legged to keep his balance on the tilting, rocking gratings of the bridge.

A mile ahead *Altmark* vanished and reappeared as she sank into a trough between waves then lifted again on a crest. Kurt swept the horizon with his glasses clapped to his eyes then lowered them and added his report to the unspoken negatives of the silent lookouts, saying nothing because they saw nothing: "No sign of her, sir."

Paul Brunner, *Brandenburg*'s Executive Officer, clung to the other side of the bridge. He grunted his agreement, "It looks like we've lost her, sir – or she's lost us."

Moehle scowled and swore. "A pity. She was ours for the taking. We're close to home now and we can turn a blind eye to our orders and fight an action with another cruiser. I'm sick of sinking merchantmen." He grabbed at the screen as *Brandenburg* rolled nearly on her beam ends, shoved himself upright and said, "But I wasn't going to risk a night action. The darkness could cancel out all our advantages of speed and gunnery, and luck might give the *Tommis* the edge. It's too risky." He shook his head, then admitted with grudging respect, "And that captain was damned quick in coming around to

30

bring his broadsides to bear. But if I could see him *now* . . ."


Smith still sat in his tall chair at the front of the bridge. *Cassandra* was trying to repair her damage. The carpenter could fix a patch on the bulkhead where the shell had ripped in to wreck the wireless office, but the office itself was another matter. It had to be cleaned and a party were at work on that. Then, like the main office, the burnt-out interior would be shut up, being of no further use until a dockyard could work on it.

Smith listened to Galloway's report on this and nodded. There would be burials, too, either when they reached port or at sea. He felt cold to the bone, wet and miserable. Then Buckley appeared at his elbow and said, urging, "I've got a bit o' breakfast for you, sir. Nothing hot because the galley stoves aren't working on account of this weather." Smith thought that this was the second day that he and *Cassandra*'s crew had eaten only cold food. There were likely to be more. But Buckley was going on, "You've had nothing except that cup o' coffee and that was over an hour ago."

Smith realised that he was hungry, and the thought of coffee was a pleasant one. He grinned at Buckley and his mother-hen act and said, "All right. I'll come." He told Harry Vincent, who had the watch, "Call me if anything is sighted." Then he went to the steel box at the back of the bridge that was his sea cabin. He ate, but abstractedly, preparing his report in his head to be written when the hasty meal was done. Then there were the letters to write to next of kin. And there was *Brandenburg*; he had to think about her, remember all he could because the knowledge might help him if – when – he fought her again.

\* \* \*

31

In the wardroom Chivers told the officers there grimly, "Well, this is supposed to be an unlucky ship but I think we were bloody lucky last night. If it was *Brandenburg*."

Merrick, the lieutenant of Marines, said, "You're not sure?"

"No. The Old Man is certain but he's been on the beach since before young Appleby was born and – " He stopped short then as he caught Galloway's cold eye on him, then went on, "But if it was her then we were lucky and if we meet her again, well, all right, we've got to have a crack at her, but it won't be exactly an equal contest."

Faulknor said thoughtfully, "She's bigger, two or three knots faster and has nine six-inch guns to our five."

Chivers sniffed, "And if *Calliope*'s experience is anything to go by she'll outrange us. *Brandenburg* fought her at the back end of last year, I don't need to remind you, and left her in the dockyard for a good six months with a casualty list as long as your arm."

They did not need reminding and sat in silence.


Dobson sat on the crowded mess deck, a dressing around his head, and listened to his mates. He stored up all their recollections of their parts in the fighting. He would use them later. He had known nothing of the brief action. Some members of the damage control party had found his unconscious body and carried him to the sick bay. The surgeon had discharged him from there barely an hour ago. He had seen nothing of the damage done to the ship or the bodies awaiting burial.

He was sorry to have missed the battle, as he thought of it. Still, the facts could be slightly adjusted to improve his story when he got home: "Some of the chaps copped it. I got a bash on the head but I kept going long enough to see Jerry run for it." The laceration hidden under the dressing covering his forehead might leave a scar that would show when he leaned against the bar with his cap shoved to the back of his head.

He came from a family that ran its own fruit and veg business in North London. When he left school he went straight into the business where his father told him daily that he would never be any bloody good, with his nose stuck in them flaming comics when he should have been working. Dobson was not interested in fruit and veg but he devoured the comics with their stories of heroism. The hero always triumphed and nobody got hurt. He knew life wasn't really like that, but just the same, when he joined the Navy he was certain he would return home as a hero. His father told him he was a bloody fool: "If they'd tried to conscript you I could ha' got you made exempt! What d'ye want to volunteer for?"

Dobson didn't care. He would show his father; he would show the lot of them. But now on the mess deck he knew he had just missed an opportunity to prove his gallantry. So he said yearningly, "It would ha' been something if we could ha' sunk her. Maybe if we'd had another captain . . .?" Heads nodded in agreement.

Jackman, Petty Officer, heard those remarks in passing and paused. He had a savage glare that silenced conversations and a mouth like a steel trap. He was a professional who looked after his men but now he peered at Dobson, black eyes glinting under thick, black brows as if disbelieving what he heard. "What the hell d'you know about it? What d'you think the Old Man should ha' done?"

Nisbet put in, "Well, I dunno, but he's been a long time ashore. Maybe if we had a younger feller that had been to sea lately – "

Jackman cut him off, "Like you or Dobson, maybe? Captains Nisbet and Dobson doing a double act on the bridge; what a sight!" That raised laughter and Nisbet grinned but Dobson reddened, embarrassed and angry. Jackman went on, "I'm thinking the Old Man's right and

33

that *was Brandenburg*. You spotted her, Nisbet, my son, and all credit to you, but until you did nobody, including you, thought she was within a thousand miles of us. She had the jump on us but the Old Man still got us into action and nearly into a position to fire broadsides, when the weather closed in. *And* we're still here."

Dobson asked, "What do you mean?"

Jackman shook his head pityingly, "Where have you been, sunshine? You heard about *Calliope*? So what price us to sink *Brandenburg*? We're chasing her 'cause we've got to, but Gawd help us if we catch her! Tell you what, though, I've been talking to Buckley, that big killick that's the Old Man's cox'n. Buckley's known him donkey's years and from what he tells me I think we might do better with the dug-out up there – " and he jerked his head, indicating the bridge " – straight off the beach, than some red-hot young skipper with plenty of sea-time and never any experience in action. And Buckley says that with this feller we'll see plenty of that!"

He looked around the mess, all their faces looking thoughtful now, then back at Dobson. He muttered, "Gawd give me strength!" And strode away.

Dobson still had his dreams.


*Cassandra* bucketed on through the short winter's day, the humping seas and howling gale. In the late afternoon the early dusk was already darkening the eastern horizon but briefly the rain ceased and the wind scoured the sky clear. Visibility lifted to port although to starboard the squalls still swept black across the surface of the sea – and *Altmark* was sighted again: ". . . Red Nine-Five!" The hail came from the port side lookout.

Smith spun around in his chair, searched with his glasses and found the now familiar silhouette: funnel and boatdeck aft, bridge superstructure forward and shallow well-deck between. He had one hand already below the screen and now he thumbed the button that set the alarms clanging throughout the ship.

*Altmark* was hull up on the horizon and just abaft the beam. *Cassandra* was steaming parallel to her but leading her by a mile or so, had caught up with her and passed her in the murk. But where was *Brandenburg*? Smith still held the glasses to his eyes and picked her out just as the lookout's hail came again: "Ship Red One-Oh-Five!"

There she was, again just abaft the port beam and maybe a mile astern of *Altmark*. It made sense for her captain to have stationed her there, between *Altmark* and *Cassandra* coming up astern, and ready to run down to her if she was threatened from any other quarter. Smith knew her captain, Moehle, and that he was no fool.

He ordered, "Starboard twenty!"

Kelso had charged onto the bridge and stared at that order because Smith was turning away. *Cassandra*'s bow swept around and she plunged through the big seas, widening the distance between her and the other two ships, running deeper into the squalls so she was once more enshrouded in rain and near-darkness. The other ships were lost to sight.

Now Smith ordered, "Port twenty!" And again felt the heel as *Cassandra*'s slender hull turned. "Midships! Steer that!" Now she was on a course parallel to that of the enemy. He had not reduced speed and the fact that she had overhauled the enemy showed she was making a few knots more than they. So she would be head-reaching on them now and pulling ahead. Smith thought that Sandy Faulknor up in the gunnery control top deserved a word of explanation. He picked up the telephone: "Sandy. You'll get your chance in a minute or two. Enemy should be on the port quarter."

He put the phone down. All the time he had been listening to the "Ready" reports coming in. Now the decks had cleared of running figures and the ship was quiet, waiting. Smith waited, judging the right moment, and when it came: "Port twenty!"

*Cassandra* heeled once more then settled on an even keel as Smith's next order set the helm amidships. She ran down through the gloom of rain driven on the wind, the sky slowly lightening around her, and then burst out of it into that last light of the day.

It was as Smith wanted it. The sun was now down below the western horizon while to the east the dark band had lifted to a high back drop against which *Cassandra* would be nearly invisible to *Brandenburg*'s gunnery staff. There she was, still a mile or so astern of *Altmark* but now much further astern of *Cassandra*.

Smith reached for the telephone: "Sandy. How do you see them?"

Faulknor almost shouted his excitement, "Beautiful! Clean – hard – black!"

The ships were etched in outline against the afterglow of the sunset and *Cassandra* was broadside to them. Smith ordered, "*Brandenburg*. Open fire!" He replaced the phone and crossed to the port wing of the bridge. In one sweeping glance from bow to stern he saw the barrels of all five guns turning, rising and falling as the bearings and ranges were transferred from Sandy Faulknor and his team in the director to the dials of the guns, the setters there each matching his pointers to those activated by electrical impulse from the director. The barrels steadied, were still, he heard the firegongs clang and then the three guns belched smoke and flame as the broadside was fired.

Thunder of discharge and the blast was another wind thrusting at his face, cordite stinking on that wind then carried away as *Cassandra* charged on. All of it was repeated as another salvo was fired. And again. Smith was watching for the fall of shot, glasses held to his eyes. He saw plumes of spray from shells exploding in the sea beyond *Brandenburg* and a hit or a near-miss, then bursts

36

of shells falling short and he guessed that Moehle had turned away to open the range and to put off Faulknor.

He ordered, "Make smoke!" And took away the glasses just long enough to rub his eyes and to see the smoke start to roll black and oily from *Cassandra*'s twin funnels, then he lifted them again. There was another hit on *Brandenburg*, Smith was sure. And then the flicker of flame showed along the length of her that meant she had fired a salvo.

He snapped, "Starboard twenty!" Yet another tight turn, deck heeling, staying in the turn as the bridge staff clung on. The after 6-inch guns that would still bear fired again, shaking the lean hull through its length. A moment later it shook again as the salvo from *Brandenburg* burst in the sea, the shells mostly astern but one close enough to the starboard quarter for Smith to feel the shock of it. Then the guns ceased firing and he ordered, "Midships!"

*Cassandra* had turned through one hundred and eighty degrees so now they were running back along the line of their own smoke and Sandy Faulknor reported, "Can't see the target for the smoke, sir!"

Smith told him, "Wait." *Cassandra* was now hidden from *Brandenburg*. He counted the seconds as she raced back along her previous course but now with the smoke standing like a range of low, black hills to starboard. Galloway reported, voice squawking over the telephone from aft, "That near-miss back here sprayed us with splinters but did no serious damage. No casualties."

"Thank you." But now Smith decided he and Faulknor had waited long enough. They had to wreak what damage they could while the light lasted. "Hard astarboard!" And then on the phone to Sandy Faulknor, "We're turning. You should find *Brandenburg* off the bow." He heard Sandy acknowledge that.

The slim grey cruiser heeled again, thrust into the smoke and for seconds it blinded them all on the bridge. It choked them as they breathed so that they coughed it out. Then

37

*Cassandra* was through it and there was *Brandenburg*, off the bow as Smith had promised Sandy, but closer now because she had driven in towards the smoke. And she was not such a good target as before because the red wash left by the sun below the horizon had faded and was fading still. *Altmark* tossing beyond her was almost invisible as the sky darkened.

"A" gun forward of the bridge bore this time and fired, cracking ears, the yellow muzzle flashes brilliant now as dusk rushed on into 'night. *Brandenburg* had been taken by surprise, her guns having to traverse around to lay on *Cassandra* when she suddenly tore out of the smoke. But Faulknor had those few vital seconds of foreknowledge, the long barrel of "A" gun steadying then recoiling as Sandy triggered it again. And Smith looked around at the sea like pitch under a dark sky and thought that *Brandenburg* would be having a hell of a job seeing them even though *Cassandra* was clear of the smoke.

He held her in the turn to starboard until *Brandenburg* was on the port beam. *Cassandra* was broadside to the enemy so that all her guns bore and he ordered, "Midships!" She straightened out, settled on an even keel again. And fired again, all five guns flashing as one, heeling her over, still pitching like a see-saw as she thrashed on.

His gaze shifted as rain rattled across the bridge once more and he saw the loom of the squall to starboard. It hung like an arras but was sweeping towards him, seeming blacker than the smoke that was now shredding on the wind astern. He turned his gaze to port, setting the glasses to his eyes, and saw the red ripple along *Brandenburg*'s hull that marked her salvo. "Starboard twenty!" He thought he had seen a near-miss fall close to her but could not be sure because of the gathering gloom. But now as *Cassandra* heeled under helm he saw the flash that he was certain marked a hit. That looked to be right aft in the other cruiser.

He heard Kelso yell, "Hit!" and that was confirmation but now the shells from *Brandenburg* howled in – fell short and astern. That last helm order had taken *Cassandra* away from them but they might have fallen short anyway because Moehle's gunners could barely see their target. And now the squall swept over the ship. One second he could still see the dim, blurred shape of *Brandenburg* and the next she was blotted out by a wall of rain that hammered on the bridge.

"Port ten!" To run down towards the enemy, try to maintain some sort of contact; he must not lose them again. There were three hundred of his fellow countrymen aboard *Altmark* and they were getting desperately close to a German prison camp. But he knew that when *Brandenburg* saw him she would open fire, so trailing her would mean a running battle. He was under no illusions as to *Cassandra*'s chances in any such long-drawn-out action.


Paul Brunner reported to Moehle on *Brandenburg*'s bridge as *Cassandra* was hidden by the blanketing squall, "That last hit aft has damaged steering and screw – "

Kurt Larsen broke in, "What about the prisoners?" And then quickly apologised to his captain as Brunner glared at the interruption.

Moehle grunted acknowledgment, but remembering that the prisoners taken from the *Orion* were confined aft, asked Brunner, "Are they all right?"

The Executive Officer nodded, "It shook them up a bit but none of them were hurt."

Kurt wondered about the lone girl among them. She had been the cause of his outburst. He wondered if she had been afraid but dared not ask. That question would bring others from Moehle and Brunner as to why he was concerned. Answering that could put both himself and the girl in danger. He feared for her.

Brunner went on, "Hessler says he will give us a full report as soon as he can, but it doesn't look good." Hessler was the Engineer Officer. "He can't give us better than fifteen knots and manoeuvring won't be easy."

Moehle swore and banged his fist softly on the bridge-screen, a demonstration of quietly cȯntrolled anger and frustration. "Very good," he acknowledged. He was silent a moment, then thinking aloud: "The captain of that cruiser will be looking for us; he has been all the time. He'll be running down to us now." He peered out into the darkness. Once again, he didn't want to risk a night action, nor any action at all while *Brandenburg* was thus crippled.

He grinned and gave his orders, told Brunner, "Make sure *Altmark* gets that, too. Speed fifteen."

He saw the dim blue flicker of the signal lamp passing the order to *Altmark* to follow as *Brandenburg* turned 180 degrees, away from the Norwegian coast and running back on her former course. He would take her circling around behind the British cruiser.


Appleby had found his corner again, backing into it as if guided by some protective instinct. As the shells fell around the ship he twitched and shook, hands to his ears and eyes screwed tight shut. He tried to go out onto the bridge but his legs would not obey him, shook under him so he thought he would fall were it not for the sheltering steel that hid him, held him up. This time he was not alone.


Dobson had not seen this fight from start to finish though he had been conscious all through this time. He saw nothing from his position in action, waiting as a member of the damage-control party in a passage below decks. But this time he heard the guns, *Cassandra*'s shaking the

40

bulkhead on which he leaned, and *Brandenburg*'s, the shells bursting in the sea and the impact on the hull like the beating on a big drum. He was aware of the sea close to him, only the thin steel plates between. He imagined them rupturing and the passage in which he stood flooding green in seconds.

The near-miss came like a hammer-blow that threw *Cassandra* aside and hurled Dobson across the passage as if he had been kicked by a giant boot. The others in his party sprawled around him but then bellowed orders jerked them to their feet and they surged back along the passage, answering the summons. Dobson went with them, running and bouncing from side to side of the passage as the deck shifted beneath his feet. But he followed them only as far as the ladder lifting to the deck above. He swerved away from them then, took the ladder on the run but did not go out onto the exposed deck. He huddled down behind a locker, head down between his knees, hands clasped over it, and stayed there, shuddering.

He had no thoughts of heroics or medals now. He was afraid and he only wanted to stay alive. Down there in the passage he could die an awful death. He knew his friends were still below, knew confusedly that he wanted to be with them, of them, but the fear held him captive in his sanctuary.

Now it was quiet on the bridge. There was tension still but with it a feeling of anticlimax. Smith felt it, faced the need for another decision and conjured up a mental picture of the chart. Then he told Harry Vincent, "Pilot! I want a course for Trondheim."

"Aye, aye, sir!"

*Brandenburg* and *Altmark* had eluded him again. Smith had to accept it after half an hour of searching with nerves strung tight at first but slowly easing as time went by without a sighting or the sudden shock of gun-fire. He had guessed wrongly. He had to be right this time. He still believed the enemy ships were bound for Norway. Trondheim would be the nearest landfall. So he would start from there and sweep southwards down the Norwegian coast.

John Galloway stood at his shoulder and Smith told him, "We'll stay closed up at action stations in case we run into them again. It would be a good idea if you could organise the galley to turn out some soup or sandwiches and have them taken to the guns."

Galloway answered, "I've got them working on it now, sir."

He would. Smith nodded approval. It was hard to fault the Executive Officer.

He saw young Appleby standing close up to the bridge-screen, his face a pale smudge in the darkness that itself darkened as Appleby became aware that Smith was watching him, and looked away.


There had been no firing for some time. Dobson uncoiled his lanky body from behind the locker, cautiously and looking to see that he was not observed. He heard the voices echoing below and realised the men of his party were returning to their post in the passage. He ran down the ladder but light-footed and quietly and was able to mingle with the other men as they streamed past the foot of the ladder. He took his first deep breath of relief and celebration of survival then, because no one had seen him.

He stood anonymous among them where they clustered in the passage, a lot of them talking all at once so he could listen and need not trust his voice. Here he would look as though he was one of them though he knew the truth was different. After a while he found himself relaxing, grinning at some of the jokes and once he laughed. It was then he saw Jackman standing a yard apart from the group. The Petty Officer's eyes were fixed on him, face expressionless.

Dobson looked away. Jackman had seen him, Jackman knew.


On the bridge Smith prayed that they would come up with *Altmark* the next day and that somehow he would be able to call for help. So long as *Brandenburg* stood in the way he could not get at the prison-ship. Besides having some three hundred captured seamen locked below her deck she also had Sarah, his daughter, aboard. Because it seemed all *Orion*'s crew and passengers had been taken off. Please God. *Brandenburg* had taken the dead from *Orion* and presumably given them burial at sea. He stared down at the cold dark sea alongside. If Sarah was not a prisoner then the alternative did not bear thinking about.

# 4

The tug sailed from Trondheim in the night. *Hauptsturm-führer* Gerhard Fritsch had chartered her, paying her captain well. Fritsch climbed down to her deck from the quay only minutes before she cast off, his greatcoat flapping about his skinny frame in the wind. Under it he wore the grey-green SS uniform and with one hand he held to his head the high-fronted cap with its death's-head badge. The Norwegian porter followed him aboard but only to hand Fritsch's valise to a member of the crew before scuttling ashore again, desperate to escape sailing in the tug with Fritsch. The porter was an instant judge of men and spat in the dirty water of the harbour as he left the tug.

Fritsch went below to the little saloon, stiflingly hot from the stove burning there. He stayed in the saloon as the tug got under way and ran down the fjord. When she met the open sea she began to lift and plunge. He scrambled up the ladders and out onto the deck and so into the wheelhouse to stand by the skipper at the wheel. Fritsch, was not seasick, only impatient. He would soon be at the rendezvous.

Fritsch was an officer of the Gestapo and it was work that suited him. He was a man of evil nature and in the last few months it had been honed, strengthened and expanded as he worked with the execution squads in Poland. So now he had a talent and a hunger for righteous cruelty "for the good of the State". Fritsch had tasted blood.

He was also a man of ambition, determined to rise in his chosen profession by whatever means came to hand. It had been his idea that *Altmark*'s prisoners should be combed for anyone who might provide a source of propaganda. If necessary he would make do with any British seaman who would go on radio to say that he had been well-treated by his captors, but he hoped for something better. A ship's captain prepared to condemn the Royal Navy for failing to protect him and rescue him from *Altmark*, that would be a catch. And he had come to Trondheim rather than wait for *Altmark* to dock in Germany because he had a shrewd idea that Goebbels, the propaganda minister, would have his people waiting for her there. Fritsch would report to his own master, Himmler, head of the SS, who would use any success to promote his own organisation in Hitler's eyes.

An hour before the dawn the tug was close to the limit of Norwegian territorial waters when her skipper grunted past the stubby pipe stuck in one corner of his mouth, "There they are." He pointed and Fritsch peered out at the heaving sea, for a moment saw nothing but then he made out the two distant, different shadows in the night and recognised them as ships.

*Kapitän-zur-See* Gustav Moehle had made his decision in the night, with *Brandenburg* crippled: "We'll stop inside Norwegian waters and transfer the prisoners taken from *Orion* to *Altmark*. Then she can potter home on her own and we'll go direct. One other thing: she made a signal not long ago that the prisoners she already has aboard are growing restless and her captain has asked for some men and an officer." He glanced at Kurt Larsen, "I want you to do it. Take half a dozen good men and a petty officer." That suited Kurt; he would have volunteered if not ordered.

So now he stood with three of his little party in the sternsheets of *Brandenburg*'s pinnace, crowded with the men from *Orion*, as it wallowed through the swell towards *Altmark*. The petty officer, Horstmann, stood in the bow with the other three men of the escort. All of the guards were watchful with rifles ready because the prisoners sitting or standing in the well between them, like those aboard *Altmark*, were restless, sullen and defiant. Any attempt on their part to take over the pinnace would be foolhardy but there might be a desperate soul or two among them.

Then there was the girl. She sat in the sternsheets by Kurt but they did not look at each other. There had been one startled exchange of glances when she had first come aboard *Brandenburg* but from then on they had ignored each other on the rare occasions when they met, she allowed on deck for exercise, he passing by.

Kurt had wondered uneasily more than once whether he should tell his captain – but what? He had paid court to the girl in Berlin before the war and had later come to suspect that she had been involved in the underground resistance to the Nazis. That was all it was, suspicion. But he did not want to point that finger at her in Hitler's Germany, for her sake and his. Mud of that sort could stick and he might be asked why he had not reported his suspicions before. But anyway, she was a prisoner now and the past was behind them. He had decided it would be safer for both of them if they acted as if they had only just met and that seemed to suit the girl. But he worried about her fate when she reached Germany.

She was blonde and blue-eyed, pretty, but there was more to her than that. Her head barely reached Kurt's shoulder and she was shapeless in the borrowed oilskin, her legs in their slacks showing below, but she had a lithe body that turned men's heads. Kurt had seen it happen. This was an attractive woman, sensual and sexual.

Sarah was glad to be out of *Brandenburg*, apprehensive about *Altmark* looming black in the night and worried about her reception in Germany. The *Gestapo* wanted

46

her. She had fled from them to Poland less than a year ago and they had murdered her mother and stepfather.

Kurt felt her shudder, glanced sidewise at her and muttered, "Are you all right?"

She was pale now but she nodded. She understood, though Kurt had spoken in German. She had lived in Berlin for fifteen years and spoke the language like a native. There was no point in pretending she did not. Kurt Larsen remembered her, as he would. They had spent a large part of that last summer before the war in each other's company. She had to trust him not to give her away, and did. At the same time she knew she could ask for no more. There was no question of asking him to help her to escape because he would not. He was fiercely patriotic and she was an enemy now.

The pinnace slid in alongside *Altmark*'s hull. Jacob's ladders dangled from the deck above and Kurt grabbed at one of them. He told Sarah, "You follow me up. I'll send a line down for your case." It stood by Sarah's knee and held everything she had been able to cram into it before hurriedly leaving *Orion* at gunpoint.

She saw him climb over the bulwark above her and seconds later a line snaked down the side of the ship to be caught by one of the guards. Sarah climbed the ladder but before she reached its head the case jerked upwards past her at the end of the line and was taken inboard. Then Kurt's hand was under her arm, half-lifting her over the bulwark and she stood on the deck of *Altmark*.

Kurt called, "Who is taking charge of these prisoners?" There were no lights showing except shaded torches held by some of *Altmark*'s crew. Kurt thought that, as they were in Norwegian waters then the two ships could have been lit up like Christmas trees. But they did not want to betray their presence to any searching British ship, particularly the cruiser that had dogged them for the last twenty-four hours. *And* they did not want the Norwegians to see any prisoners being transferred. They should have

47

been freed in neutral waters so this was a breach of the Geneva convention. Kurt did not like it but it was Moehle's decision – or was he under orders?

A voice answered out of the darkness, "I am taking the prisoners!"

Kurt found the owner of the voice and saw the prisoners from *Brandenburg* brought up from the pinnace then taken to the prison flats before the forward well. They were decks originally intended for stores and hastily converted with a few blankets and boxes, an empty oildrum for a lavatory. He had seen them before and shuddered at the thought of being locked down there for the best part of every day.

The girl had been given a cabin and as he led her aft to it, a seaman following with her case, he said quietly so only she could hear, "If I can help in any way, I will. You only have to ask." He saw a tug manoeuvring to come alongside. There was a man on her deck who appeared to be waiting to come aboard. Kurt wondered, A pilot?

Sarah said softly, "Thank you." They came to her cabin and he saw her locked in there, a sentry with a pistol on his belt standing outside. Then he went to report to *Altmark*'s captain.

Fritsch was given a large cabin on the upper deck. Two of *Altmark*'s officers had been turned out of it to squeeze in elsewhere. A folding table came down from the bulkhead and he sat behind this and read the list of the three hundred prisoners now held aboard *Altmark*. It was only faintly promising. There were more than two hundred seamen, engineers, stewards – including Indian sailors from SS *Huntsman* – and a number of officers but only three captains. Fritsch sent for them one by one and each captain in turn told him to go to hell.

Fritsch did not believe it with the first, persisted in his wheedling and threats but neither shook the stolid

48

ship's captain before him. He wasted less time over the other two. When the last had gone Fritsch cursed in exasperation. Had this entire trip been for nothing? He had been certain that one at least, and probably more, would have agreed to co-operate. Could he salvage something from the wreckage?

He bent over the list again. The final sheet carried the names of those prisoners taken from the *Orion* but he had already seen her captain. He turned over that last sheet and tossed the list aside. Then he saw that there was one more name on the reverse of that last sheet but it was headed: Passengers. Then came a solitary name: Sarah Smith.

No good.

He leaned back in his chair and his fingers drummed impatiently as he scowled at the list. It was useless. But . . . His fingers ceased their tapping and he picked up that last sheet again. Sarah Smith. The name reminded him of someone . . . For several seconds the connection eluded him but then he remembered. Could this be the same girl? It was not an uncommon name. Doubtless there were hundreds of women with the name "Sarah Smith".

He shuffled through the stacks of seamen's discharge books that had come with the list and found the British passport. The date of birth looked right. The passport had been issued when the girl was seventeen, two years before Fritsch first met her. The small photograph was that of a solemn schoolgirl. It could have been that of the young woman he had known but was flat and lifeless.

There was an easy way to find out.

He felt a rhythmic shudder start in the deckplates beneath his feet and heard the low beat of *Altmark*'s engines. She was under way.

Sarah sat slumped on the bunk in her cabin, for a moment despairing. She had only exchanged one prison for another. From the time of her capture by *Brandenburg*'s boarding-party she had hoped for rescue.

She knew the Royal Navy was sweeping the seas in search of *Altmark* and the cruiser. She was under no illusions about the risks she would run if they were caught and brought to action. There would be dead and wounded in any battle. But they were risks she was prepared to take rather than be carried back to Germany. Her hopes had risen when she twice heard distant gunfire and felt *Brandenburg* shake as she fired her salvoes, shudder when she was hit. The Navy had caught her! But then the fighting had ceased and Sarah was still a prisoner. Now she was aboard *Altmark* and nearer to Germany.

Remembering the fighting led to thoughts of her father. When she had left Montevideo aboard *Orion* he had just been made captain of *Cassandra* and was preparing to sail in her that same day. She was sure he would be involved in the search for the two raiders.

She looked around the cabin. It was smaller than the one she had been given aboard *Orion* but comfortable enough. She would not be in it long, only for the time it took *Altmark* to run down the Norwegian coast then across the Skagerrak and so to Germany. Three days?

She thought that the men battened down below in the forward hold were destined for a prisoner-of-war camp but that her fate might be different. She shivered, then remembered her father again. He would not have given up hope. Nor would she. Sarah sat straighter.

Kurt Larsen felt and heard the engines' throb as he stood on *Altmark*'s upper deck. The tug had long since steamed off into the night, headed for Trondheim. *Brandenburg*, his ship, was also under way, her gun-bristling silhouette merging into the darkness as her course and that of *Altmark* diverged. He would not see her again until he rejoined her in Germany. He watched until she was lost to sight then reluctantly turned to go below. He was proud of *Brandenburg* and of being one of her officers. He could feel no such emotion for this prison-ship. He had welcomed this duty only for the sake of the girl.

50

The seaman found him as he reached the door of his cabin: "Herr Fritsch wants to see the woman prisoner, sir"

Kurt asked, "Fritsch?"

"A Gestapo man come aboard from Trondheim to interrogate the prisoners."

The tug's passenger. Kurt thought, Fritsch? Surely not! He had known a Gestapo agent of that name in Berlin before the war, a nasty bit of work. Aloud he said, "Where is he?"

"I'll show you."

Minutes later Kurt tapped at the door of another cabin and pushed it open. He stood aside to let Sarah precede him and looking over her head saw the man in the chair behind the table and facing the door. The same one.

Kurt had warned Sarah but she was still shaken at sight of the narrow face behind the desk, the thin hair brushed flat from the knife-edge parting, the slitted eyes. She saw her passport on the desk in front of him. She had grown up in Berlin using her stepfather's name of Bauer for simplicity's sake. But when she was seventeen her mother had got her the passport in her own name, wanting her to keep her British nationality.

Fritsch looked at Sarah first and recognised her as the girl he had known as Sarah Bauer. He saw instant recognition and shock in her eyes, the colour drain from her face. He took a great breath of relief and triumph; this was the woman he wanted. Only then did he turn his gaze on the naval officer who had escorted the woman to this cabin and now stood with his back to the door. It was Fritsch's turn to be startled, but then he quickly recovered and smiled thinly, "Well, well."

Sarah stood before the desk but Kurt Larsen picked up a chair with either hand. He set one behind her and put his hand on her shoulder, gently seated her. Then he sat in the other chair beside her.

Fritsch watched this, saw the challenge in Kurt Larsen's

eyes but ignored it. He waited until they were seated then
said, "How extraordinary that we three should meet again
like this."

He thought that it was much better if these affairs
could be conducted in a civilised fashion. Besides, he
could not use the rough stuff aboard this ship. But he
was sure it would not be necessary, anyway. He leaned
back in his chair, eyes closed, recalling all the details and
thinking how he could use this gift that had dropped into
his lap.

He said dreamily, "We met in Berlin last summer. It was
not Sarah Smith but Fraülein Bauer then, your stepfather's
name. I introduced you to each other and privately advised
Herr Larsen that we in the Gestapo believed that you
were mixed up with enemies of the State. Later we
caught one of them and when we interrogated him in
*Prinz Albrecht Strasse* he told us a great deal." He was
talking of Gestapo headquarters. "He gave us a number
of names and one of them was yours. We looked for
you in the house of your mother and stepfather but
you had left Germany for Poland only a few hours
before."

Sarah whispered, "You murdered them." Kurt saw she
was white-faced.

Fritsch murmured, "There was a fire."

"My mother and Ulrich Bauer were in there!"

"So I understand. But it was an accident."

Sarah said, her throat tight, the words choked out of
her, "You bastard!" Kurt laid his hand on her arm, a
warning gesture; she was a prisoner and once ashore
in Germany Fritsch could claim her. Sarah shrugged
free.

Fritsch's thin lips had tightened but his eyes stayed
closed as he went on, "So it seemed we had lost you
but we kept digging." He smiled at Sarah, showing big
yellow teeth. "We dug up quite a lot of history. For
example, that your mother obtained a divorce from your

52

father and that he is an officer, a captain, in the Royal Navy."

"What about it?"

Fritsch was not going to elaborate on that at this time. He changed his tack: "Another of the names your young friend gave us was that of a Frau Rösing. I understand you were quite close, old friends from schooldays. You got away but she didn't. Her husband was shot while attempting to escape arrest but he had carelessly made her pregnant not long before." He paused.

Sarah demanded, "What have you done to her?"

Fritsch spread his hands to show them empty. "Nothing. She is in a camp of course: *Sachsenhausen*." Sarah knew it: a concentration camp. Fritsch raised his hands and laced the fingers together behind his head. He smiled at Sarah again and it sent a shudder through her. Fritsch saw it, savoured it and said softly, "You know, I think we are going to be friends." He saw her stiffen in the chair and her head go up, her lips tighten. He thought, She will be stubborn but she will co-operate. If not here, then in *Prinz Albrecht Strasse*.

The dawn had broken when Kurt finally escorted Sarah from the cabin and led her towards her own. Her feet dragged and twice she stumbled and he had to take her arm. The sun was hidden still behind the overcast of low cloud and *Altmark* butted southward through a lumpy grey sea. The coast of Norway lifted a scant mile to port, snow-covered but the white splashed here and there with the brown and green patches of forest.

Kurt asked sombrely, "Will you agree to do it?"

"He knows I will," Sarah said bitterly, "I have no choice."

Kurt was silent for a pace or two. He was a patriot and a regular officer in a proud service. He regarded the SS as another but he was uneasy about part of it – the *Gestapo*. And he had known Fristch of old in Berlin, knew he was evil. He had known this girl, too, was still fond of her

53

though her country was at war with his. He said, "I must warn you. If you think to agree and then renege, they will be – cruel."

"I know the kind of torture they inflicted on the man who betrayed me, and the others, and I don't blame him for breaking. I know what they may do to me."

"They disgust me." His voice was thick with revulsion; he felt physically sick.

A lookout bawled on the bridge, "Ship starboard beam!"

They both paused and turned to look out across the grey sea to where it met the clouds in a blurred horizon. Kurt said, "It looks like the British cruiser that's followed us since the night before last."

Sarah stared out at the distant ship. It stirred no feelings of hope. She knew very well that *Altmark* was inside Norwegian territorial waters and so out of reach of any pursuit. She turned away and Kurt Larsen took her to her cabin and locked her in.


The officers and men of *Cassandra* had stood to for dawn action stations but now the day had come and Galloway said, "That's *Altmark*, sir."

"Yes." Smith slowly turned, glasses moving from the prison-ship to sweep the horizon all round that port side. He stood on the port wing of the bridge with a little group of officers, all of them searching now as he was.

Kelso crossed from the starboard wing with his rolling walk and reported, "Nothing in sight to seaward. Looks as though *Brandenburg* has gone home." He sounded, if not cheerful, then relieved. He peered out at the distant, mountainous coast beyond *Altmark*. "I spent a month's leave in Norway. Summer of '37. Had a damn good time sailing and I met a cracking girl. Tried my Norwegian on

54

the people in the bars. That was Oslo, though. The year before that I had two weeks in Hamburg when my ship was in there. Had a few runs ashore. Now I could tell you a few things about – "

Smith lowered the glasses and shot a glance at Ben that shut him up. But Harry Vincent did not see that glance and said, "*Altmark* is tucked away inside Norwegian waters where we can't get at her and doubtless she'll stay inside them all the way to the Skagerrak."

Smith rasped, "We're all capable of working that out, Pilot!"

Harry shut his mouth and swallowed. The group became quiet. Smith was unaware of the reaction, preoccupied. *Altmark*, her holds crammed with British prisoners, had got away from him. It might be that his daughter was among those prisoners. Strictly *Altmark* could not carry them through neutral waters but if the Norwegians challenged her, asked if she carried prisoners, then her captain would deny it. Smith was certain of that. And if he was reckless enough to follow her out of Norwegian waters into the Skagerrak, Germany's backyard, there would be more than just *Brandenburg* to deny him.

He went over the events of the last two days in his mind but did not see what else he could have done. *Brandenburg* had been the stumbling-block, she and the stroke of bitter luck that had wrecked *Cassandra*'s remaining wireless office and thus her communications with Admiralty and other ships. Momentarily he wondered, had there been an obvious, better course of action and had he been too long "on the beach" to see it? Then he told himself not to be a bloody fool. What was he to do *now*?

He ordered curtly, "Starboard ten!" He heard that passed by Kelso and told Vincent, "I want a course and speed to take us down the coast but out of sight of her." He nodded bad-temperedly towards *Altmark* as *Cassandra*'s head came round.

Buckley, misjudging his captain's mood for once, came to him with the steaming mug and said, "Coffee, sir."

"No!" Smith snapped at him. Buckley looked down at the coffee then sniffed, walked away – but left the mug on the shelf below the bridge-screen and in front of Smith's tall chair. He retired to the back of the bridge just in time to avoid Smith as he came striding rapidly across the bridge to pivot on his heel on the starboard wing and then retrace his steps. The other officers quickly got out of his way. *Cassandra* thrashed out to sea and then turned again when *Altmark* had slipped below the horizon. The two ships were now out of sight of each other. The routine work of the ship went on and she ploughed steadily southward as Smith paced back and forth across the bridge.

Buckley watched him for a time then went below and scrounged a mug of tea from the galley. The cook who gave it to him said, "The buzz is that we've lost her, then."

Buckley sipped at the tea. "I wouldn't bet on it."

"Why? What d'ye think your bloke will do?"

"Don't know. But he's thinking about it."

But he returned to the back of the bridge and stood there an hour before Smith suddenly halted in his pacing and stared sightlessly out to sea. Buckley nodded to himself, recognising the signs. A moment later Smith called, "Pass the word for Mr Kelso." And when Ben Kelso came panting to the bridge, "How much Norwegian did you learn while you were in Oslo?"

Kelso blinked at him. "Well, I learned a fair bit before I went there and I took a phrase book. I got along." Then he scented danger and hedged, "I'm not fluent, you understand – "

"Still got the book? Is it aboard?"

"I've got it somewhere, but – "

"Good. What about your German?"

"Just a few words. I only got ashore half a dozen times so I didn't get time to – "

56

"We'll have to manage." Smith left Ben open-mouthed and turned to Galloway, "Let's see that chart. And bring a pad." In the chart-room with Galloway, Kelso and Vincent he bent over the chart, measuring and calculating, then tapped it with his finger. "There!" And then he gave his orders.

Jackman stood on the mess deck with notebook and pencil in big, stubby-fingered hands. He said, "I'm looking for volunteers. Harrigan, you'll do for a start. Bennett, Nisbet . . ." He wrote down the names as he picked them out, glinting black eyes under the black brows scanning their curious, wary faces, ignoring the calls of: "What's it for?" All in good time. They would find out soon enough. His eyes rested on Dobson for only the time it took to blink, then moved on. Dobson's name did not go in the book. He knew why and could not look at the others.

Smith sat in his chair and saw the fresh mug of coffee Buckley had brought, unseen, only a minute before while Smith was in the chart-room. The old, cold one was also still there. Was Buckley making a silent point about foul-tempered captains? Smith grinned.

Galloway returned to the bridge after passing on Smith's orders. He saw that grin, as did Kelso, who muttered, "He's in a little better temper now."

Galloway looked at his captain with a new respect. "There's nothing wrong with his nerve."

Kelso muttered again, "I'll grant you that. But what about his sanity? This caper . . ."

# 5

Smith strapped the holstered Colt .45 pistol around his middle then shrugged into his oilskin as Buckley held it for him. A swell was still running and *Cassandra* lurched so they staggered together like some couple in a clumsy dance, cannoning off the desk and the side of the bunk. The sea cabin was crowded with the pair of them in there. Smith cursed but mildly, absent-mindedly, his thoughts already running ahead.

Buckley grumbled for the third time, "I don't think you should go yourself, sir"

"Mind your own damn business," Smith told him absently.

Buckley sighed with mingled patience and exasperation, and gave up. "The motor boat is ready, sir. Paint's still a bit tacky in places but she'll do."

Smith merely grunted acknowledgment. He jammed on his head a cap without cover or badge and shoved out of the cabin into the night. He waited then for a few minutes, peering out at the heaving, black sea under a starless sky, until his eyes became more accustomed to the darkness.

*Cassandra* had closed the coast again and was on the edge of Norwegian territorial waters but he could not make out the loom of the land in the night. He could see dimly the red and green navigation lights of some craft inshore and to the south, heading northward on a course for Trondheim. There was nothing in sight to the north. He reminded himself that there was still ample time, that *Altmark* would only be making the ten or twelve knots she was showing when last seen. The weather had still not wholly relented, his ship rolling under him as she lay hove to, a spit of rain sweeping over her on a bitterly cold wind. He thought it was a fine night for what he had to do.

He dropped down the ladder, Buckley trailing him, and strode rapidly aft. *Cassandra*'s deck was crowded. There were parties of men carrying rifles by three of her boats, other men lined up and gripping the falls of the boats, waiting to lower them. The men watched him as he passed, silent and curious. Kelso and Chivers waited with Galloway on the starboard side by one of the two motor launches carried by *Cassandra*. Behind them was ranked a party of seamen, swaying to the motion of the ship.

The two lieutenants were talking with Galloway, their heads turned to watch for Smith, voices lowered so the men would not hear. Galloway said, "I can't fault his handling of the ship in those two actions. He's hung on to *Altmark*. *Brandenburg* could have eaten us alive but she didn't."

Kelso, bulky in oilskins, carried a megaphone and wore a cap like that of Smith: without cover or badge. He muttered impatiently, "All right, he's better than we expected. But this! It could wind up as an international incident! *If* it works, and it's a bloody big 'if'. I know a bit of Norwegian but I'm not fluent or anything like it."

Galloway put in, "You don't have to be. You won't be trying to fool Norwegians."

Kelso would not be comforted and warned Galloway, "If this blows up in our faces he'll wind up on the beach again and this time for good. And he might not be the only one!"

But then Chivers saw Smith approaching and said crisply, "Shut up!"

\*     \*     \*

Galloway reported, "All ready, sir." Smith scanned the seamen ranked by the first motor launch and saw that each of the twenty men had a white armband and a rifle slung over his shoulder as Smith had ordered. The white armbands were for identification in the night. He had told the men earlier, "I don't want you shooting each other."

He moved on to the second motor launch on the port side and then to one of the cutters. He inspected the men drawn up by each of them as he had those manning the first launch. Then he returned to that first one on the starboard side. He put a finger to the fresh paint on the launch and found it tacky but he agreed with Buckley: it would serve. He ordered, "Lower away!" The men at the falls let them run out hand over hand and the boats dropped down to the sea. The armed parties started to climb down the scrambling nets and into the boats.

Smith cocked an eye at Kelso, "And you?"

"Ready as I'll ever be. As I told you, sir, my knowledge of the language is limited – "

Smith cut him off: "But it's more than anyone else can boast. Besides – " he grinned at Kelso " – I believe you always doubted the existence of *Altmark*. Now you'll be able to satisfy yourself that it's really her."

Kelso said glumly, "Sir." And went down into the launch.

Smith told Galloway, "When we've got her you'll see our signal. Come in to us then."

"Aye, aye, sir. And good luck." Galloway watched as Smith followed Kelso.

Smith knew Galloway was still worried about this operation. He had objected earlier in the day, "It's a hell of a risk, sir, mounting an operation of this kind in neutral waters." He meant that Smith was putting his career on the line, and that was an understatement.

Smith had told him, "*Altmark* is an enemy ship and she's carrying British seamen she should have released

60

as soon as she entered Norwegian waters. She's already in breach of international law."

Galloway had argued, "She may have transferred all her prisoners to some other ship for all we know."

Smith had shaken his head, "I don't believe she has and I can't give her the benefit of the doubt and let her go back to Germany with our men aboard. That's a risk I won't take."

Now Smith found Buckley already in the sternsheets of the launch with Kelso. The second launch, with Chivers in command and towing the cutter, came up astern. Both were filled with armed men; there were just over sixty of them in the three boats. Smith tucked the tiller under his arm and the line of boats curved away from *Cassandra*'s steel side. Galloway saw them become furred outlines and then merge into the rain and the night.

Smith was out to free the prisoners from *Altmark*.


"Ship right ahead and running down on us, sir!" That call came from a keen-eyed lookout in the bow, uttered softly but carried back on the wind to Smith in the stern. He shoved up to his feet and stood, balancing against the roll and pitch of the motor launch. He blinked away the rain and the spray that flew inboard from seas breaking at the bow and saw the lights of the ship coming down from the north. The launch was heading to meet it. Both ship and boat were within a mile, or two at most, of the coast.

Kelso asked, "Do you think that's her, sir?" He sat beside Smith in the sternsheets, oilskins around him like a tent and the megaphone clutched on his knees. But most of the men carried aboard the launch were hidden in the cabin and only half a dozen showed as crew.

Smith nodded. They would know for certain soon enough. He looked astern at the other lights coming up from the south that he had seen when standing on

*Cassandra*'s bridge. He judged them to be better than a mile astern of him now and belonging to a small craft, probably not much bigger than the launch. A fisherman? That seemed likely. And unlikely that it would interfere or affect this operation. His eyes came down to the boats following him, Chivers' launch with the cutter in tow. They, too, were taking a lot of water inboard but the conditions were good enough.

He borrowed Kelso's megaphone to hail: "Wait!" He saw the white bow-wave fall away from the stem of that other launch as Chivers threw out the clutch. It lay with engine idling, the cutter drifting astern, as Smith in his launch pulled away. Chivers knew what to do and would wait there for Smith's signal.

The ship ahead was closing quickly now, the gap between ship and boat narrowing at their combined speeds. Kelso shifted in his seat and there was a general restless stirring among the men in the boat, a tensing for action. Smith called, "Be still! But check your weapons, make sure safety catches are on. No one moves or fires unless I give the word. Hear that, Jackman?"

"Aye, aye, sir!" He was the petty officer in charge of this party and answered from his post at the entrance to the cabin, his face a pale mask in the darkness. From there he could see the men inside the cabin and out of it, could be relied upon to see Smith's orders carried out.

The ship was lifting close now, could be seen and not just in outline but as a three-dimensional hull, black in the night and with a white bone of a bow-wave in her teeth as the ten thousand tons of her drove down on the little launch at twelve knots. There was the bridge structure forward and then further aft the main superstructure where the boats hung in their davits.

Kelso said hoarsely, "That's her!"

It was *Altmark*. Smith took a breath. Now for it. He ordered, "Signal her!"

62

The signalman in the well of the launch lifted the Aldis lamp and worked the trigger, sending in flickering morse a U and an L, the international signals for "You are standing into danger" and "Stop". A lamp blinked acknowledgment from *Altmark*'s bridge and then seconds dragged by until the bow-wave subsided. But her screws still churned slowly giving her bare steerage way, she still slid down on the launch.

*Altmark*'s bow was passing the launch now and Smith eased over the tiller so he came around in a hairpin turn. He ran level with her but quickly closing her side and just below her bridge. There was a man out on the wing, leaning over to peer at the boat bouncing in *Altmark*'s bow-wave and close alongside.

Smith ordered, "Hail him!"

Kelso stood up, cleared his throat and lifted the megaphone. He bawled the message he'd carefully prepared in his laboured Norwegian, "*Altmark*! Stop! Mines ahead! You must take a pilot!"

It would be no surprise to *Altmark*'s captain that there was a freshly-sown field of mines on this coast; there were others, also needing the services of a pilot. Smith and Kelso wore plain uniform caps such as pilots might wear, while on the upperworks of the launch and the roof of the cabin was painted, and still drying, a Norwegian flag. Would it work? Smith held his breath.

The man up on the wing shouted down to them and Kelso groaned, "Oh, hell! He says he doesn't understand Norwegian."

Smith snapped, "Tell him you speak little German!"

Kelso muttered, "That's a fact!"

"And get over the message of mines!"

Kelso tried again, his stretched nerves raising the pitch of his voice as he shrieked his warning. Possibly that apprehension came over to the man on the bridge, or it may have been Kelso's gestures as he wailed,

"*Minen!*" He pointed ahead and threw up his arms, "*Boom!*"

The man on the bridge wing shouted back unintelligibly then disappeared. Kelso blew out his cheeks and said weakly, "I think he's got it."

Smith said, "Well done." *Altmark* was slowing further still, her screws had stopped and just the last of the way on her was shoving her through the water. More men showed on her deck below the bridge, lifting some heavy bundle onto the bulwark, throwing it over. It unrolled as a Jacob's ladder dangling down the side, its foot trailing in the sea.

Smith eased the tiller over again. The launch's engine died and she slid in towards the ladder. "Signal Mr Chivers!" The Aldis flashed again, briefly, and that would bring the second launch and the cutter down on *Altmark*. The sooner the better. *Altmark* would have a crew of a hundred or more. Smith and the score of men with him could only hope to gain a foothold by surprise and hang on for a few minutes until the reinforcements arrived. But it could be done. He had stopped *Altmark* and the crucial element of surprise was almost within his grasp.

Kelso waited to take the tiller. Smith unfastened his oilskin, ready to throw it off. Then he would be able to get at the big Colt .45 and it would be easier for him to climb. He was going to be first up the ladder. Jackman and the boarding-party in his launch would follow him, then Chivers and his two boatloads of men as soon as they could get alongside. In minutes the ship would be his.

Kelso said, "Jesus!" A flame licked up over the sea to the south and a second later there came the muffled *thud!* of an explosion. Smith saw the flame had its source in the fore part of a fishing boat, a craft little bigger than the launch with a wheelhouse and mast set aft. She seemed to be carrying some sort of cargo stacked on her deck and now the yellow flame from the front of this was broadening at the base, lengthening as the wind blew the flame back towards the rest of the cargo, leaping higher.

This he only glimpsed from the corner of his eye, intent on taking the boat in to the foot of the ladder. But he was aware that the fire out there was bright enough to shed light this far and it was casting shadows of the boat against *Altmark*'s black side. Worse! It had lit up the launch and cutter that had been lying off and now were heading towards *Altmark* in response to his signal. They were between *Altmark* and the fishing boat and could be seen against the light cast by the fire, packed with men, and the rifle muzzles poking up above some of them were only too obvious. They were unmistakeably naval boats with armed parties aboard.

Kurt Larsen woke when *Altmark*'s engines stopped. He jammed his feet into boots, grabbed his oilskins and ran out on deck. He saw the knot of seamen below the bridge, lowering the Jacob's ladder, and heard their explanation: "It's the pilot coming aboard, *Herr Oberleutnant*." He leaned over the bulwark and saw the launch in its Norwegian colours sliding in towards the ladder. Then he raised his head as the *thud*! of the explosion came flatly over the black sea. He saw the leap of flame and its spread – then a launch and cutter silhouetted against its light.

He shouted, "*Tommis!*" Then bawled it again up at the bridge, "*Tommis!*" He heard an answering yell from up there then the clang of the engine-room telegraph being put over; they were starting the engines again. The seamen around him gaped, then tried to haul in the ladder but failed. A man in the launch below was holding it fast.

Kurt spun on his heel and saw on the bulkhead behind him a fire-hose, an extinguisher and an axe. He pulled the axe free from its clips and turned to the ladder. The blade gleamed in the firelight as he lifted it above his head, then he brought it down on the rope of the ladder where it was stretched taut over the bulwark.

Smith swore at the firelight but then the launch ran in and banged against *Altmark*'s black side, ground along it. Jackman seized the ladder and Smith threw off his oilskin and plunged towards it as Kelso grabbed the tiller. That was the signal for two ratings to shake out a big white ensign and spread it over the Norwegian colours on the launch. There came a yell from the deck of the ship above and Jackman was suddenly straining to hold the ladder as the men up there tried to haul it in: Smith saw one of them pointing; they had seen Chivers' two boats. Jackman shook his head and growled at Smith through clenched teeth, "No good, sir!"

There was the glitter of steel above the bulwark and Smith saw it was the blade of an axe, heard the *chunk*! as it severed one of the two side-ropes of the ladder so it sagged lopsidedly. The axe flashed again and cut the second rope. The ladder collapsed, falling onto and over the launch, wooden rungs clattering, men cursing as the rungs struck them. *Altmark*'s screws were turning again and she surged ahead as the launch veered away from her side.

Smith watched her draw away then turned and went back to take the tiller. He followed *Altmark* south but diverged from her course at an angle to make for Chivers and the fishing boat, now dead in the water and ablaze from bow to stern.

Kelso said, "Sorry, sir."

"Not your fault," Smith told him. "You did very well."

"But of all the *bloody* luck! For that boat to catch fire just at the moment when – "

"All right." Smith broke in, silencing him. There was no sense in wasting time bemoaning lost opportunities. "Use that loudhailer of yours again. Tell Chivers I'm going to look for survivors and he is to follow us."

They were passing the second launch and the cutter now and Kelso bawled that message, voice echoing tinny from the megaphone. Chivers' answering hail came: "Aye, aye!" The fishing boat was only a cable's length ahead now and its towering flames lit the launch bright as noonday. Smith felt the heat from the fire scorching his face. He ordered Jackman, "Get the men out of that cabin and tell them to look out for survivors." He thought bitterly that there was no point in them hiding now because *Altmark* was gone. As he glanced quickly that way he saw her blending into the darkness outside of the ring of light shed by the flames. Kelso had been right: *bloody* luck!

The sea was on fire now, a growing pool of flame spreading out from the bow of the stricken fishing boat. The men lining the sides of the launch were holding their arms up to shield their faces from scorching. Smith altered course to swing around the outside of the pool and come no closer to the source of that blistering heat. As the launch passed down the side of the fishing boat he saw the fire on the surface of the water was edging aft but had not yet reached the stern. The after part of the boat itself, however, wheelhouse and mast, was a pyre with flames soaring higher than a house. And there was the blazing frame of what had been a small dinghy hanging from davits over the stern.

Smith shouted, "Look out for heads in the water!" No one could have survived aboard the fishing boat nor in the lake of flames rapidly surrounding her. The dinghy had not been launched so if anyone had got off her alive he would be swimming in that narrowing neck of sea right astern and between the closing wings of fire. He would not be swimming long. Smith turned the bow of the launch into that smoke-wreathed neck.

It was like entering an oven. The heat seared them all aboard the launch, had them gasping for breath in that airless tunnel running into the fire. The smoke caught at their lungs and set them coughing and the roar of the flames deafened them. So the call when it came back to Smith was choked and passed from man to man back along the length of the boat: "Swimmers off the starboard bow!" Smith saw the man standing in the bow, one arm lifted to shield his face from the heat, the other outstretched, pointing.

Smith saw them and turned the launch. As it closed the swimmers he saw they were a group of three. One of them held on to something in the water to support himself – an oar? The other two were shoving at either end of it. The launch ran in alongside them, engine idling, and arms reached down to grab them and haul them out of the sea and inboard, starting with the man holding on to the oar. Smith quickly glanced around him and didn't like what he saw.

Kelso shouted above the crackling din of the fire, "It's closing fast, sir!"

Smith nodded. His way out was closing too fast. The burning sea had now locked around the stern of the fishing boat and was spreading still. The walls of flame towering on either side of him were sliding in on the surface of the sea. The gateway between them and behind him was pinching in rapidly, would soon be gone. They had to get out and soon. In the last seconds the heat had intensified beyond what he had already thought insupportable. His face and hands burned, his eyes streamed tears that dried on the lids. But the three men were now aboard and another gasped message came back to him as the engine's beat quickened again: "No more! That's the whole crew!"

Smith gave thanks for that. He shied away from the

thought of leaving men to die in this hell but a further search would have put them all at risk. They might already have left it too late. He turned the launch tightly but even so she went closer still to the fire as she made that turn. The men had turned their backs to it and tried to protect hands and faces. The three survivors lay in the bottom of the boat, exhausted. The paint, both fresh and old, was blistering and peeling from the launch's upperworks. In places the timbers smouldered and Buckley had got out a bailer, was dipping water from alongside to douse them. Jackman set other men to do the same.

Then the launch straightened out from the turn and her stern dug in as the engine went full ahead. The way out of the flame-locked pocket was frighteningly narrow now. The walls of flame reached out for them in the boat and the heat gripped and tormented them for interminable seconds longer, sucking the air from their lungs, roasting them so they swayed and fell. Only Smith stayed upright, the tiller under his arm. Then they were out of it.

Buckley dragged himself up from the bottom of the boat and croaked at Smith, "Are you all right, sir?" Smith nodded. Kelso was clambering up to drop heavily into his seat again, gasping. The prostrate bodies littering the boat stirred and rose. They leaned over the side to lave their faces with cupped handfuls of seawater. Until Jackman called huskily, "Come on you lot, you've had your time – get inboard."

They turned into the boat and he went to the survivors still lying on the bottom. Some of the men who had posed as crew on the foredeck of the launch stripped off the oilskins they wore and handed them to Jackman. He wrapped one around each of the survivors as he persuaded them to sit up. Seamen took two of them into the cabin but the third staggered aft to slump in the sternsheets beside Smith.

Chivers, with the cutter in tow, was close now and Smith eased over the tiller to fall into station ahead of them. Then he looked at the man beside him, lit clearly by the flames from the fishing boat still blazing a cable's length away and burned down to the waterline. He was tall and broad in the heavy clothing he wore, thick woollen jersey and trousers, that would have drowned him soon if he had not been pulled out of the sea. He had a full beard and his hair was grown long so it reached down to cover his collar. Both hair and beard dripped salt water. He studied the men in the boat and looked past Smith to the other launch and cutter astern. He obviously heard the orders barked by Jackman and the talk of the men as they tended the other two survivors, because when he spoke it was in English: "You are the captain?"

"I am. David Smith. And you?"

"I am captain also. Per Kosskull." He held out his hand.

Smith shook it. "You were unfortunate. That was petrol?" He jerked his head in the direction of the fishing boat.

"Petrol, ya." Kosskull nodded. "I was paid for bring this cargo from Bergen, better than for fish. I was going for my – " he searched for the phrase, then remembered "– home port, ya? Trondheim. Then there is the fire. Why? I don't know, but I think one man, he smoke. Damn fool." He threw up his hands. "But burn very quick. We try to get out boat but no time. Too hot, so we jump in the sea. Very happy when I see your boat." He patted Smith's arm.

"Pleased to be able to help." Smith thought he would have been better pleased if Per Kosskull's boat had not wrecked a carefully planned operation when it was on the brink of success. But he commiserated, "I'm sorry you lost your boat."

Kosskull shrugged, "It was – insured – you understand? And I have another in Trondheim, motor boat like this but not so big. So I can fish still."

Smith said, "I understand. Your English is good."

"I was seaman ten years. Many times in English ships.

70

I know English ports. And Royal Navy. I have seen many times." He went on, not looking at Smith, "Before the fire I saw you alongside a ship. I think maybe it was a German ship with iron ore from Narvik. And now these – " he cocked a thumb at the armed men in the launch and then in the boats astern " – with rifles. I think maybe my fire spoiled something for you."

Smith heard Kelso seated on his other side mutter under his breath, "Too bloody true!"

Kosskull said, "This is sea of my country." He stopped and groped for the right word but only came up with: "Place for no fighting."

Smith supplied the word for him: "Neutral." Kosskull was no fool. Unfortunately. He knew very well that Smith and his men had attempted some action against *Altmark* in Norwegian waters, were still in those waters. It looked as though diplomatic cables concerning violation of neutrality would soon be flying between Oslo and London.

Ben Kelso muttered again, "Throw the bugger back over the side!"

But now Per Kosskull ran his hand along the blistered and peeling upperworks of the launch and turned to face Smith. "You came into the fire to get us. We will say nothing."


The signal was flashed to *Cassandra* somewhere out in the night and there came an answering wink of light. Smith pointed the bow of the launch towards it and headed out to sea. Some minutes later his ship lifted out of the darkness, at first a bare shadow without even the white blaze of a bow wave to mark her as she lay hove to. But then the shadow hardened, grew as they closed it, overhung them as the boats ran in alongside, rose and fell against the grey and rusting steel.

Smith climbed up the waiting ladder and was met by a relieved Galloway. He gave the Executive Officer a brief account of the night's failure – because that was how he saw it – as the survivors were hauled up one by one on a line and then taken below to the sick bay, the boats were hoisted inboard.

Galloway said, "You had rotten luck, sir."

Smith did not answer that but said, "We'll try again tomorrow." Another way. There had to be another way. "We haven't much time."

Galloway said without enthusiasm, "*Altmark* can't stay in Norwegian waters forever, sir."

"She can until she's in the Skagerrak. Then it will be too late."

"You think Jerry will come out to protect her, sir?"

"He will. And he doesn't have to use ships; U-boats will do. And there'll be air cover from bases in Germany."

Galloway said doubtfully, drawing the word out, "Ye . . . es."

Smith eyed him. "You don't consider that a threat?"

Galloway shrugged, "The U-boats, yes, but aircraft? In theory, I know, they pose a threat, but it's one thing practice-bombing an anchored wreck as a target. Hitting a manoeuvring ship that fires back is something else."

Smith recalled the bombing he had seen in Spain in the Civil War, the reports of the dive-bombing in Poland. He said harshly, "Not theory, John. In those waters without our own air cover we'd be a dead duck!" But he saw Galloway was not convinced.

He called together the men of the intended boarding-parties from the launches and cutter. He scanned the dark mass of them in the night and told them, "It didn't work but that wasn't your fault. You all did well." He thought that might make them feel a little better after the bitter disappointment of this night. But then an anonymous voice said, "You did pretty well yourself, sir." And that brought laughter and a grumble of agreement.

It heartened him. But his plan had failed. They had not rescued the prisoners from the *Altmark*. When he got to his sea cabin his hands started to shake in his usual reaction. He dragged off the oilskin and with fumbling fingers unbuckled the Colt .45 from around his waist. As he fell onto his bunk he thought, Tomorrow . . . Then he lifted his wrist, peered at the luminous dial of his watch and saw it was past midnight . . . Today I'll try again. Another way . . .

And as sleep claimed him: "Sarah . . ."

# 6

"It's like a scene from a Christmas card," Ben Kelso
murmured it softly.

It was two nights after the failed attempt to board
*Altmark* and Smith sat again in the sternsheets of the
motor launch. On either hand lifted snow-covered hills,
dull silver in the moonlight. This was the Jössingfjord,
near the southernmost point of Norway. The black boxes
of houses were scattered here and there across the slopes,
each marked by the yellow squares of lit windows. Smith
thought Kelso's description was apt, but the peace of the
Jössingfjord had not long to live.

He had not had another chance to act against *Altmark*.
On the morning after he had tried to capture her he
had met a Danish coaster bound for Trondheim and
transferred Per Kosskull and his two-man crew to her.
He also found a Norwegian patrol-boat cruising to seaward
of *Altmark*, escorting her. All he could do was follow and
wait on opportunity. That came when Philip Vian arrived
this day, with his 4th Destroyer Flotilla and the cruiser
*Arethusa*, hunting for *Altmark*.

Vian, as Captain (D) commanding the flotilla, was in
the destroyer *Cossack*. He was in wireless contact with
Admiralty and Smith had reported *Cassandra*'s damaged
wireless and her presence.

He put himself under Vian's command. *Altmark* had
turned away at the sight of the destroyers and run into
the Jössingfjord. Churchill was at the Admiralty now and
at his order Vian was going to root her out.

74

"She's a beauty." Kelso said it admiringly. He sat beside Smith and was there again in case his meagre knowledge of German and Norwegian were needed. He was talking of *Cossack*, leading the way now, two cables' lengths ahead of the motor launch and on the port bow.

"She is." Smith nodded ready agreement. He could see her plainly in the light reflected from the snow. Set against that background, long, low and slender, slipping quietly through the ice-dotted waters of the fjord, she presented a picture in herself. He thought she was a lovely ship, but he would not exchange her for *Cassandra*.

The Norwegian patrol-boats, there were two of them now, had refused to accompany Vian and tried to oppose his entering the fjord, but he had persuaded them that honour would be satisfied if they yielded to superior force. Now they lay astern at the entrance to the fjord. *Altmark* was hidden somewhere ahead.

*Cossack* had an armed boarding-party of thirty men and three officers marshalled ready on her fo'c'sle. Smith carried in the launch the same twenty men he had taken two nights before under Jackman. They were tensed ready for action. He had told them before they went down into the boat, his voice harsh and urgent, "We're going to bring out three hundred of our own, British seamen. This time nothing will stop us! Nothing!" And they knew this was not bragging nor bravado, understood the warning that lay behind the words. He and they would carry out the rescue even if few of them survived. And they found they were with him, would follow him.

Buckley was there, of course. He had tried again to persuade Smith to stay aboard *Cassandra* and let Kelso or some other junior officer command the launch, and he had failed again. So he had grumbled and come along without orders. As he would have climbed into the boat with Smith even if ordered to stay aboard *Cassandra* himself. Smith grinned, feeling his face muscles numb with the cold.

Kelso saw that grin and wondered, What the hell is so

75

funny now? They could come under fire from *Altmark* at any moment. She had not used her rumoured 6-inch guns so far and that suggested the rumours were no more than that and she probably did not have any. Probably. But not certainly. Kelso thought, If she's saved them for now and she's waiting with them ready around the next corner . . .

The fjord bent ahead of them and *Cossack* was starting into the turn now. Smith eased over the tiller and the bow of the launch came around, the next reach of the fjord slowly opening before them.

The lookout right in the bow said quickly, "Christ! There she is!" And a fraction of a second later she came into Smith's view. He saw her a piece at a time as if the headland he was rounding was a curtain being drawn back. First the stern and the after superstructure were there, with the boats in their davits and the big single funnel, then the long well before the bridge superstructure lifted. Forward of that was another well and then the fo'c'sle. Now he saw her whole. She lay bows on to the shore and loomed huge in comparison with *Cossack*. Her grey hull stood stark black in the night against the snow slopes of the hills and the ice that locked her in on both sides. The channel she had smashed for herself through the ice was a ragged scar of white-seamed water like black marble.

A searchlight's beam lanced out from her, bathing *Cossack*'s bridge with light, meant to dazzle and blind Vian and the helmsman, the other men there. And *Altmark* came astern. Kelso yelled, "She's trying to ram *Cossack*!" That was obvious. The big, black ship charged out of the lane in the ice stern first and under full power. For one awful second Smith thought the attempt was going to succeed and *Cossack* would be cut in half. But somehow her captain and navigator managed to turn her out of the way and *Altmark* missed her.

She swept past *Cossack* and now bore down on the launch. Smith shoved it around in a tight turn to starboard as that huge stern rose like a house on his port bow. Kelso said, "Bloody *hell*!" Then the boat was rolling wildly and pitching in the wash as *Altmark* crashed past close alongside to port. She left them astern and with a deafening crunching and screeching smashed herself a new channel through the ice and snow on the right-hand shore of the fjord.

Smith looked over his shoulder and saw *Cossack* sliding in on the other side of *Altmark*, heard the destroyer's bow scrape along *Altmark*'s poop and the yells of the boarding-party. Kelso shifted in the seat alongside him and said excitedly, "I reckon they're aboard her, sir!"

So did Smith. He sent the launch sliding in towards *Altmark*, at first heading for the bow as that towered closer. He called, "Grapnel men get ready!" The grapnels had been hastily fashioned by *Cassandra*'s engineers earlier in the day. The four "grapnel men" had the job of hurling them up so their hooks lodged aboard *Altmark*, and the lines they trailed hung down her side. Then Smith and his party could climb them. He hadn't liked the idea but had seen no other way of getting aboard.

The men were standing ready to throw as the gap of water between boat and ship narrowed. But then Smith shouted, "Stand fast!" And as their faces turned towards him, "There looks to be a ladder aft!" There was, and it proved to be a Jacob's ladder when they came to it, the boat scraping along between *Altmark*'s grey, rust-streaked side and the thick, fractured ice through which she had forced her way. And now Smith realised that she was at rest. Her desperate manoeuvrings had only resulted in her running aground stern first.

He stopped the launch under the ladder and jumped for it. For a second he wondered why it was there, then saw the reason: there were men scrambling across the ice towards the shore and they had obviously come from *Altmark*. He started up the ladder, hearing Buckley shout behind him, "Look out up there, sir! Sounds like a hell of a fight going on!"

There was shouting on the deck above Smith as he climbed and the drumming of running feet. The ear-splitting crackling of pistol and rifle fire was continuous and echoed back flatly from the walls of the fjord. He reached the head of the ladder, threw a leg over the bulwark and then he stood on *Altmark*'s deck. Now he could see that *Cossack* had withdrawn so as not to run aground like *Altmark*, but there was no doubt she had put her boarding-party over. The deck was alive with running figures and he remembered at last to draw the Colt pistol from its holster. Kelso appeared beside him and then Buckley's head showed above the bulwark. Smith said, "Come on!"

He was close to the after superstructure and led the way to it, finding that the hurrying figures were all *Cossack*'s men. He searched the superstructure but found no prisoners. In one cabin there was a suitcase holding a woman's clothing, a neatly folded blouse and a skirt. Sarah's? He stared at them and shook his head helplessly. He did not know. Another five men of his party joined him now and he ran at the head of them, along one of the catwalks crossing the after well deck and so to the bridge. Here, again, he found *Cossack*'s men in control, *Altmark*'s captain and his bridge staff held under armed guard. There were no prisoners in the bridge superstructure, either.

Smith wondered uneasily if the captured seamen had been transferred to *Brandenburg* and somehow crammed into her already crowded hull? It was possible, for the short passage from Trondheim to Germany. But then from the vantage point of the bridge he saw some of *Cossack*'s boarders grouped in the forward well and working on the hatches there. He ran down the ladders and forward, reached them just as the clips were freed.

The officer there was Turner, leader of *Cossack*'s

78

boarding-party. As his men opened the hatch he bent over it to call down, "Any British there?"

And a roar came up out of the darkness, a disjointed chorus but a common thread of a message running through it: "Yes! We're all British down here!"

Smith grinned at the men with him, saw them laughing, then remembered he had not found Sarah. She could be in the hold and if she was then Turner's men would soon have her out of it. But if she wasn't? Somebody aboard this ship would know if she was held prisoner and where. He started aft again, his men at his heels, and had just reached the ladder leading up to the bridge when Buckley said, "What's that lot ashore, sir?"

Smith looked across the ice lying between *Altmark*'s stern and the snow-capped rocks lining the bank of the fjord. He saw the figures slipping and sliding from the ice to start the climb up the white-draped hillside. And then he ran.


Kurt Larsen was on *Altmark*'s bridge when *Cossack* swung around the bend in the fjord. A second later *Altmark*'s searchlight lit up the destroyer's bridge – and he saw the men crowded on her fo'c'sle, knew at once they were a boarding-party. He slid down the ladders to the deck, bellowing for the six men he had brought from *Brandenburg*, dragging his pistol from its holster. He realised *Altmark* was under way and charging astern through the channel she had cut in the ice. He guessed her captain was going to try to ram *Cossack* and hoped he would succeed but doubted it; Kurt had known British destroyer captains.

*Altmark* rushed down on the destroyer but she slid out of the way. The big tender drove on and crashed into the ice reaching out from the other side of the fjord. By then Kurt had gathered his men in the well deck forward of the bridge, thinking that looked to be where

*Cossack*'s boarders would come across. Fritsch appeared, in a grey-green greatcoat that reached down to his ankles and carrying a Luger. The coat was unbuttoned and his hair stuck out from under his cap as if he had jammed it on hastily on waking from sleep. He demanded, "What the hell's going on?"

So he had been asleep. Kurt told him shortly, "That's a British destroyer and she's about to put an armed party aboard us."

Fritsch stared, at first incredulous but then outraged. He complained, "But this is *piracy*!"

Kurt agreed, "That's right." But he remembered the prisoners battened down in *Altmark*'s hold. When she entered neutral waters she should have declared she was holding them and released them in Norway. He said, "What's more to the point is: What can we do about it?"

Fritsch rubbed his free hand across his twitching face, "You'll throw them off, of course."

"I'm not so sure." Kurt suspected that *Altmark*'s crew were not organised to deal with this kind of situation. His eyes were now fixed on the British destroyer. She was sliding in towards the prison-ship. Was her bow pointing directly at him or –

Fritsch felt a surge of fear that dragged at his guts but he swallowed and told himself there was too much at stake for him now. The opportunity of a lifetime was in his grasp and he would not let it go. There had to be a way out. He looked for it, desperately, and finally leaned over the bulwark. Some distance still separated *Altmark* from the shore, a strait not of water but – He burst out, "By God! That ice is thick!"

Kurt tore his eyes away from *Cossack* just long enough to glance down at the ice now enclosing *Altmark*'s stern, the huge slabs of it like concrete cracked and tip-tilted where the pressure from the ship driving slowly into it was ripping it apart. "It's mid-winter; what do you expect here?" His gaze snapped back to the destroyer now nosing in towards the ship and he saw she was going to come alongside *Altmark*'s stern, nearer the shore.

He yelled to his men to follow him and ran aft, became aware of Fritsch at his elbow and the SS man shouting, "Where is the key to the woman's cabin?"

Kurt glanced at him then away. He would not trust the girl to Fritsch. They were passing the after superstructure that held the cabins and he could see to his right the slim grey hull of the destroyer, its bow only feet away from *Altmark*'s poop that lifted up ahead of him from the after well deck. Then Fritsch seemed to stumble, cannoned into him and Kurt fell to the deck, Fritsch sprawling on top of him.

At that instant *Altmark* grounded. Her progress checked and she shuddered as her keel grated on the bottom of the fjord, then she was still. Some of Kurt's men staggered and fell, that grounding shaking them from their feet. But Fritsch shouted, "Keep going!" He gestured with one hand, urging Kurt's men on towards the stern. "And you keep still!" He said that softly, for Kurt's ears only, but there was no mistaking the menace in his voice. His other hand held the Luger and its muzzle was jammed into Kurt. Who wondered: Would Fritsch dare? And had no doubt of the answer. The men had run on, he and Fritsch were alone and a lot of men could be shot before this night was over. One more or less would not be questioned.

Fritsch stood up and jerked the pistol. "On your feet." He shoved Kurt ahead of him at the point of the Luger. "You may think this is a matter of *honour* – " the word came out as a sneer " – but it is a matter of State. So lives, particularly yours and hers, are unimportant. I'm not going to be captured by the British and neither is she. Where is the key to her cabin?"

81

Kurt led the way to his own cabin. They were barely inside the after superstructure when *Altmark* shuddered and heeled. They heard the destroyer grinding alongside, the yells from the deck outside as the boarding-party from *Cossack* fought its way aboard and *Altmark*'s men tried to stop them. Fritsch cast a quick glance over his shoulder and Kurt saw that, despite the cold, he was sweating. But the Luger still pressed hard into Kurt's back. He had no alternative but to take the key from its hook in his cabin and open the door to that which held Sarah.

She was dressed and on her feet. Wide-eyed, she started to ask, "What's happening – "

But Fritsch told her, "Shut up!" He snatched her overcoat from where it hung on a hook behind the door and threw it at her. "Put that on. We're getting out of this."

She looked to Kurt but he said, "Do as he says." Then she saw the pistol held to his back. Her hands shook a little as they pulled on the coat but she watched Fritsch steadily and he saw that defiance. She said, "I'll bet we're hiding in a river or a fjord – Norway? And I'll bet that's the Navy out there that's putting the fear of God into you."

"And you think they're going to save you." Fritsch grabbed her with his free hand, threw her towards the door and warned, "Stay two paces in front. Try to run and I'll shoot you through the leg. And there's another reason you should do as you're told." He spelt it out for her as they made their way along the passage.

Fritsch hesitated before stepping out onto the deck and held them both under the threat of the Luger as he peered cautiously out around the steel door. His eyes flicked rapidly back and forth between them and the deck, never leaving them for more than the blink of an eye. He gave them no chance to resist or escape. Looking past him Kurt saw that the destroyer had hauled off so as not to go aground. He also saw some of *Altmark*'s crew marched past under the guard of a British seaman armed with a rifle.

Fritsch muttered, "The cowards have surrendered."

Kurt believed they had simply lacked organisation and leadership but he said nothing; Fritsch would not understand, did not care, was concerned only for his own skin and his prize prisoner. Kurt watched the girl, saw her face in the dim light that filtered in from the half-open door, and it was calm. Then she became aware that his eyes were on her and she smiled faintly. This in spite of the way Fritsch had dashed her hopes of escape with a few savage words.

They waited there for some minutes, each one stretching out and racking the nerves of all of them. Fritsch sweated and his hand holding the pistol twitched but he was still determined, his glare told them that. Then at last the afterdeck outside seemed quiet, the shouting now coming from the bow where it stuck out into the fjord. Fritsch gestured with the pistol, "Out!"

He herded them ahead of him across the deck towards the bulwark on the starboard side but just before they reached it a bullet droned overhead and he ducked into its steel shelter. "Get under cover!" He shouted that at Sarah but Kurt was already dragging at her arm to pull her down. That first shot was followed by others and now they saw the muzzle flashes up on the snow-covered hillside. Fritsch called shakily, "Some of them are already ashore!" He was talking of *Altmark*'s crew, armed with rifles and now firing at *Cossack*. That fire was now returned, the air above them alive with the din of crackling reports and buzz of shots that passed close overhead, the clangour and howl of ricochets.

Fritsch grovelled still lower below the bulwark but soon the firing from the hillside ceased. He raised his head cautiously and looked around him. Opposite him on the port side there was a Jacob's ladder hung over the bulwark. He said, "That's how they went. And that's our way." But then he changed his mind and turned away from that ladder. Unknown to him it dropped down to Smith's launch, with a man at the helm and two more at bow and stern to guard her, all of them armed. Instead Fritsch saw a similar ladder on this starboard side and realised he did not have to cross the open deck to reach it, had only to crawl along in the cover of the bulwark.

"No. Better this way," he corrected himself, and waved the pistol. The other two crept along to the head of the ladder and Fritsch pointed the Luger at Kurt Larsen. "You go down first. Wait for her and then you both wait for me. If you try to run you won't get far."

They obeyed him. He crouched with his head just lifted high enough to watch Kurt as he descended the ladder. The hand holding the pistol rested on the bulwark so he was ready to use it on Kurt or an enemy inboard. Kurt stepped down onto the ice packed and tilted against *Altmark*'s hull and held the ladder steady for Sarah. Fritsch shoved her at it, "Go on! And remember!" He did not need to repeat his threat.

Sarah rose to climb over the bulwark then hesitated as a voice called, "The Navy's here!" But the voice was distant, from the bow. There was no help for her. The firing from the shore broke out again as she started down and momentarily she froze on the ladder, face pressed in against the cold steel of the ship's side, heart thumping. Fritsch flinched but this time did not recoil and stayed in his place. He yelled, voice high and near to breaking, "Keep going!"

But it was as much Kurt's deep tones from the ice below her that set her moving again, as he said, "You haven't far to go and you'll be safer down here than hanging up there." So she took a breath, unclamped one hand, moved it. From then it was easier and soon she stood on the ice by Kurt Larsen. He seized her by the arm, steadying her as her feet slithered and he muttered, "Keep out of the way." He pushed her behind him.

Fritsch was on the ladder and scrambling down it with the haste of near-panic as the firing went on. But he paused when ten feet from the foot of the ladder to show them that he still held the pistol ready in one hand. "Back off!" Kurt had hoped to jump Fritsch while he used both hands on the ladder but now he swore silently and retreated with Sarah until Fritsch said, "That's far enough." He still lived with his fear but his obsession drove him and he made no mistakes.

He joined them, pointed their way to the shore and stayed a few feet behind them as they all slipped and slid over the cracked and sometimes up-ended ice, skirting the breaks where the water of the fjord glittered. Then they were on snow that crunched under their feet and was already trampled by the boots of those of *Altmark*'s men who had come ashore ahead of them. Sarah saw some of them crouching behind rocks higher up the slope with only their heads showing. The firing had ceased for the time. Fritsch gasped, "Wait!" He halted to catch his breath before starting up the hillside and they all three panted with the exertion, their breath steaming.

Sarah gave silent thanks for the overcoat but wished she had some sort of hat to keep out the awful cold. That was a minor, insignificant worry, but she told herself bitterly she should concentrate on it because she could do nothing about the dread that possessed her now. It was snowing. She shook out her hair and saw the flakes fall from it. Fritsch said, "Move!" And they set out on the climb up the hillside.

\*    \*    \*

85

Smith saw that flourish of the blonde mane above the dark shadow of the overcoat against the snow, and ran as if he had shed twenty years. He left Buckley and Kelso behind. Only Jackman and two of the ratings were with him when he came to the Jacob's ladder hanging right aft on the starboard quarter. He was first down it, then his feet flew from under him as he tried to run on the ice. He stumbled and fell again and again as he charged towards the shore and that may have saved him from some of the shots that came from the hillside, buzzing and ricochetting from the rocks on the shore or slamming into *Altmark*'s hull. He ignored them, gaze fixed on that small figure climbing the hill with two others.

He shouted, "Sarah! *Sarah!*"

She heard him and turned as he reached the shore. He heard her call down to him and recognised her voice though he could not believe the words, "I'm staying with them! Leave me! I want to stay with them!"

He kept on after her, the snow being kicked up around him as the firing from the hill became heavier. He was climbing now but Sarah had turned from him and was still working higher up the hillside. Not believing, refusing to believe, he shouted once more, "*Sarah!*" Then he was falling face down in the snow and the darkness rushed in.


He surfaced for a few seconds to see Kelso close by at the tiller of the motor boat. He realised he lay in the sternsheets and the boat was under way, bucking over the water at full speed. Buckley was bending over him, swearing and anguished, wiping at Smith's face. He could taste the blood that had run into his mouth before Buckley started his cleaning. Jackman's voice in the background said, "I couldn't catch up with him, but I got him back as soon as I could."

Smith faded away then. He returned to brief consciousness some time later when the launch ground against

*Cassandra*'s steel side. Jackman was saying, "That's a hell of a head wound he's got. Will he be all right?"

And Buckley said, "Shut your bloody trap!"

He was being hoisted aboard *Cassandra* on a stretcher, spinning slowly at the end of a line above the deck then lowered into a forest of arms reaching up to him from a spread of faces white in the darkness.

Galloway's voice came, anxious, "Will he be all right, Doc?"

So the surgeon, Kilmartin, was there.

And Kelso: "He was terrific! Bloody terrific!"

Smith knew vaguely that he wanted to talk to them, but he could not. There was something about his daughter that troubled him but he could not remember what it was. Then he drifted away from them all.

# Part Two

# *Narvik*

# 7

"*Ah!*" Hannah's eyes were closed. She lifted under him, quivering, then collapsed. Her body went slack and he lay on top of her, felt her legs slide down to lie outside of his. For a while they were still and she kissed him, arms around him, then let him go as he rolled away.

He sat on the edge of the bed and looked at his watch. He had plenty of time. But he meant to catch that early train to Scotland. He would be aboard *Glowworm* when she sailed. The light was growing outside, the cold pallid light of a winter's day. The curtains were drawn back and he could see Hannah's clothes scattered in a trail across the floor where he had dropped them last night.

This was her service flat, rented when she came to London from the States. He no longer had a base in London and anyway, this was a far cry from the spartan cell he had rented until he went to Montevideo. Hannah Fitzsimmons had brought him here as soon as she could get him out of hospital, though the doctors would not pass him fit for sea. She told him that first night, mumbling, her mouth on his, "I don't want you fit for sea. But fit? Let's see . . ." Her hands seeking and finding . . .

Now he had persuaded Admiralty that he was fit to join his ship. They had sent her to sea, with Galloway in temporary command, a week ago. Smith had raged but the war would not wait for him. *Cassandra* had gone to patrol off Norway and the destroyer *Glowworm* would take him there to join her. He hoped he had persuaded Admiralty to his way of thinking on another matter, John

Galloway's application for transfer, but he would have to wait and see.

Hannah watched him now. Her mouth had gone down at the corners but when he turned to her she smiled. She pushed up to kneel behind him where he sat, arms around him, long fingers gently stroking the new, pink scar tissue on his leg. The head wound had appeared dramatic but proved minor. It was the bullet that ripped through the thick part of his thigh that kept him in hospital.

He reached for her but this time she pulled away. "I'll grab a shower and cook you some breakfast." She swung her legs off the bed and walked away from him. She wondered, Why did you get involved with this guy? And remembering, This is 1st April. That figures. You sap. But I won't make it tough for him. I won't drag along to the station or beg him to come back because that's goddamn stupid. He'll come back if he can. Please God.

And she wouldn't cry until she was in the shower.


Smith rolled out of the bunk as the alarm rattlers sounded. He had left Hannah's arms and bed a week before. Now the grey steel walls of the tiny box of a cabin, rust-streaked and sweating with condensation, closed him round. The deckhead above him was lined with snaking steel pipes. This was the destroyer *Glowworm*, 1300-odd tons and soaring and plunging like a lift in this storm off the coast of Norway. He had slept, fully dressed, for only a few minutes after standing down from dawn action stations. Now he threw back the blanket and yanked on his seaboots, grabbed cap and oilskins from their hook and ran.

*Glowworm* had sailed from Scapa Flow as a member of the destroyer screen escorting the battlecruiser *Renown*, flying the flag of Admiral Whitworth. He was leading a mine-laying flotilla to the Vestfjord, the approach to the Norwegian port of Narvik. The mines were to be laid in the "Leads", the narrow strip of sea running down the Norwegian coast. They were intended to stop the passage of ships carrying iron ore from Narvik to Germany. *Cassandra* would rendezvous with *Renown* and her escort in the Vestfjord when Smith could transfer to her. That had been the plan. But *Glowworm* had separated from the rest of the force to search for a man fallen overboard and had not yet rejoined. She was alone and now about to go into action.

The destroyer's narrow passages and companions were filled with running men, but not crowded and elbowing. They avoided each other and collisions automatically out of long practice so the streams of them went their different ways without check. They hurled bawled comments at passing familiar faces, joking and on edge, snatched from sleep and thrown into this disciplined stampede – to what? Hours of boredom closed up in a gun team on the exposed and freezing cold upper deck or in a magazine far below – or awful wounds and death?

"I'd just come off watch!"

"If you can't take a joke you shouldn't ha' joined!"

"Roll on my bloody twelve!" The end of the twelve years he'd signed on for, but he wouldn't get out now until the war was over.

Smith slipped into the stream going his way and as he ran pulled on the oilskin over the thick sweater he wore, his jacket left hanging in the cabin. He came out on the deck and headed forward to the bridge. At the foot of the ladder he met Buckley, who asked, panting, "Know what it's all about, sir?"

Smith shook his head. "Come on, but keep out of the way." He started up the ladder to the bridge that would be crowded and where spectators who got in the way would be unwelcome. He was a spectator as he was a passenger aboard the destroyer, with no post to fill in action, no orders to give. He had to heed the warning he had given to Buckley and on the ladder he thought that it had been a waste of breath; the leading hand knew already.

And Buckley, climbing at Smith's heels, muttered to himself, "Does the bastard think I was born yesterday?"

Roope, Lieutenant-Commander and captain of *Glowworm* was already on the bridge with his staff, binoculars to his eyes. Smith did not disturb him but asked a sub-lieutenant, whose wind-reddened face hid inside the hood of his duffel coat like a cowled monk, "Good morning. Why the alarm?"

The monk blinked at that "Good morning" but answered, "Destroyer sighted off the port bow. You can just see her without glasses. We think she might be enemy." And he raised his own binoculars to peer out at the distant, blurred ship.

Smith could barely make her out. The storm still raged so he looked out over towering crests of waves, through driving sleet and snow. Visibility was down to three or four miles at best. The other ship was a grey blur in the middle distance. Was she a destroyer? An enemy? He borrowed the glasses from the Sub and as he lifted them to his eyes heard Roope order the turn to port that would point *Glowworm* at the destroyer, and: "Challenge!"

The searchlight's shutter clacked as the signalman flashed the challenge at Roope's order. And that was a destroyer out on the horizon, no doubt of it, and Smith thought she was an enemy. He lowered the glasses. An answering light now flickered from the upperworks of the other destroyer and the signalman, now with telescope to his eye, reported, "She claims she's Swedish, sir."

Roope shook his head, "I saw that but I don't believe it. Open fire!"

There was a pause while *Glowworm* pitched and plunged through the big seas then the salvo gongs clanged and her 4.7-inch guns fired. Smith lifted the borrowed glasses again to watch the fall of the shot, thought he saw splashes lift near the far-off grey ship and heard confirmation come down through the speaker from the Gunnery Officer controlling the firing up in the director control tower: "Short!"

The guns fired again but the grey ship had narrowed as it turned away, blurred further as it slid off into the murk. It was seen for a few seconds longer then was lost in the dark background where sea merged with lowering sky without sign of the join.

The Sub grumbled, "Gone away."

Smith returned his glasses. The guns had fallen silent. He stared with the others on the bridge at the place where the enemy destroyer had vanished as *Glowworm* shoved through the big seas towards it. The other ship did not reappear but they waited, Smith uneasily.

He wondered if that was because of some premonition but then told himself that was nonsense. Or was it because of the continuing worry and bewilderment over Sarah? God knew he could not understand what was happening – had happened – to her. He remembered her shouting to him in the Jössingfjord: "I want to stay with them!"

Why?

While he was in hospital he had been visited by an official from the Foreign Office who had told him that representatives from the British embassy in Oslo had sought out Sarah. The Norwegians had held her with the crew of the *Altmark* but she had not gone with them when they had returned to the ship and sailed it back to Germany. She had stayed in Norway, first at the German embassy in Oslo but only for one night. She had then travelled north with one German SS officer to a remote village, Heimen. The representative from the British embassy who went there to see her gave it as his belief that the village had been selected by her escort for its remote position. He thought that Sarah had gone there, or been taken there, so he would be able to contact her only rarely. But he said that she had still insisted that she wanted to stay with the SS officer escorting her.

Again – why?

Smith had already worried long and fruitlessly at that question and now had time to brood over it once more as *Glowworm* searched. He stood wedged in a back corner of her bridge where he had some protection from the howling wind, driving sleet and rain, and would not be in the way of Roope and his bridge staff.

But he had another visitor while he was in hospital, Hannah Fitzsimmons leaning over him and smiling. "I warned you I would track you down." She gave him some ease of mind: "I know Sarah, maybe better than you do. Remember we were together in Poland and for weeks – no, months – after that before she found you in Montevideo. And this business smells. Sarah would never sell out. There has to be something we don't know."

She also brought ease to his body, her arms locked around him, her voice husky and breathless in the dark, "Was that good? That was good!" And finding each other again later in the night. Night after night.

A big sea broke inboard and hurled icy spray into his face. But he had left Hannah as soon as he could get to sea. He could have been with her now. He laughed at that and at himself then, but stopped when he saw the Sub staring at him.

Buckley had disappeared but now came staggering to Smith's side, balancing precariously against the pitch and roll, clutching a steaming mug in each hand. He held out one: "Kye, sir."

Smith said, "A poor substitute."

Now Buckley stared at him. "Sir?"

"Never mind." Smith took the cocoa, wondered how Buckley had conjured it up with the ship at action stations but did not ask and said only, "Thank you." He sipped then gulped at the sweet heat of it as he went back to his thoughts.

They were not of Hannah now and the moment of wry humour had passed. Sarah had no apparent reason to go back to Germany and a very good one for staying away: just before the outbreak of war she had been involved in an underground organisation in Berlin that was engaged in smuggling out of Germany people persecuted by Hitler's regime. She knew the SS and was afraid of them; she had told Smith how they worked, how they had treated some of her friends. If she went back to Hitler's Germany she would be executed – or worse, sent to a concentration camp where dying took longer.

In the early sedated and bemused days in hospital he was haunted by one possible reason and he had forced himself to face it. In his years spent in Intelligence he had encountered more than one double agent. Suppose Sarah had infiltrated the rescue organisation and betrayed it to the Gestapo? Then pretended to "escape" herself through Poland and used her British passport and the name of her father, a Royal Navy captain, to carry out some spying mission for German Intelligence? She had told him that she had been happy in Germany for a long time, that she had been fond of a young German naval officer, Kurt Larsen. It was a possibility, that could not be denied.

But he did not believe it, could not believe it of the girl he had come to know, however briefly, in Montevideo. She was *his daughter* . . .

And later, cold logic told him that was not a possibility. Because Sarah had been on a British ship, *Orion*, bound for a British port. She could not have known that she would be captured by *Altmark*.

But still he was left with the question: Why did she want to stay with the enemy?

"Ship! Fine on the port bow!" That yell came from the masthead and the glasses on the bridge swung onto the bearing. Smith cursed his lack of a pair of binoculars and stood waiting behind the Sub, shifting from one leg to the other with impatience. He could see another darker smudge on the dark frieze of the blurred joining of distant sea and sky. A ship, but that was all he could make of it.

97

Then the Sub said jubilantly, "Looks like we've found her!" He shoved the binoculars reluctantly into Smith's outstretched hand.

Now the ship leapt out at him, a picture still furred at the edges but recognisable as a destroyer. The same? The mottled camouflage of her paint looked similar but – he thought the ship first sighted had more sheer to her bow than this one and a clipper stem.

His unspoken thought was echoed by Roope, who said, "That's another one of 'em. Open fire!"

So there were two enemy destroyers now and Smith knew their types. Either one of them was bigger and a shade faster than *Glowworm*, but Roope was going to fight them. Of course. There was always a chance, a very, very slim chance that he would win or anyway survive. He could certainly hope to cripple one or both of his adversaries for *Renown* and her destroyers to finish off, or for them to be out of action for a long time. Meanwhile *Glowworm*'s wireless operator was busily sending out signals to the Fleet reporting the presence of this enemy force.

And Roope was expected to fight, by Admiralty and the public. That was tradition, and Smith also lived and was ready to die by it. Roope turned then and his face was expressionless but his eyes met those of Smith who saw determination – and a shared understanding?

*Glowworm*'s guns fired again and this time they kept on firing. The enemy destroyer replied. Neither scored a hit on the other despite the range being barely three or four miles now but conditions for gunnery were appalling. Both destroyers bucketed, pitched and rolled over the huge green seas, the barrels of the guns now pointing at the sky then down into those same heaving waves. Smith thought *Glowworm* was close with several salvoes. Roope was closing the range. Then the other ship turned away, though still firing and with *Glowworm* in pursuit. Smith clung to a stanchion to stay upright, narrowed his eyes against the spray, sleet and rain that lashed his face and wondered: Where was the other destroyer? Was *Glowworm* being led onto her?

He thought he saw her, farther still beyond the fleeing ship, looming out of that grey haze of sleet, rain and wind-whipped spray that fogged the middle distance. Then he became aware of Buckley staggering up to his side and the big leading hand's hoarse voice saying, "That's no bloody destroyer, sir!"

Smith looked again and now she was a little nearer, a little clearer. She was not a destroyer. Could she possibly be friendly? Smith did not think so and that was confirmed when he saw the stabs of flame from the big guns in her turrets. Then after thirty-odd long seconds the shells fell short of *Glowworm*. The spouts of dirty sea water they threw up dwarfed those lifted by the enemy destroyer's guns, looked to tower high above Smith where he stood on the bridge. He said, "That's a heavy cruiser. Firing eight-inch guns." She could be one of two: *Blücher* or *Hipper*.

He listened to his own voice, calmly commenting. He wasn't putting on an act to try to impress Buckley with his coolness. He did not try to create impressions with Buckley, anyway; they had known each other too long. He felt calm – or stunned? He thought that he had reason to be in shock. He knew he was looking at the doom of *Glowworm* and probably staring his own death in the face.

Roope was turning *Glowworm* away. His duty now was to send another signal to the Fleet, not to try to fight a cruiser like this, with her 8-inch guns and heavy armour, twice the length of a football pitch and ten times the tonnage of *Glowworm*. But he was already too late. The next shells from those big guns struck home on his ship and she staggered under them. Then she was hit again and she could not survive long under the hammer of those guns. Smith knew *Glowworm* could not escape – and so did Roope. He turned her again now and headed once more towards the cruiser. And into her fire.

"We're doing no good here!" Smith shouted that at Buckley as *Glowworm* was hit repeatedly. He gave a jerk of his head and with Buckley following him he clawed his way down a shell-twisted ladder to the deck. There they found a gun that was short-handed through men lost to wounds. The pair of them stripped off their hampering oilskins and filled the gaps, a leading seaman and a captain passing ammunition to the loader.

He bawled, "We've got another couple o' hands, Jim!"

The layer swung around in his seat long enough to blink at them, at first without recognition because of Smith's lack of badges of rank, but then identifying this captain on passage. He was not amused nor impressed; this was no time for either. The gun had got badly needed replacements and that was enough. He shouted, "We'll be getting an admiral next, Brummy." And he turned back to his dials.

The men at the gun got some protection from the gun-shield that covered front, sides and top of the gun but it was open at the back. So they were left vulnerable to the scything splinters hurled by shells bursting behind them. Some of those splinters were as big as a fist and all of them were ragged steel. They slammed and screamed around the gun but Smith and Buckley were not hit.

*Glowworm* was taking this punishment because Roope was working her into a position to fire his torpedoes. Smith, squinting around the gun screen with eyes smarting from cordite smoke, coughing from the reek of it, tried to estimate the distance between him and the cruiser. He thought it was about three thousand yards away when Roope turned *Glowworm* broadside to the cruiser and fired his torpedoes. The "fish" leapt from the tubes in the waist and dived into the sea. Smith thought he saw the tell-tale bubbles marking the trail of them but could not be sure because of the big seas that were running and churned into foam by *Glowworm*'s manoeuvring, the tops of the waves blown off in spray spread like a blanket over

100

the tossed water. The torpedoes might have gone on diving to the bottom of the ocean or surfaced uselessly. Or they might run straight and true to their target.

They did not. There was neither sight nor sound of any torpedo striking the cruiser and Roope turned *Glowworm* away. Then smoke swirled around her as her funnels belched it out at Roope's order. The few guns that were not mangled into scrap and still in action ceased firing because their crews and the Gunnery Officer in the director control tower had no sight of the enemy and they were hidden from him by the smoke. When they turned again it was to haul clear of the smoke but on the side away from the cruiser. Now *Glowworm* wallowed along, lower in the sea from the weight of water in her, tossed heavily by the huge green waves. She did not run away under cover of the screen.

Smith knew what Roope was going to do. *Glowworm*'s captain was lying in wait to ambush the cruiser. But for the moment Smith was just glad of the respite like the others. Keeping upright on the heaving deck was an effort in itself, but passing ammunition at the same time, with each round weighing a half-hundredweight, was exhausting. He panted, leaned against the shield to steady himself against the pitching and rolling – and to snatch some rest.

"Bit o' nutty, sir?" Brummy had got out a bar of chocolate, broken it up and was sharing it around the gun's crew.

"Thank you." Smith took a piece from the broad hand blackened by smoke and oil from the gun. He and the others sucked chocolate and stared out over the bow as the minutes passed. Their ears, plugged with cotton wool, rang in the sudden comparative silence. It was only comparative because there were still the pounding of the sea and shriek of the wind. The engines still thumped under their feet and the fans thrummed. And there was a mounting roar from the flames – there were many fires now. The cries of men sounded faint and far-off to their ringing ears.

101

Then Jim shouted, "Jesus! It's like a block o' flats!" They saw the cruiser coming through the smoke, huge, drably gaudy in her daubed camouflage paint. And close! Smith thought she was a bare half-mile away. The 8-inch guns in her turrets looked enormous to the men standing on the deck of *Glowworm* and her bridge structure towered high above them.

They were in action again, the gun slamming and recoiling, the breech knocked open to eject the shell-case that clanked and rolled across the deck. The cordite smoke jetted again to set them coughing. They looked out over the bow that now turned to point at the cruiser. She was broadside on to *Glowworm*, the guns in her turrets laid forward and aft, only now starting to train around towards the destroyer. Not so the lighter armament of 4-inch and anti-aircraft guns. They poured in a hail of fire and at that short and still closing range it was almost impossible to miss. The shock of the hits were a continual hammering, shaking *Glowworm* and underneath it was the rapidly increasing beat of her engines as she surged towards the cruiser.

"Stand by to ram!" The speakers squawked out the warning, barely heard through the gunfire and bursting shells. The men of the gun's crew threw themselves down on the deck and clung to whatever handhold they could find. Smith only went down on one knee – he had to see – and braced himself against the shield. The cruiser was trying to turn away but was too late. She lengthened and grew before Smith's eyes as *Glowworm* rushed down on her, speed still increasing, closing through a barrage of shell that hosed her from stem to stern.

"Hang on for Christ's sake!" Jim howled it. The cruiser filled all their vision now and the firing stopped; *Glowworm* was too close for the enemy guns to depress to hit her. That was the bow of the cruiser stretching across in front of *Glowworm* and only yards away now. Smith could see the faces of men peering down from her lofty bridge structure that lifted to the gunnery control top. And he knew her now, had seen her before in days of peace. This was the *Admiral Hipper*.

Then they struck.

*Glowworm* charging in at thirty knots was stopped dead as she slammed into the bow of the cruiser. Smith was hurled against the steel of the shield, bruising and winding him. *Hipper* heeled over to that shock but was still steaming ahead so that *Glowworm* ground her way aft along the cruiser's bow, ripping away forty yards of the armoured belt. Smith gripped the shield for his life through that tearing, lurching progress. The deck tilted beneath him, threatening to throw him into the sea boiling alongside. He was deafened by the clangour and shriek of battered, torn steel.

Until *Glowworm* finally fell away from *Hipper* and a gap of churned sea opened between them. The cruiser was stopping and the destroyer drifting away from her. There was no firing now. Smith turned his head stiffly and saw that the ready-use ammunition had gone and he did not think any more would come from the magazine below decks. The other guns would be in the same position. *Glowworm* lay ominously low in the water now, her bow crumpled right back to her bridge. Her rigging, cut by splinters, hung uselessly. Her decks were cratered and many of the holes gouted roaring flames from fires beyond control. He thought the probability was that *Hipper*'s gunners did not think her worth the waste of further powder and shot. She could be left to sink. And she was sinking.

She blew up. He thought later that fire had got through to one of the magazines. But now he knew only the huge kick as the deck lifted under him, the deafening explosion and the leap of flame far higher than any other, reaching above *Glowworm*'s topmast. She rolled underneath him and he turned, saw Buckley's lips moving as he cursed. Smith could read the obscenities and shouted, "She's going!"

His voice sounded in his ears as a whisper. It was as a whisper that the order came to him, passed along the deck by men who mouthed: "Abandon ship!" Smith went with those few of the gun's crew still living. With others, stokers and signalmen, they launched a life raft, dropped down into the sea and climbed onto it or clung to it. They were only just in time to see *Glowworm* dip her bow under, lift her stern and slide down beneath the waves. She left a scum of wreckage and oil. And, swimming or clinging to rafts, only thirty-eight out of her crew of a hundred and fifty.

Brummy croaked, "We'll have to swim for it." Their raft, with a dozen of them hanging on to it, was some way apart from the others and a freak of wind or current was widening the gap. Smith saw *Hipper* had stopped and was picking up the other survivors.

Then Buckley gasped beside him, "No, we won't. Here's somebody come for us." Then he choked as a sea swept over the raft, spat water and finished incredulously, "Would you believe it? Look who she is, sir!"

Smith turned and saw the ship steaming towards them through the heavy seas, then slowing, stopping to drift down to them as the wind thrust her. She had scrambling nets hung over her side, her deck was lined with men and others were climbing down the nets to be ready to help the men on the raft. This was a light cruiser, a smaller ship than *Hipper*, though bigger than *Cassandra*.

Buckley said, "It's *Brandenburg*."

Smith nodded. It was not such a remarkable coincidence that *Brandenburg* should be here. Germany had only six light cruisers of which *Brandenburg* was one. The sea was freezing him. He knew that neither he nor any of the others clinging to the raft could live for more than a few minutes in this sea. He feared for his life. Yet the thoughts came: Why was this force at sea, and in these waters?

Norway?

But then the raft surged against the side of *Brandenburg*. Within minutes he and the others were snatched from the raft and helped up the nets by brawny, cursing German seamen, to stand on the deck of the cruiser. Buckley had worked his way into the middle of the little group of survivors. He stood with his knees bent and shoulders hunched to make himself look shorter, and kept his face turned away from as many of the enemy around him as he could. He was worried about being identified. He and Smith had been prisoners aboard this ship and escaped from her only months ago.

Smith did not think they would be recognised unless they were very unlucky. They were soaked to the skin, hair plastered to their heads and faces smeared with oil. The other men in the group wore working dress of overalls or anything old they had put on to go on watch, hoping it would keep them warm and dry. Smith was just another of them in his trousers and sweater, without cap or jacket or any badges of rank. He covertly examined the Germans around him but saw no one he remembered, no flicker of recognition on any of their faces. He thought he saw one man who would have known him instantly but he was high on *Brandenburg*'s bridge: *Oberleutnant-zur-See* Kurt Larsen. So long as he came no closer he was no threat.

But if he saw Smith he would recognise him as the man he had first met in Spain a year ago, then later in Berlin and Brazil. He would bear witness that Smith had been an Intelligence agent – a spy. He would no longer be treated as a prisoner of war. Under Hitler's regime he would be lucky if he was shot.

*     *     *

105

Gustav Moehle told Kurt Larsen, "A job for you again, Kurt, interrogation of prisoners." Because his English was good. He had learnt a lot from Sarah Bauer, as he had known her then, in Berlin before the war. Moehle grinned at him. "Talk to them tomorrow. We may be in action at any time today."

"Sir!" Kurt acknowledged the order. He had returned to Germany in *Altmark* after she had been hauled off the shore and all necessary repairs made. He had rejoined *Brandenburg* in Kiel just as the repairs to her screws and steering were completed. Before she sailed on this operation, *Weserübung*, the invasion of Norway, he took a week's leave. When he returned to his ship he was bitter and depressed by what he had learned.

Smith and his bedraggled and shivering group were taken below under guard. As they stumbled stiffly and wearily down a ladder and along a passage, Buckley muttered, "See that lot, sir?"

"Don't call me 'sir' here," Smith answered. One of their escorts might know that much English to identify him as an officer. And all the prisoners would be interrogated. He would have to give a false name and rank to avoid being identified. Then he acknowledged Buckley's remark, "I see them." He and the other prisoners were passing mess decks holding a few off-watch seamen but crowded with soldiers. Their packs and rifles were stacked under or between the tables and the men themselves sat on the benches around the tables or sprawled on the deck. They looked to be in various stages of seasickness, from the prostrate and seemingly unconscious to those holding their heads in their hands.

Down another ladder and there were more mess decks, more soldiers. He wondered how many men could be packed aboard this cruiser, the bigger *Hipper* and the two escorting destroyers – if there were only two? Experience

106

told him from 1500 to 2000. But what other ships might be in this force? Where were they going and to what purpose? There could only be one answer to that. They were bound on the invasion of Norway, and specifically – Trondheim? They were off that port now. There would be other groups of ships, laden with troops, further north and south, intent on making landings at other key ports. Bergen? Narvik? Hitler was out to ensure his supplies of iron ore from Norway.

A rifle butt urged Smith along another passage to a sickbay where a doctor quickly but thoroughly examined the survivors. He repeated, "*Gut! Gut! Gut!*" as he worked through them, then left them to his sickberth ratings and the guards.

One of the sickberth ratings, middle-aged and tubby, told them, "I worked in England before the war. *Ja?* So – you want, you speak to me. *Ja?* Tomorrow *Herr Oberleutnant* Larsen *komm*. Speak good English. Ask questions. But now you eat and sleep."

Smith thought bleakly that if *Herr* Larsen was going to interrogate the prisoners then inventing a false name and rank would be a waste of time.

The prisoners were given blankets and their clothes taken away to be dried. A cook brought them soup and bread that they ate at a mess table. No one had much to say. Two of the men pushed their empty plates away and slept at once, their heads on the table.

Smith knew that was shock or battle fatigue and he would fall victim to it no less than the others. He crawled into the bunk he was given and closed his eyes. Now the reaction started and he hid it as he always did, huddled down under the blanket so his shaking hands could not be seen, his body held taut to keep from shivering. He told himself that he had to escape, he worried about his daughter and his ship, his career. And then he grinned at himself: he was lucky to be alive at all to be able to worry.

He looked across the sickbay and saw Buckley in a bunk over there, watching him. He asked, "All right?"

Buckley had seen the tension in his captain's face ease away, the clamped jaw relax, the rigid body loosen under the blanket. Now he, too, could let go. "Yes, sir." He turned over, sighed and settled down.

Smith closed his eyes. He slept.

But his last thought was that he had to escape or die.

# 8

"She's in action! Must be wi' some of our ships! Mebbe
*Renown*!" Brummy looked hopefully around the sickbay.
The deep-throated booming of the guns was deafening
even below decks in *Brandenburg*. Their firing shook the
ship so that loose gear on the shelves rattled and slid, only
held in place by the "fiddles", the lips running along the
edge of each shelf. It was three in the morning and the
dozen prisoners stared at each other and wondered.

They had come a long way on the road back to normality
in a short time; *Brandenburg*'s men had hauled them out
of the sea only eighteen hours before. Their clothes had
been returned. They had washed though not shaved, eaten
and rested all through the day. So now they showed signs
of life although they were still quiet, were alert and not
half-drowned, exhausted flotsam.

Jim said, drily but watching the deckhead, nervous and
voicing Smith's thoughts, "But if it is, and *Renown* drops
some fifteen-inch bricks on her and sinks her, what the hell
happens to us?"

But then the firing ceased and the armed guards in the
passage outside the sickbay looked as relieved as the
prisoners. They grinned at each other, all in the same
boat, literally, listening to the silence. That was only
comparative. There was still the thrum of the ventilating
fans and the rapid beat of *Brandenburg*'s engines. Smith
thought she was doing well over twenty knots – and not
pitching and rolling. So was she no longer on the open sea
but in sheltered waters?

One by one the men turned over in their narrow bunks and drifted off to sleep again. But Smith stayed awake, busy with his thoughts, restlessly but fruitlessly seeking a way of escape. Tomorrow – or rather today?

When *Glowworm*'s survivors had first stirred from sleep in the middle of the day, the tubby sickberth attendant had brought their food. He told them they would not be allowed on deck for exercise because: "Sea is a pig. Big green bastards come inboard. You go on deck maybe tomorrow. No soldiers then."

Buckley had asked, "Why no soldiers?"

The SBA glanced quickly at the guards outside in the passage, saw they had not heard but said, "Never mind." He had obviously been sworn to secrecy concerning the soldiers and was afraid even telling the prisoners they were aboard would get him into trouble. But now he stared at Buckley and asked, "I see you before? In England?"

He had doubtless seen Buckley with Smith, walking the deck of *Brandenburg* off the coast of Brazil only four months ago. They had both been prisoners aboard her then. Buckley rubbed at his face to hide it and answered, "You might ha' done. I kept a pub in Newcastle. Or it might ha' been my brother. He went to sea."

The SBA frowned, "Not in Newcastle." But he let it go, shaking his head.

Smith had warned Buckley later, "We'll have to be careful. He remembers you."

But now, as the hands of his watch edged slowly around the dial, Smith recalled the words of the SBA: "No soldiers tomorrow." So presumably they were to be disembarked tonight?

Two hours later the engines slowed and stopped. *Brandenburg* lay still and the men imprisoned in the sickbay woke again. Smith wondered, Were they in a port? Deep down in the bowels of the ship below the waterline, as they were, there was no question of looking out of a scuttle. But he thought again,

110

Trondheim? The most important port on this stretch of the Norwegian coast?

Those questions were soon answered. The tubby little sailor waddled into the sickbay, round face beaming. He announced, "We are at Trondheim. We *komm* in past the Norwegian guns very fast and they miss. All is well."

So the gunfire had been *Brandenburg* replying to shelling from the two forts at Brettingen and Hysnes on the shores of the fjord. Now the Norwegians had changed from nervous neutrals to reluctant, and probably bewildered, belligerents. The two thousand or more troops embarked in *Hipper*, *Brandenburg* and the other ships – how many? – would be swarming ashore to overwhelm any small garrison.

Not from *Brandenburg*. An hour later Kurt Larsen climbed to her bridge and his captain Gustav Moehle told him, "We've just had a signal from *Hipper*. She's putting the last of her troops ashore now and all goes well there." Kurt looked across at *Hipper*, anchored in the harbour like *Brandenburg* but closer to the port. The four destroyers of her escort lay close by. The sun had risen but not yet showed its face and the harbour lay under a low ceiling of thick cloud. In that early half-light the ships were almost in total darkness but Trondheim was sprinkled with lights being used by the troops still on the quay, though some were marching off inland and others had already gone. More were going in from *Hipper* and the destroyers, packed into the warships' boats or commandeered tugs.

"Worked like clockwork, sir." Kurt grinned at his captain and Moehle returned it, both celebrating a job well done. But Moehle said, "We aren't finished. The soldiers of the *Herr Oberst* we have aboard, and those in *Wilhelmina*, aren't needed here so we are ordered to go on with her to the secondary objective."

The secondary objective was Bergsund, further north.

111

The colonel, *Oberst* Klaus Grundmann, stood at Moehle's side, tall, lean, his grey-green field uniform neatly pressed, forage cap cocked jauntily on his grizzled head. He commanded the regimental combat team embarked in *Brandenburg* and the transport, *Wilhelmina*, lying a few hundred yards ahead. Now he put in, "Except for the pioneers. They are to be landed in Trondheim; they are needed here." And smiling at Kurt, "You'll know them when you see them. They are a law unto themselves. Their uniform is whatever they find comfortable to work in and they look like a bunch of vagabonds!"

Moehle nodded, "Just so. We have aboard a company of pioneers and engineers, about a hundred of them, to be landed here first. There's a tug coming out to take them ashore. And I've spoken to *Hipper* about our prisoners and she's going to take them." He said drily, "There was a bit of an argument but she's got the room now she's landed her troops and Heye is taking her back to Germany tomorrow night." *Kapitän-zur-See* Hellmuth Heye was *Hipper*'s captain. "He's sending a boat for them. See to their transfer, Kurt."

The guards bawled in at the door of the sickbay and the fat little SBA scuttled about among the prisoners. "They want you on deck. You go now to *Hipper* and you will soon go in Germany. Wish it was me!"

Smith glanced at Buckley, both of them still only in sweaters, and said softly, "We need some more protective clothing." They needed a lot of things for an escape attempt but clothing came at the head of the list for now.

They moved out, one guard with his rifle going ahead, the other bringing up the rear with the dozen prisoners strung between. As he climbed the ladders Smith saw the mess decks still packed with soldiers, some sleeping with their heads on tables or curled up on the deck, others peering lifelessly, queasily at the bulkheads. He came

112

on one pile of packs and equipment stacked close by the ladder, green-grey field jackets tossed on top of it. Before he could say a word Buckley had stepped briefly aside, picked up two of the jackets and was back in the line, without a soldier turning his head and neither guard any the wiser.

Smith took one of the jackets when Buckley handed it to him. He wondered if wearing it would annul his right to be treated as a prisoner of war? But they would execute him for espionage anyway, he knew that. As he stepped out onto the deck he shrugged into the field jacket and buttoned it up against the icy wind. Buckley had stolen two large ones. His jacket was only a shade tight but the other hung on Smith, the sleeves almost hiding his hands so he had to turn back the cuffs.

A drizzle was falling now so the other ships and the shore were only furred silhouettes. The prisoners stood huddled, anonymous shapes in the early morning gloom. Smith and Buckley once again worked their way into the middle of the group. They waited until all of them were there, one of the guards counting, "*Eins, zwei* . . ." Then they were marched towards the solitary light burning dull yellow in the waist.

It hung at the head of an accommodation ladder rigged against the cruiser's side and a crowd of soldiers stood close by. They were waiting their turn to descend the ladder and wore a motley collection of clothing. Some were in the grey-green service dress, many wore overalls with the uniform tunics pulled over them and a few were muffled in greatcoats reaching down to their ankles. Many of them humped big packs slung from their shoulders and high on their backs. There was a stack of canvas sacks and stencilled wooden crates and Smith thought, Tool-bags? Crates of supplies? Engineers?

The prisoners were halted on the fringe of the crowd. An officer standing under the light at the head of the ladder turned and nodded as one of their guards reported their arrival. Smith recognised Kurt Larsen. And he would remember Smith.

Kurt peered at his watch and swore softly. *Hipper*'s boat had not arrived. He told the petty officer overseeing the embarkation of the soldiers, "The prisoners are here. I'm going to find out what's happened to their boat." *Brandenburg* was ready to sail, only waited to be rid of these soldiers and prisoners. "I'll only be a few minutes. If it turns up while I'm away, load 'em."

Kurt Larsen strode off towards the bridge and Smith drew a breath of relief. He looked about him. The other survivors from *Glowworm* and their guards all stood with backs turned to the bitter wind that drove across *Brandenburg*'s deck. Smith nudged Buckley and gave a jerk of his head. The signal was understood and together they inched sideways until they merged with the soldiers. The guards did not see them go and the soldiers stood uncaring in a dark, wet dawn mood, cold and turned in on themselves, eyes on the queue ahead of them waiting to descend the accommodation ladder.

There was an eddy in the crowd as they started to shuffle past the stack, each man stooping, grunting, to lift a tool-bag or crate onto his shoulder then moving towards the ladder. Smith eased forward and Buckley followed. They allowed themselves to be sucked into the line and as they passed the stack first Smith, then Buckley lifted a tool-bag and swung it onto his shoulder. There was a minute of shuffling and jostling as they queued for their turn, tense seconds as they passed the petty officer under the light, the tool-bags on their shoulders between him and them. Then they were stepping down the ladder to the tug lying alongside, rising and falling gently on the swell.

Aboard her, they stood shoulder to shoulder, packed in among the others and once more in sheltering shadow. The last of the soldiers stumbled down the ladder and the tug

114

swung away from *Brandenburg*'s side, headed towards the scattered lights marking Trondheim.

It ran in between two breakwaters, slowed and eased to starboard. Her engines stopped then briefly went astern, taking the way off her, then she neatly rubbed against a quay with a creaking of her rope fenders. The soldiers were able to step ashore from its deck. They swarmed over the guard-rails, each carrying his tool-bag or crate and started to build a new stack, forming a new group.

Smith and Buckley went with them, set their burdens down on the stack and worked through the group to its inshore edge. Before them was a row of sheds lined along the quay, and beyond them lay the cat's-cradle of railway lines that was a marshalling yard. Here, away from the scattered lights at the quayside, they stood in shadow again, looking at the backs of the group. After a moment they just sidled away from the backs and walked off into the deeper darkness.

Buckley took a great, gulping breath then muttered, "Never thought we'd make it."

Smith found he, too, had been holding his breath. Now he was panting and warned, "We're not in the clear yet, by a long way." But at least they had escaped from the ship. It was a beginning.

There were alleys turning off from the quay between the sheds and they took one of them. They wended their way through the web of railway lines and more buildings. German soldiers were everywhere but all of them were busy. None of them questioned two more "soldiers" like themselves who moved briskly now, purposefully, as if they knew where they were going and were bent on some duty. And there were Norwegians, staring at the troops, bewildered and glaring impotently.

Buckley muttered, "Think we should ask one o' them if he can hide us, sir?"

Smith shook his head. He was well aware that they had a long way to go and were without food or money. They could not hope to hide behind their makeshift disguises for long. They had to have clothes. They needed help. A stranger might give it – or turn them over to the *Wehrmacht*. So they would only take that risk later and if forced to it. Besides, he did not want to hide – yet. He knew who he was looking for. But he had to find that someone soon.

And had he found the place now? Here was a fish quay but were there more than one? Would the man he sought be here? Fishermen stood about in their jerseys and heavy jackets, thick trousers sprinkled with fish scales, their legs stuffed into the tops of seaboots. There were boats tied up to the quay and Smith's hopes rose faintly but briefly, died as he saw the armed German sailors put aboard to guard them. It was no more than he had expected.

Kurt Larsen reported to Moehle on the bridge, "The pioneers have gone ashore and the prisoners have been transferred to *Hipper*. But two of them are missing. I – "

Moehle swore and broke in, "Have you started a search? How the hell did they get out of the sickbay? They were under guard!"

Kurt answered, red-faced, "They came up on deck with the others. The senior rating commanding the guard swears he counted them and they were all present on deck." There was no sense in wasting time on excuses. Kurt went on, "I think they mixed in with the pioneers and they'll be ashore by now." They had escaped right under his nose and Kurt waited for his captain's just wrath.

Moehle scowled at him, then grinned. "It's good for the soul to feel a bloody fool sometimes. And whoever they are, they've got their nerve."

Kurt answered, "Yes, sir."

"Nothing we can do about it, but they can't get far. Send a signal to the military ashore. I can't see them searching now – they've got their hands full at the moment – but tomorrow, maybe . . ."

And the major in Trondheim who received the signal in his newly requisitioned office glanced at the flimsy sheet and promptly tossed it aside to be dealt with later. "Right now we're carrying out an invasion," he muttered, "not searching for escaped prisoners. First things first."

Smith kept on walking around the fish quay, glancing at faces, seeking one. It was long odds against him finding it but there was a chance . . . He and Buckley skirted grumbling or silent groups, getting hostile glances from the fishermen because of the uniforms they wore. They had almost run the gauntlet when a hoarse voice called, "Hey!" They did not look around but they heard running feet coming up behind them. A suspicious sentry from one of the boats? Or were they being hunted already? But then the hand seized on Smith's arm, halting him and pulling him around. And he saw the face he sought.

Per Kosskull, big, blond and bearded, ran a hand through the hair that grew long to shag over the collar of his jacket. He stared disbelievingly at Smith and whispered, "I think sure it was you but – " He fingered the *Wehrmacht* field jacket.

Smith explained, "We stole them to escape. We were prisoners aboard *Brandenburg* out in the harbour."

Kosskull nodded, then said quickly, "We must better walk." He fell into step at Smith's side and jerked his head at Buckley, "He was in your boat, ya? Who is?"

"My cox'n." Which meant his servant but not his lackey, his right-hand man, a score of things. Then Smith told Kosskull about *Glowworm* and his capture. As he talked and they strode on along the quay he remembered how he had saved this man when his boat had exploded and burned. Per Kosskull had shrugged off the loss then with the words, "I have another in Trondheim." Now Smith

117

said, "I remembered you." He came straight to the point, "You said you had another boat here."

Kosskull glanced at Smith, then halted, asked, "You want it to get away?"

"I have to escape." He returned the fisherman's stare, not pressing his case, sure of the kind of man he was dealing with and letting him remember that night weeks ago when Smith had saved his life.

Kosskull nodded, "Yes, I have a boat."

"Is it under guard?" Smith gestured back towards the fish quay.

Now Kosskull shook his head. He set off again still heading along the quay with the railway tracks on his left. "I went out with the boat last night for the fish . . ."

He said he had found the weather bad, had caught nothing and so had run for home. He was inside the fjord and past the Norwegian shore batteries in the Narrows when he heard them open fire. He steered inshore and then was overtaken by the two cruisers and their destroyer escorts as they charged in at over twenty knots. "Like all the Norwegian Navy at once, but I knew they were not Norwegian."

He had not suspected an invasion, let alone German sentries being set to guard the fishing boats of the Trondheim fleet. But he had been wary of bringing his boat back to the port where the warships had gone. He had heard gunfire and knew something odd was going on. If there was more gunfire he didn't want his boat involved. Instead he tucked it away in an inlet near the town and then came in on foot. "Is not far."

They walked for almost an hour, the first ten minutes of it in the town. They left the quay, crossed a cantilever bridge and followed a road lined with factories. In these streets through which Per Kosskull led them they met few people and only once a file of *Wehrmacht* soldiers. They were marching rapidly and scarcely spared a glance for Smith and Buckley, marching equally rapidly in the

118

opposite direction, with Per Kosskull between them like a prisoner under escort, or a guide.

Then came empty country roads, and for the last half-hour a track that wound along the side of the fjord through firs with branches heavy with snow. It crunched under their feet. Then Kosskull turned off the track to skid down the steep drop to the fjord, clutching at saplings as he went to slow his speed and keep his balance. And at the bottom they found the boat, tucked into a little inlet and tied up to the trunks of firs whose branches overhung it like a screen.

It was a motor launch, with a cabin set into a half-deck forward, aft of that a well that held the engine housed under a hatchcover, and piles of fishing nets. The steering position was a wheel mounted just aft of the cabin. Kosskull pointed to the electric torch tied on a loop of string and hanging from a hook by the wheel, "In case you need at night. If the engine stop."

Smith said, "We'll pray to God it doesn't." But he was grateful for the torch, tried it and found the battery good. Kosskull laughed, then took them into the cabin. There was room for another half-dozen men in there but the three of them were bent almost double under the low deckhead. He showed them the primus stove and the cupboard with his stores, bread, butter, cheese, tinned meat and condensed milk.

Out in the well again he slapped the engine housing and said, "Enough gas for two hundred miles, maybe. Maybe more?" He shrugged and explained, "The weather."

Smith nodded. They would use more fuel and time in adverse conditions.

The fisherman cocked an eye at them, "It is bad out there now. And tomorrow, maybe next day. Where I fish last night – " he grimaced "– is bad, but out at sea is *very* bad and this is little boat."

Smith said, "We have to go. Are you coming?"

Kosskull shook his head. "This is my country. There

will be Norwegians fighting the Germans. I will find them."

He showed them how the engine worked and watched while Buckley started it. Then he stepped ashore and cast off the lines tied to the trees. He called, "Good luck!"

Smith answered, "Thank you, for everything." He had given them a chance for freedom and life.

And Buckley waved to Kosskull, "Good luck to you, mate." Then he muttered, "We're all going to need it."

Smith silently agreed as he eased the launch away from the bank, cautiously getting the feel of her. He knew there would be British ships off Narvik, trying to stop the iron ore ships sailing south to Germany, and that was about three hundred sea miles north. Kosskull had said the launch had fuel for two hundred, more or less. Well, they would go as far as they could on that. And then? He would face that later. Now he was free and at sea.

That freedom was soon at risk. As the launch puttered out of the inlet Buckley called urgently, "Ship right ahead!"

Smith saw her at once, just the vague shape of her out in the channel in the centre of the fjord. It was full day now by the clock but the leaden sky still hid the sun and seemed to hang even lower than before. A drenching rain mixed with big, wet flakes of snow added to the gloom. He turned the launch to run along the shoreline just out of the shallows and at the foot of the hillside that rose steeply from the water. He hoped that as she was showing no lights she would be hidden in the darker shadow there.

He looked again at the ship, seen only like a ghost in that bad light but he did not need Buckley to tell him, "*Brandenburg* again, sir." The bulk of her slid past in a beat of engines and swash of screws, showing no more light than the launch. Behind her came a transport, a carthorse following a thoroughbred, lacking the warship's grace but also devoid of its menace. She ploughed through the water of the fjord that the cruiser slit with her sharp stem. But

Smith thought they were both making about fifteen knots or more.

The lookouts on *Brandenburg* and her consort did not see the launch. Smith relaxed as the two ships sped on down the fjord towards the sea. But that had been close. If he and Buckley had sailed ten minutes earlier they would have been further out in the fjord, seen, stopped and questioned. The questions would not have taken long and that would have been the end of it.

Smith and Buckley exchanged glances when they heard gunfire again. From *Brandenburg* or the Norwegian shore batteries in the forts guarding the entrance to the fjord? They did not know and the firing was brief. Buckley said, "Looks like she's slipped past 'em again, sir." Smith nodded agreement. When they passed the forts themselves at noon, only dimly seen through the rain, they drew no fire. Either the little launch had not been seen or the gunners did not think it worth ammunition.

They found rough going even there in the sheltered waters of the fjord; the waves still kicked up and the wind rocked them. When they finally left it and embarked on the open sea they set their lives at risk. The little launch was tossed about like a cork, now climbing a wave that hung over it like a cliff, then sliding bow-first down the green, glassy slope on the other side. The tops of the waves often broke over her and as often she dug her stem into them. Her well filled with water nearly to the gun'ls and Buckley had to bale her out with a bucket.

They had no oilskins but he had earlier found some tarpaulins he fastened around their shoulders. They kept out some of the weather, the freezing spray and the wind that cut to the bone. Before they left the fjord he had wedged himself in the tiny cabin and made coffee. They had drunk it and chomped on bread and cheese from Per Kosskull's stores. Smith reflected wrily now that it was as well Buckley had prepared that rough meal because they would not be using the primus stove in this sea.

The last of the day passed without sight of the sun. They fought their way northwards all through it under a darkening sky, standing watches at the wheel in turn, and in between bailing out the water they shipped in the well. They got their heading from the compass by the wheel but Smith wondered uneasily if it was any good. He suspected Per Kosskull used it rarely, if at all, preferring to rely on his knowledge of these waters gained over a lifetime. He thought they might be making six knots over the ground. They had no chart, log or sextant. He decided navigation was going to be difficult.

As the early dusk closed in he took over the helm and asked, "Can you see what fuel we have left?"

Buckley peered at the gauge on the engine and reported, "The needle's swinging about between a quarter and three-quarters full. Say half full, sir?"

Smith nodded. He would have to be content with that. It would see them through the night, anyway. If they survived the night. The sea was as wild as ever, the wind as strong. A heavy rain mixed with sleet was falling now, rattling on their tarpaulins, drumming on the cabin roof. Smith was numb where he stood at the wheel. All day he had tried to keep moving, even when at the wheel, but it was not easy. He had no feeling in his arms, legs, hands, feet. He knew Buckley was in little better shape. They were both exhausted.

Night fell about them like a shroud as the rain and sleet became snow, swirling blindingly around the launch. Smith had to meet each wave as it came, could see no further than that wave, and toppled over each and every crest into a black ravine. It took all his strength and skill to keep her head to the sea. Waves broke over the bow and the roof of the cabin to burst on him where he stood at the wheel. The well filled again and again; Buckley was continually bailing. Yet he still found time and breath once to shout at Smith, "We've come through worse than this, sir!" He grinned, teeth showing white in the darkness.

122

Smith grinned back at him and nodded. But – worse than this? He could not believe it. Buckley was trying to cheer him. The leading hand had tended the engine and done most of the bailing. Smith was certain he himself would have collapsed if he had done so much work but the big man laboured still. If Smith had been able to choose any man to go with him on this launch he would still have taken Buckley and without hesitation. And if they got out of this it would be due to his efforts.

The night dragged on interminably. They changed places again and again, but only exchanged one exhausting, agonizing labour for another. They were soaked, frozen, but still could have closed their eyes and slept where they stood at the wheel or knelt in the well to bail.

Smith was at the helm close to midnight and at first he thought what he saw was just a trick of the storm, a thickening of the snow so that it now showed as a white wall stretching across ahead of the launch. But then it seemed to take shape . . . He yelled at Buckley, "*A ship!*" And, "*Use the torch!*"

Buckley snatched it from its hook and the beam sprang out, probing weakly yellow at the muffling snow. Smith's first thought was that they were not going to drown and he felt relief wash over him, warming, giving him life. Then he wondered what ship this was, remembered that he had seen *Brandenburg* put to sea and there would be other enemy ships out and bound for other ports – Narvik? For a moment he was on the point of yelling at Buckley to put out the torch until they had found out whether this ship was friendly. Then realised that was nonsense; there was no way he could find out and anyway it was too late.

The ship had passed but a searchlight's hunting beam found and held them in a pool of light. Smith turned to follow the ship, steering the launch to run up the beam which was blinding him. She would also be slowing and turning. Then the searchlight's beam twitched away to cast its light alongside the launch, no longer blazing into

123

his eyes. He saw the ship ahead once more, stopped to windward of him to give him a lee.

He closed her, ready to turn and try to run if she proved to be an enemy. And Buckley bawled, "I'd sooner take my chance with the sea than be took prisoner again!" Smith nodded, his face set, blinking away the water that streamed down from the hair plastered to his skull. But he thought he knew the ship ahead, could not believe it but then was certain as Buckley yelled in confirmation.

There was a scrambling net hung over her side and as he eased the boat in against it a voice bellowed above him, "Do you speak English? Do you need help?"

Smith said, "Tell them." Buckley's voice would carry further and more clearly than his own in this gale.

Buckley answered both questions, roaring, "Yes!" Then he added, "*Cassandra!*" And grabbed at the net.

Smith managed to laugh through his pain and exhaustion. Buckley's was the correct answer from a boat carrying a ship's captain when challenged by that ship. What would they make of it aboard? But now a light shone down on the boat, picked up Smith and he knew that those on deck would recognise him. He shouted, "I want to save this boat!" He would not be able to return it to Per Kosskull but there might be a use for it.

A voice burst out, disbelieving, "Bloody *hell*! It's the *captain*!" But then the lines came down and two seamen with them, jumping into the leaping boat and hooking them on. Buckley was grabbing at the net to hold the boat in against the ship's side as they both seesawed, the boat now almost level with the ship's deck then plummeting twenty feet below it. Smith saw men on the net, waiting to help Buckley and himself. He let go of the wheel and threw himself at the net, hooked his stiff fingers like claws into its wide mesh and started to climb. Buckley and the two seamen from the boat were already fighting their way up *Cassandra*'s side.

The boat dropped away and sheered off then the sea

came up and washed over him. Smith clung on and then he was lifted from the roaring black world and out again into that of swirling white. Buckley had hold of one of his arms and one of the seamen on the net had the other. Another was working lines around the two half-drowned men.

They climbed again, at first slowly then more quickly as the hands above hauled in on the lines and drew them up to safety. At last they stood on the deck, still in darkness but close enough to see their rescuers – and be seen. The long and long-faced, lugubrious Chivers was commanding the party that had brought them aboard. He gaped at them now.

Per Kosskull's boat was being swung inboard. And Buckley told Smith simply, happily, "I knew you'd get us through, sir."

Smith could not understand that but did not try. He was up to his knees in water as the sea washed over *Cassandra*'s deck but it was enough that he was aboard his own ship.

It was like coming home.

But there would be desperate work for all of them now.

# 9

*Brandenburg* rocked over in the turn and Kurt Larsen grabbed at the mug of coffee before it could slide away across the glassily polished surface of the wardroom table. He swore with sleepy pre-dawn irritation. Then he wondered at the reason for the turn? He was about to go on watch and now drained the mug, headed for the bridge.

*Brandenburg* had fought her way north with the transport *Wilhelmina* through the storm of the previous day. She disembarked *Oberst* Klaus Grundmann and his troops at Bergsund in the late afternoon. He had first landed a company a mile or so north of the port then waited for them to make their way overland. They cut the telephone lines running inland from the little town and then surrounded it. When *Brandenburg* and *Wilhelmina* entered the fjord and anchored off Bergsund they found there was no garrison, no one to oppose them.

That was not surprising. Bergsund was a small port, little more than a fishing village. Grundmann and his men were there because it offered access to the hinterland. From there he could drive north towards Narvik, though there was no road all the way to Narvik, or south to Trondheim. He could cut the fragile Norwegian communications and pose a further threat at the backs of Norwegian forces trying to organise resistance to the invasion.

Gustav Moehle had waited with *Brandenburg* until all Grundmann's troops had disembarked and then to see if they needed the support of his ship's guns. By the early hours of the morning Grundmann had confirmed that support was not needed. So Moehle left *Wilhelmina* to complete discharging her cargo of stores, transport, guns and ammunition, and sailed south with *Brandenburg* to rejoin the Naval Group at Trondheim. But now she had turned northward again.

Out on deck in the last of the night, Kurt was glad to see the weather had moderated. There was still a rough sea but not as mountainous as during the storm. *Brandenburg* smashed through its peaks and valleys, pewter-grey in this light just before the dawn.

On the bridge he took over from Paul Brunner, the Executive Officer, who told him, "Change of course was due to a signal. We've been ordered north to Narvik in a hurry. Commodore Bonte is in there with a destroyer force and it sounds as though he may need some help to get out." Bonte's ships had escorted or carried the troops sent to take Narvik.

So they were not going back to Germany at once. Kurt's first thought was that now he might see the girl, Sarah. She was still in Norway, as far as he knew. When he had learned of this planned invasion he had hoped he would find her. But he did not know where she was in Norway; he had not been able to go ashore at Trondheim or Bergsund, could well not set foot in Narvik. The chances were a million to one against their meeting – but there was still that one chance. He knew he would not have it in Germany, knew what would happen to her if she went there.

He stared out unhappily at the heaving sea as *Brandenburg* steamed northward and the sky grew lighter though the clouds still hung heavy. The day came with squalls of snow sweeping in under that lowering sky. *Brandenburg*'s crew stood down from dawn action stations and Kurt paced back and forth across the bridge. It was desperately important that he should talk to the girl, and not just because he was fond of her.

\*     \*     \*

127

Smith was torn from sleep by the clamour of the alarm rattlers. His body reacted quickly, far ahead of his mind. He was out of the cabin before he realised it was his day cabin. He was back aboard *Cassandra* and he had eaten a meal last night then collapsed into the bunk in the day cabin because Galloway was using the sea cabin abaft the bridge. But Smith was still captain and his place was on the bridge now.

He looked at his watch as he brought up at the front of the bridge, fastening his oilskins that were flapping in the wind, leaning on the screen and wriggling his feet more comfortably into his seaboots. He had slept for just six hours and his body told him that was not enough, but it would have to do for now. His weary mind dredged up his last thought of the previous night, seconds before exhaustion felled him: What would happen to Sarah now that Hitler was into Norway? She no longer had the protection of neutrality around her. They would send her to a concentration camp . . .

He recoiled from peering into that chasm, looked around the bridge and asked, "Where?"

Galloway answered quickly, "Enemy cruiser fine on the port bow, sir. She's already in action against one of our destroyers to starboard. At least we think it's a destroyer. Enemy is five miles away and t'other more than six so you can hardly see her." He wore an old duffel coat and cap like others on the bridge yet he stood out, seeming immaculate as always.

Smith grunted acknowledgment as he saw the ships then took the glasses Galloway handed to him, saw they were his own from the sea cabin and said, "Thank you, John. And good morning."

Galloway blinked at him, then grinned, "Good morning, sir. And it's good to see you here. I still can't believe it." Then he dived down the ladder, heading aft to his station in action, commanding the damage-control parties.

Ben Kelso, breathless from his race up to the bridge, panted, "Bloody incredible!"

Smith glanced around and saw the same look on all their faces, Harry Vincent, Appleby, the signal yeoman and his signalman, the bridge messenger. The look was one of admiration and respect. Smith had given Galloway a brief account of his and Buckley's escape from *Brandenburg*. Ben Kelso, along with the rest of *Cassandra*'s crew, would know all about it now. They remembered the earlier actions with *Brandenburg* and his attack on the *Altmark*. Now there was this escape from the enemy. They had known nothing of the loss of *Glowworm*, or the taking of Trondheim by the *Wehrmacht*, until Smith told his story.

He turned away from them and spoke into the voice-pipe, "Full ahead!"

He heard that acknowledged, "Full ahead, sir!" That was Taggart, *Cassandra*'s cox'n, who ran the lower deck and took the helm when she was in action.

Buckley handed Smith his steel helmet and he put it on. Then he set the glasses to his eyes and looked out over the bow. He agreed with Galloway; in this visibility of low cloud, sunless, one snow squall following another, the enemy cruiser was hard to make out and the further ship little more than a very small shadow in the murk. But the weather had eased and maybe they were moving away from the storm of last night.

The two ships in the distance ahead sparked with yellow light, the muzzle-flashes of their guns. But one of them, the destroyer off the starboard bow, trailed another, continual flame from her after end. She was on fire. Why was she engaged in a hopeless battle against the cruiser, instead of keeping her distance and calling up support? Smith swept with the glasses, checked and moved back, steadied them. He said, "The destroyer is escorting someone. I think I can make out another ship to starboard of her." Just. Or was it a distant squall making that extra shadow on the horizon?

129

But Ben Kelso, after a few seconds' hesitation, agreed. "Seen, sir. A merchantman?"

They could only speculate on that. And all the time *Cassandra* had been working up to her shuddering full speed and the reports had streamed in to the bridge as departments were closed up for action. Now the ship was silent, waiting. Smith ordered, "Open fire." And then, slowly, "She looks like *Brandenburg*." It could well be her in these waters.

Only "A" gun forward of the bridge would bear but now that flamed and recoiled, shaking *Cassandra* and all on her bridge. Then Ben Kelso answered sombrely, "Yes, sir. Agreed." And there was a heightened tension on the bridge now. It seemed the grey phantom ship out there returned time and again to haunt them.

He turned, looked for Buckley at the back of the bridge, saw him and said, "Wonder if they've missed us?" Buckley grinned and as Smith swung back he saw a copy of that grin on Ben Kelso's face. But the problem for Smith was unchanged: *Cassandra* was little better fitted to fight the bigger, newer cruiser than was the destroyer. She was inferior in armour, firepower and speed. So she had to win – or survive – through some other quality. He ordered, "Port twenty."

The bow swung to point at the distant cruiser and still moved on: "Midships . . . steady on that." Now all *Cassandra*'s guns would bear and they fired. She was steaming out to haul up on the bigger cruiser's port side. *Brandenburg* looked to be matching her speed to that of the destroyer which in turn had to keep station on the slower merchantman. Smith nodded to himself. *Cassandra* was overhauling *Brandenburg*. Soon he would have her between him and the destroyer. They were able to take her in crossfire.

There were jets of flame and clouds of reeking cordite smoke as another salvo hurtled away from *Cassandra*. He felt the blast on his face and the concussion of air in his ears. *Brandenburg*'s two after-turrets had trained around and were now laid on *Cassandra*. Shells from those guns crashed into the sea, ahead and to starboard, hurling up tall columns of dirty water that stank vilely as *Cassandra* steamed through the slow-falling spray from them. Close. Soon the three ships would be pounding each other, locked in a death grapple. Smith's face was set. So be it.

On *Brandenburg*'s bridge Gustav Moehle read the signal brought from the wireless office, swore savagely then passed the flimsy to Paul Brunner and Kurt Larsen. "Bonte's destroyers have been attacked at Narvik. It sounds as though they are in trouble. We are ordered to assist and this takes precedence over all other operations." He pounded the top of the screen softly with his fist in exasperation.

Brunner had passed the signal to Kurt and now had his glasses set to his eyes. A salvo from *Cassandra* fell in the sea off the port quarter and *Brandenburg*'s after turrets fired, heeling her over. He shouted, "I think she may be the same cruiser we fought off Iceland in February."

Moehle shrugged, "Possibly, but they have several of those old ships still in service."

Now Brunner warned, "She's steering to take us in a crossfire between her and the destroyer."

Moehle nodded, but said bitterly, "We could gain a victory here and sink all three of them." Then he sighed, "But we have our orders. File that signal. Full ahead."

Harry Vincent reported, "She's cracked on speed, sir. We're not gaining on her now. In fact, I think she's pulling away."

Smith was sure of it. *Brandenburg* was widening the gap between her and *Cassandra*. A manoeuvre? She had

131

no reason to run. Her captain must know he had the advantage in this unequal contest. The destroyer looked to be badly damaged now, with several fires and only one gun in action. But –

Harry burst out, "She's running!" His voice rose on a mixture of disbelief, relief and frustration. *Brandenburg* was making smoke now that rolled down astern of her to hide her as she retreated.

*Cassandra* held on in pursuit, firing salvoes when *Brandenburg* could be seen under the smoke, swerving at Smith's order when the enemy shells fell close. But the bigger cruiser shrank as she drew away, became vague, then was lost in the distance and bad light. The guns fell silent and Smith decided, "We've lost her and we'll be needed back there, I think." And he ordered the turn that sent *Cassandra* racing back towards the other ships.

He found them both stopped. Galloway, returned to the bridge, said, "The destroyer is *Hornet*." He could read her number now, painted below her bridge. He referred to the list of Naval Appointments he held in one hand, "Captain is Lieutenant-Commander Miller." He used his glasses again, "And the merchantman is the *Ailsa Grange*. Looks as if she's being used for trooping. I can see soldiers on her deck."

The destroyer lay right over on her beam ends, was down by the head and burning fore and aft now. She was being abandoned. The *Ailsa Grange* was close by, lowering some of her boats to take off *Hornet*'s crew. The destroyer's boats and rafts could all be matchwood; Smith remembered the destruction wrought on *Glowworm*. "Tell the doctor to be ready for casualties." Surgeon Lieutenant Kilmartin was a young heavyweight with huge hands and dark eyes that glowered out cynically from under bushy brows at any man who tried to shirk by reporting sick. "Kilmartin?" *Cassandra*'s crew would say gloomily, "More likely kill *us*!"

Ferrying men in boats from the destroyer would take

132

too long. Smith ordered, "Stand by to go alongside. I'll lay her bows to and I want a party forrard to take her people inboard." He edged *Cassandra*, nets hanging down her side, close to *Hornet*. He manoeuvred to lay his bow against the destroyer's waist because her fires were in the fo'c'sle and right aft. It was tricky work in the high sea running and at the back of everyone's mind was the fear the fire might leap to *Cassandra* – or *Hornet* might blow up. Smith knew eyes were on him as he gave his succession of helm and engine orders, heard the unanimous intake of breath on the bridge when a big sea looked set to slam *Cassandra* into the destroyer and he stopped her just feet short.

Miller, *Hornet*'s captain, still stood on his bridge but he was without his cap and his arm was in a sling. The bridge had taken a hit and he was surrounded by the tangled wreckage of compass, voice-pipes and his own chair. Smith spoke to him on the loud hailer, "Can I offer you a lift?"

Miller used a megaphone to reply because his ship no longer had power for the hailer: "That's very decent of you. I seem to have a mechanical problem."

"Happens in the best of families." *Cassandra* now rubbed against the destroyer, fenders hung between them to cushion that rubbing. Kelso was in command there in the bow, harsh-voiced and urgent. He'd got his party of seamen, under Jackman and another petty officer, organised and working efficiently. Lines were thrown over and made fast to hold the two ships together. The men waiting in *Hornet*'s waist, low in the water now, started clambering up the nets hung against *Cassandra*'s side to reach the higher fo'c'sle of the cruiser. Smith saw there were soldiers among them, two officers, both wearing holstered revolvers on their belts and packs on their backs.

Smith called down, "Look out for those soldiers, Mr Kelso."

The previously stone-faced, barrel-chested Lieutenant

turned and laughed up at Smith, teeth showing white through his beard. "I'll keep an eye on them, sir!"

Smith grinned and eased back from the screen into his chair. From the first moment of his return to *Cassandra* the previous night he had detected a different atmosphere in the ship. Glancing aft, he saw that Per Kosskull's boat had been squeezed into the waist abaft the cutter. It looked small and fragile. He thought he and Buckley had been very lucky. And there, at the back of the bridge, was Midshipman Appleby. He also looked small and fragile. Smith remembered there was a question mark over Appleby. He would have to do something about the boy.

Now an officer climbed to *Hornet*'s shattered bridge, spoke to Miller and he nodded. They both went down to the destroyer's waist.

In ten minutes all of *Hornet*'s crew had transferred, Miller crossing last of all, struggling one-handed up the net with the aid of a big, boiler-suited stoker black with oil. He came to the bridge as Smith completed the orders that backed *Cassandra* away from the destroyer and turned her to steam away from the wreck. Miller arrived just in time to see his ship lift her stern and slide down into the deep.

Smith said, "Sorry."

Miller grimaced, "Thanks." His face was pallid under the black stubble from long hours spent on his bridge. He tore his eyes away from the scum of oil and wreckage that marked *Hornet*'s grave and faced Smith. "I need to talk to you, sir. Urgently and in private. I had orders that I won't be able to carry out now and I must turn them over to you."

"Where were you bound under those orders?"

"Bergsund."

Smith glanced at Vincent and asked, "Pilot?"

The navigator answered, "Small fishing port by the look of it, sir. It lies about thirty miles south of here."

"Thank you. Mister Galloway, she's all yours. Resume course. Make what speed *Ailsa Grange* can keep up. Tell her to follow us. She may as well have our protection until we know what's going on."

So ten minutes later three of them were crowded into Smith's sea cabin abaft the bridge. A girl's photograph hung above the bunk and a book lay on the pillow: Nevil Shute. They belonged to John Galloway. He had not had time to move them out.

One of the two soldiers rescued from *Hornet* was in the cabin at Miller's request. Major Vivian Ellis was short and chesty, with a red face, bristling moustache and hair to match that showed when he took off his cap. He and Miller sat on the bunk while Smith leaned against the bulkhead. Ellis had a map-case with him and now he took from it a map and spread it on the little folding table.

As he did so he explained rapidly, "I was second-in-command of the battalion. I took over command when we were embarking and the colonel fell from a ladder and broke his leg." He shot a glance at Miller, "Right!" He was obviously impatient, urging some action.

But first Smith asked, "How is the arm?" He nodded at Miller, now with a clean white sling holding the damaged arm, his jacket hung around his shoulders.

"Fine, thanks. I was blown off the bridge but your chap Kilmartin thinks it's just a bad sprain. I was damn lucky, really." His face was as white as the sling.

Ellis cleared his throat irritably and Miller glanced at him, then turned to Smith with a wry twitch of the lips. "Well, don't know if you are aware of it, sir – I wasn't, it was all very hush-hush – but the government have been worried about a German invasion of Norway for some time and they prepared a force to get in first. There were five battalions embarked in four cruisers and three transports. *Ailsa Grange* was one of them, with Major Ellis's battalion aboard. Most of the force was to sail when there was clear evidence that Hitler was about to invade Norway. They would occupy Narvik, Trondheim, Stavanger and Bergen before the enemy got to those ports." Miller paused to ease his arm in its sling.

He went on, "But *Ailsa Grange* is slower than the other transports and the cruisers so she sailed early with Admiral Whitworth and his minesweepers. They were to lay mines in the Leads." Smith nodded; *Glowworm* had originally been part of that force. Miller saw that nod: "I see you know about that. Well, the *Ailsa Grange* was to stay with Whitworth off Narvik until the signal came for her to go in. Narvik because that's the port that Hitler's iron ore comes from."

Smith queried, "Narvik? You said you were bound for Bergsund."

Miller said, "Sorry, but I am coming to that. The idea was that if he tried to invade because we'd mined the Leads – and it was expected he would – we would be there to get in first. It was also expected that the rest of the cruisers and transports would be off Stavanger, Bergen and Trondheim by then." Miller grinned sourly, "But it didn't turn out that way. Early yesterday Whitworth sighted *Scharnhorst* and *Gneisenau* – "

Smith broke in, startled, "What!" They were battleships.

"That's right," said Miller. "He set off after them and we were left behind. That was when the signal came and it wasn't the one we'd been waiting for. Hitler had jumped the gun and got into Narvik and Norway first."

There was a tap at the door and Smith called, "Come in!"

A steward entered, tray balanced dexterously on one hand, the flexing wrist keeping the tray level despite *Cassandra*'s pitching and rolling. He beamed at Smith, "You wanted some coffee, sir."

Smith nodded, "Thank you." He watched as the steward filled two cups from the pot but then said, "Not for me." The steward's beam, Kelso's laugh, the expressions he had seen on Galloway's and other men's faces – there was a

136

definite change in the attitude of *Cassandra*'s crew towards him. Were they simply getting used to him? But what about the overheard charges of womanizing and being an armchair dug-out? Were they making allowances for him now? He didn't want people making allowances for him.

But the steward had gone. Miller sipped gratefully at the coffee but Ellis gulped his hurriedly then sat on the edge of his seat, tapping a pencil on the table. Smith prompted again, "Bergsund?"

*Hornet*'s young captain took an envelope from the inside pocket of his jacket and handed it to Smith. "The signal, and another with new orders for myself and Major Ellis. You'll see they are headed 'Most Secret' and are for the eyes of Commanding Officers only, that's just the three of us. But cutting it short, I was to escort the *Ailsa Grange* and give Major Ellis any assistance I could. He and his troops are now to be landed at Bergsund to hold that port. But he is also to accept delivery of a cargo that will come down to him from a village inland. I was to load it aboard *Hornet* and return to Rosyth at once, leaving Major Ellis to hold Bergsund. We had to carry out those orders at all costs. We were on our way to do just that when we ran into this cruiser. We turned to run but I'm afraid the *Ailsa Grange* is no sprinter. *Cassandra* was a very welcome sight, sir."

Ellis had been shifting impatiently and broke in now: "Captain Smith! It is absolutely essential this mission is now carried out by you and your ship. You can come to no other decision!"

Smith held up a hand then and his cold eye stopped Ellis. "As you say, this is my ship. And it will be my decision." Miller smiled faintly but then Smith asked, "What was this cargo? And where is this village?"

Ellis stood up to jab a finger at the map, "There." Smith stared at it, hearing Ellis go on, urgent, staccato: "The cargo is described as eleven tons of machine tools. They could be enormously valuable to Hitler's industry and his war machine if he got hold of them.

137

They'll be waiting for us there." And he tapped the map.

Smith slowly looked up from the map and saw them peering at him curiously. How long had they waited for him as he stood there in silence? For a time the words had not registered but now he concentrated on what Ellis had said because it touched on his duty. He was responsible for the lives of every man aboard this ship and must not risk them wantonly. He had to put personal emotions aside.

And machine tools? He granted that Ellis was right and they could be valuable to Hitler, but to be brought out 'at all costs'? That meant putting at risk his ship and the men in her, the *Ailsa Grange* and the battalion commanded by Ellis. Another eight hundred men. For *machine tools*?

And now the responsibility had fallen on his shoulders but the orders were clear and he had no choice.

He spoke through the voice-pipe to Galloway on the bridge, "John – will you come back here, please." Then he told Miller and Ellis, "I'll do it." He picked out another phrase from the orders and asked, "You maintained wireless silence?"

"Until we were attacked," Miller said bitterly. "Then it was pretty obvious we wouldn't reach Bergsund. I informed Admiralty."

Smith wrote on a signal pad. When another rap on the door heralded Galloway, Smith tore off the top sheet and handed it to him. "For Admiralty." And to be copied to Whitworth, advising them of the loss of *Hornet*, and that he was proceeding on her mission. "And from then on, wireless silence." He did not want *Cassandra*'s wireless transmissions giving away her presence to the enemy. "I'll tell you all I can about this later."

He nodded at the other two, "Mr Galloway will have found you places to sleep. I suggest you get all you can."

Galloway led them out of the cabin. Smith followed and went to the bridge. He told Harry Vincent, "Pilot, I want a course for Bergsund. Then see I'm called a half-hour before we make a landfall. I don't want to be seen from the shore."

Sandy Faulknor had the watch and Smith said, "I want that fishing boat made ready."

"Aye, aye, sir!" A grin accompanied the words and Sandy went on, "Nice to have you back, sir."

"Thank you." Smith wondered again at that grin, and that of Kelso and others. But he went back to his sea cabin and found the girl's photograph and the book had gone now. There was no longer any sign of Galloway's occupation. Smith lay down on the bunk and pulled the blanket over him. He knew he would not sleep, had plenty to keep him awake, God knew. But he had forgotten the exhaustion of the past thirty-six hours. Inside of a minute oblivion claimed him.


Smith laughed, "Not so wet this time!"

Per Kosskull's boat eased away from *Cassandra*'s side. The sky was still lowering, threatening rain or snow but the huge seas of yesterday had gone. He felt rested, wondered that he had slept through the forenoon since altering course for Bergsund, but was glad.

There was no sight of land. When the mountains some miles inland of Bergsund were sighted from *Cassandra*'s masthead Smith had turned her back; he did not want to be seen from the shore.

Buckley was at the wheel of the fishing boat this time and in this quieter weather she was shipping little water. One of the two seamen aboard only had to bail occasionally for a minute or two to keep the well dry. Also in the boat were Ellis, Lieutenant Merrick who commanded the platoon of marines carried by *Cassandra*, Sergeant Phillips and Corporal Lugg. Phillips and the corporal both carried holstered revolvers and small packs with emergency rations and water. Ellis had thought *Cassandra* would lead the *Ailsa Grange* straight into the harbour of Bergsund but

Smith had other ideas. He had told the soldier, "If they're in Trondheim then they could also be in here."

Ellis argued, "This is hardly Trondheim – just a few houses and a handful of fishermen working out of the place. And we can't waste time."

But Smith quoted the old saw at him, "Time spent on reconnaissance is seldom wasted." And he would not risk his ship needlessly. Ellis sniffed at this caution but held his tongue.

*Cassandra* dropped away behind them as she turned away to patrol with the *Ailsa Grange* and await their return. After a while, as the boat chugged in, the shoreline lifted into view. Off the port bow was the entrance to the harbour of Bergsund and now at Smith's order Buckley turned the head of the boat towards it. They would soon know what they faced.

They closed the mouth of the fjord on a diagonal course, the fishing boat puttering from south to north up the coast but gradually edging in towards it. They were within a mile when they passed it. Smith, Ellis, Merrick and Phillips crouched on the narrow strip of the half-deck, only inches wide, that ran along the side of the cabin roof. Nets were piled on the roof and they used these as cover as they peered through binoculars into the fjord. Buckley stood at the wheel in oilskins and all the others were hidden inside the cabin.

Smith said, "There's a lookout on the headland to the left." There were two soldiers on the high ground above the steep fall to the shore. They were seen clearly through the binoculars, outlined on the crest, rifles slung over their shoulders. He thought they would have a field telephone up there though he was too far away to pick out any tell-tale wire. But he could make out the distinctive steel helmets. He said, "German soldiers."

Merrick said, "Seen." Ellis and Phillips muttered agreement then they were all silent. The enemy had got to Bergsund first, as he had to Trondheim and Narvik.

The port was a little town lying on that left-hand shore of the fjord behind a sea-wall. Coming up from the south at this angle, Smith and the others could see behind the wall to the quay beyond and into a square formed by buildings on the other three sides. Roofs showed behind the square and lifted with the gradient that soon climbed steeply from the fjord. A gun – Smith thought it a light anti-aircraft weapon like a 40mm. Oerlikon – was mounted on the sea-wall.

The square was busy with soldiers, their trucks parked along one side of it. The barrels of more guns showed, parked here and there among the trucks. A flag with a black cross flew from one of the buildings at the back of the square, confirming German occupation.

Smith said, "Well, somebody's home." It was as he had feared, why he had brought along Sergeant Phillips and Corporal Lugg. There would be work for them now.

There were other things to see and note. A road apparently ran inland along the side of the fjord, the line of it marked by telegraph poles. It seemed to be narrow and in places cut out of the wooded hillside. The last building on that inland side of town looked like a squat hut. The tiny figure of a sentry stood there.

A big ship, a transport or a trooper, lay in the fjord outside the harbour. Scrambling nets hung down her sides and her derricks were at work. They swung cargo nets out of her holds and lowered them to boats waiting alongside. Some of the boats were bigger, sea-going fishing craft. Smith thought that they had been requisitioned from the fishermen of Bergsund. They were being used to carry the bigger items, like guns, to the shore.

Pulling boats were piled with crates. The water was dotted with the creeping craft, oars swinging, like so many beetles. It was a laborious, time-taking process, presumably forced on the transport's captain because his ship drew too much water to go alongside the sea-wall or the quay.

Ellis, momentarily subdued at Smith being proved right

in his cautious approach, muttered, "Blast it!" And he would be wondering about the machine tools – as was Smith. His orders had said his cargo would come down to Bergsund. Had it already arrived there? Did the enemy hold it now? And what should Smith do? But he had anticipated this, one of several possible situations, and had a rough plan ready to be polished.

He told the others now, outlining his intentions in a few short sentences as he peered through the binoculars. They heard him out in silence, busy with their thoughts and not looking at each other, apprehensive.

One of the men on the headland had gone down on one knee. Using a telephone to report the presence of the fishing boat? Smith said, "We'd better keep an eye on that gun. If they get suspicious they might use us for target practice."

So now, uneasily they checked back quickly and frequently to see if that slender barrel had foreshortened as it pointed at them. But soon the quay and the town were lost to sight, hidden by the sea-wall as Per Kosskull's boat trudged steadily northward across the mouth of the fjord. Smith had seen enough anyway, pictures stamped on his mind. The others scribbled notes, shifting uncomfortably on their damp perch as the sea slopped inboard or cramp locked their muscles. Smith suffered with them but stared at the passing shore, and thought.

When they were out of sight of the watchers on the headland Buckley turned the boat at Smith's order and ran in towards the shore. He was working from the chart now, saw the inlet he wanted as they closed the coast and pointed Buckley towards it. Ellis, Merrick, Phillips and Lugg had been huddled in the cabin, comparing notes and planning, since Smith had ordered the turn to close the shore. Ellis was still in there, drafting orders now, but the others were out in the well.

Smith asked Phillips, "You know what you have to do?"

142

The sergeant was young for his rank, broad and stocky, confident but not cocky. "Ascertain enemy strengths and dispositions . . ." He recited the orders Smith had given him before they left *Cassandra*, then finished, ". . . and to see without being seen, avoid action."

"Don't forget that. Understood?" Smith addressed Phillips but cocked an eye at Corporal Lugg, tall and muscular, hatchet-faced and pugnacious.

Lugg caught the eye on him: "Yes, sir. Softly, softly."

The pair of them landed on the southern shore of the inlet, that nearer to Bergsund, and started the climb up the snow-covered hillside towards the ragged crest. They would approach the port over the high ground. Smith watched them go as the boat headed out to sea and prayed they would be all right. He had set them a large task and sent them into enemy-held country. But now Ellis and Merrick claimed his attention, wanting to discuss their plans.

Ellis was serious. "I think, from what I saw of the stores, guns and transport going ashore or already there, and from the size of that troopship, there could be a couple of battalions in there, fifteen hundred men or more."

That was double the force that Ellis commanded. Smith thought that now the soldier was remembering that phrase "at all costs" and thinking of what it might mean in terms of the lives of his men. Because they would not be just occupying a friendly, undefended port. Smith did not like the idea, either, but – He said slowly, "There weren't many soldiers to be seen in the town. There was no barracks, no sign of any garrison being stationed there. It's a small town and I think it was probably taken by very few men. It may be held now by only a company or two while the rest have gone inland. So if we can achieve surprise, and using the fire-power of *Cassandra*, we can take the port."

"But that's only what you think," said Ellis, eyes on Smith, "your opinion." Smith had to agree and nodded.

143

Ellis pressed, "It looks like they've got the – " He hesitated, remembering that his orders were for the eyes of Commanding Officers only and Merrick was present, then finished: "– the cargo. But suppose they haven't?"

"We'll cross that bridge when we come to it," Smith replied. He was in command here. What risks he took to seek out and seize the 'cargo', that would be for him to decide. The orders he had inherited from Miller had not envisaged that Bergsund would be held by the enemy, but they had not said that he could back off if it was. Also the attack on Bergsund and the manner of it would be his decision, too, and to be taken in just a few hours.

There was *Cassandra* ahead, turning, running in to pick them up, and the *Ailsa Grange* staying out on the patrol line. The troops in her, and Smith's own men in *Cassandra*, would be wondering what lay ahead for them. He felt a moment of self-doubt. Was he being influenced by emotion? But his orders were clear and permitted no divergence. In his mind he had already taken the decision and if he was wrong the awful burden would lie on his conscience. His face was bleak as he climbed the ladder to the deck of his ship.

# 10

A dark night and now snow was falling, but lightly, tossed on the wind. The inlet should lie ahead, over the nodding bow of the fishing boat, but darkness and the whirling white flakes hid it. Smith looked at his watch using a torch, held in his cupped hands so there would be no leakage of light. There was always the possibility of an enemy patrol on the dark shore. It was time. He said quietly, "Look out for their light. They should show it now if they are there." If. And if this boat was in the right place and he and Harry Vincent, standing beside him now, had not made a balls-up of their navigation so that the inlet was a mile away. He licked his lips.

He was using Per Kosskull's boat again because he was ready to try to bluff if he found a German patrol waiting for him at the inlet. There was silence in the fishing boat except for the low putter of its engine as it crept in towards the unseen shore. They all tried to pierce the darkness and the blinding snow. The same team was in the boat as earlier in the day but with the addition of Harry Vincent and the other soldier rescued from *Hornet* with Ellis.

He sat in the sternsheets of the boat now, wrapped in a borrowed oilskin, a young second-lieutenant attached to the battalion as interpreter. Tall, gangling, relaxed, he had explained: "My father was in the timber business in Bergen from before I was born." He had grinned at Smith, "The old man had the right name for it – Woodman. I lived in Norway until I was nine years old and then I went to school in England. But I still came back for vacations up to

1938. Father was promoted and moved back to the London office then."

When he climbed into the boat Smith had asked him, "Are you being looked after all right, Mr Woodman?"

"Yes, sir, thank you. Mr Kelso lent me this oilskin and really made me welcome."

"I'll bet he has."

Dry humour there because Ben Kelso would greet an interpreter with heartfelt relief, and Harry Vincent had laughed. But they were all serious now. Phillips and Lugg were missing from the team, the two men they had put ashore and had come for now, the men Smith worried over. But –

"There it is! Port bow!" The low call came from one of the two seamen acting as lookouts, standing in the bow with one arm outstretched, pointing.

Smith had seen the three short flashes, yellow sparks in the night. They had gone now but he told Buckley at the helm, "Port ten . . . steady . . . now steer that." The boat crept on in and now Smith saw the looming shadow of the shore, the black lift of the hillside on either side of the inlet. The boat rode more easily as they slid into the sheltered water, the way came off her as the clutch was thrown out and then the bow grounded gently on the southern shore. He called softly, "Quickly now!"

The voice of Phillips drifted back to him, "We've got an extra one, sir." Now Smith could see the two figures that would be the stocky marine sergeant and the taller corporal, standing in the surf that washed the beach. They were shoving a third man up into the bow where one of the lookouts hauled him in and passed him to the other seaman who brought him aft into the well. Phillips followed, thickset body dropping springily into the well, and introduced the man he had brought, "This is Harald Olsen, sir. He only has a couple of dozen words of English and most of them aren't fit for mixed company. But we got him to understand who we were

146

and what we wanted and he agreed to come of his own free will."

Smith saw the corporal still waiting on the shore and asked, "So it's all right?"

Phillips answered, "All set, sir. Lugg knows what he has to do."

The fishing boat was going astern out of the inlet and Lugg fading rapidly into the gloom as he watched them go. Smith gave Buckley the course he had to steer back to *Cassandra* then left Harry Vincent with the conn and told Phillips, "Come on." He led the two, Phillips urging Olsen, to the cabin and ducked in through the door. They walked into total darkness that fled as Smith closed the door behind them and its automatic switch triggered the light. The men of *Cassandra*'s torpedo branch, the ship's electrical experts, had installed the light and switch at Smith's order.

They squeezed in around the little table where Ellis and Merrick sat already with the lazily grinning Woodman. Young Phillips was grubby, face sweat-streaked despite the cold. He fumbled now at his pocket, pulling out a notebook. "I found Mr Olsen at his house, up on the hill about a half-mile behind the town. I didn't want to risk getting any closer – I could see a few soldiers patrolling the outskirts."

"Quite right," Smith agreed. Harald Olsen was a man in his sixties wearing an ancient overcoat and suit. Before he sat down Smith saw the bottoms of the trousers were tucked into thick socks and he wore heavy boots. He had come dressed to walk on the hills. He had pulled off a woollen hat and now clutched it in one hand. A fringe of grey hair stuck up wildly around a pink pate over a weather-beaten face.

Smith said, "Tell him who I am and that I would like some information." He smiled at Olsen while Woodman spoke, pleasantly, also smiling. Smith saw the old Norwegian relaxing in the light and nodding his bald head as he was addressed in his own tongue.

147

He spoke to Woodman who confirmed, "He says he will help in any way he can, sir."

He interpreted as Smith put his questions. Olsen said he had been born in Bergsund and lived there all his life. He had been a fisherman for many years plying out of Bergsund, running a one-man business, selling fish on the quay there and also carrying it upriver by boat, stopping at every village to sell. But his wife had become ill a few years ago and he had given up the boat and bought a smallholding outside of town. His wife was dead now but he would not go back on the water. He had a cow and grew vegetables. Some of these, and most of the milk from the cow, he sold. "I want to live quietly, in peace."

Ellis was showing signs of impatience yet again but Smith needed to know the background of this man, to judge his worth as a source of information. He thought Harald Olsen would be sound.

The old man had heard shooting the previous day and seen the transport and a German warship outside the harbour. Smith thought, That could be *Brandenburg*. Olsen said he had not gone into town because of the shooting, but a man coming out and hurrying away inland to safety had told him what was happening. About two thousand men and some guns and vehicles had been landed. Shots had been fired but only as a warning. No one had been hurt.

Ellis scowled at Smith, but in answer to his next question Olsen said he didn't think there were so many soldiers to be seen now. Some of them may have gone but he didn't know when or how. He thought possibly in trucks or more likely on foot. When pressed he refused to elaborate, spread his hands and said he could only speak of what he had seen.

Smith liked that and nodded approval, then asked about the road leading inland. Olsen said it was narrow but a good metalled surface. At present it was snow-covered and treacherous for vehicles. It led to the next village some fifteen kilometres inland.

"That's Heimen, sir," Woodman explained.

148

Smith nodded, expressionless but taking it in, then said thickly, "Go on. What about the fjord? To what extent is it navigable?" He went on with his questions and Woodman with his translating. The fjord was navigable for thirty or forty kilometres from its mouth. There was a buoyed channel with a depth of five to six fathoms and ships regularly used it to go upriver.

"In fact," said Woodman, "he says a ship goes up every month to load timber. There's a sawmill at Heimen and a few houses belonging to the people who make a living from it."

Smith's questions went on as he tried to build up a picture of Bergsund and its defences. Ellis drummed his fingers on the table and looked pointedly at his watch. He was reminding Smith of the warning he had given to Ellis and the rest at that afternoon's briefing. Smith had told them baldly, "Time is short." When – if – they attacked Bergsund the enemy would call for help and it might not be long in coming. There were German ships active all along the Norwegian coast and Smith did not want to be caught in Bergsund.

But Olsen's information could be valuable and they could not take any action until they got back to *Cassandra*. Smith stole a glance at his own watch, asked two more questions of Olsen and then finished with him. He told Woodman, "Give Mr Olsen my thanks. I may ask him for more help later but I will return him to his home as soon as I can."

Olsen shrugged at that, a gap-toothed grin cracking his red face. Woodman translated, "He says no one will worry over him now and you only have to put him ashore. An old dog like him will always find his way home."

Smith turned to Phillips, who recited the results of his reconnaissance, detailing enemy positions and strengths, reading from his notes, his pencil marching over the map. ". . . we located the telephone lines, both the one running inland along the side of the road and the other field telephone line Jerry has run up to his lookouts on the hill. They won't be any trouble, sir – " He grinned at Smith, "Not the lines nor the lookouts . . ."

When the fishing boat finally ran in alongside *Cassandra* they had done. Ellis scowled dubiously at his notes but Smith's plans were complete – or as complete as they could be. "Events might dictate changes and we'll have to be ready for them. I never knew one of these amphibious operations that didn't go wrong somewhere." He spoke with the bitter knowledge of a veteran of a dozen such ventures. Ellis kept the silence of a man embarking on his first.

There were other boats alongside, from the *Ailsa Grange*, that had brought two companies of Ellis's battalion. The last of the men of one company, awkward with slung rifles and girded with ammunition pouches, were climbing up the nets to *Cassandra*'s deck. The other company still sat on the thwarts of the pulling boats, rifles, Bren guns or mortars held upright between their knees. The major commanding them called from the sternsheets of his boat, reporting to Ellis, "All correct."

Ellis passed on to him the orders drawn up by Smith then looked over the white faces turned to him. He bawled a few cheerful words of encouragement, clearly so all of them could hear him: "Well done! They look fine!" Then he muttered, "God help them. They've got over their seasickness, anyway."

He transferred to one of the empty boats vacated by the soldiers now aboard *Cassandra*. It carried him back to the *Ailsa Grange*, there to brief the two companies still aboard her. He would not have long.

Smith boarded *Cassandra* and ran up the ladders to her bridge. Phillips would take Olsen below and see he got a meal and a cabin where he could rest. When Smith leant over the screen on the wing of the bridge he saw Harry Vincent, still in the fishing boat. Harry had taken in tow the boats from the *Ailsa Grange* carrying the company of soldiers. As Smith watched Harry got under way, the boats dragging astern, headed back to the inlet where Lugg waited. The Corporal would be showing a light briefly every ten minutes, as Smith had ordered – he glanced at his watch – starting about now.

Smith briefed his own officers, with Miller and the other officers from *Hornet*, and those from the company of soldiers now aboard *Cassandra*. Then he set them and their men to making their preparations, drove them all, striding rapidly among them: "Come on! We haven't got all night!" But he was on his bridge when Harry Vincent returned in Per Kosskull's boat and towing the now empty pulling boats rising and falling on the swell. Harry took them to the *Ailsa Grange* then brought the fishing boat back to *Cassandra* and reported to Smith on the bridge: "All the soldiers safe ashore and on their way, sir."

"Very good," Smith acknowledged, grateful for that one crumb of comfort. All manner of disasters might have befallen that first party; Harry getting lost or the soldiers landing only to be ambushed . . . But that had not happened. And now he glanced at his watch again and told Galloway, "I want all our boats inboard and quickly. Tell *Ailsa Grange* the same. As soon as she's ready we'll get under way."

He took a deep breath and sat back in his chair. There was a huge prize at stake this night. His orders demanded he should make this attempt to recover the cargo of – machine tools? But he would be lucky to come away with it. The bigger prize for him was out of his reach except for a miracle. But he could pray for that. He looked around at the ships, seen through the snow as shadows in the night, and the men like smaller shadows hurrying about their decks. He would pray for all of them.

*     *     *

151

It was quiet on the bridge now, all of them silent because they would soon be in action and no one could be sure he would survive. *Cassandra* slid into the mouth of the fjord at a creeping five knots, not a light showing except a red pin-prick in the night, like the glow from a cigarette, at her stern. That was a marker for the *Ailsa Grange* following her in. This was not like entering the Jössingfjord, with a moonlit sky and the yellow squares of lit windows. All was darkness and Smith could just see the loom of the headlands. The snow-shrouded slopes rose steeply from the water on either hand, the glassy surface of the fjord between.

Smith called softly into the tension, "Mr Appleby!"

The young midshipman jerked into life and hurried to his side, breathless. "Sir?"

Smith told him, "You're coming ashore with me, I want a minner and a signalman with his lamp to go with us. Get 'em."

"Aye, aye, sir!" Appleby scurried away and Smith faced forward again. That would keep the boy occupied.

He thought the snow was falling more thickly. Peering through it he could just make out the enemy troopship bulking large. She lay at anchor in the fjord off the little harbour. There was no need to worry about the lookouts on the headland because Lugg and the soldiers would have dealt with them. The snow had probably hidden *Cassandra*'s approach from the lookouts on the trooper, but now –? The men over there, with watering eyes on this bitterly cold night, might miss the slender cruiser, but not the bulk of the *Ailsa Grange*, standing high out of the water and broad in the beam.

He would not wait for them to raise the alarm. He wanted complete surprise. "Lights! Engage!"

They were the only orders needed. The searchlight above the bridge ignited with a crackle of carbons and shot out a long beam that found the end of the sea-wall, then ran along it like a questing finger and stopped on the

152

Oerlikon gun. It was not manned. Only a sentry, in a greatcoat reaching down to his ankles and with a rifle slung over his shoulder, stood beside it. "A" gun fired from *Cassandra*'s bow, was laid fractionally low and the shell burst below the sea-wall. The next was on target and the Oerlikon was hurled over onto its back. By then the sentry was off the sea-wall and running for his life across the quay. The snow spurted up from his boots and the long skirts of his coat flapped like wings.

Smith told Galloway, "Bring up the soldiers on the starboard side." That was the side away from the firing that started now, one machine-gun rattling from the shore then another. *Cassandra*'s replied, tracer-like fireflies arcing lazily across the dark sky. "Starboard a point:" to bring the ship's head around a fraction further towards the troopship, setting *Cassandra* gliding in across this sheltered water that lay still and reflective as a dark mirror.

The searchlights aft of *Cassandra*'s twin funnels were burning now. That sweeping the quay and square showed them now bare of guns and trucks. Smith wondered briefly at their absence – but first things first. The beams of the other two searchlights flooded over the troopship so Smith could see her name: *Wilhelmina*. She was a ship of around ten thousand tons with a single funnel and a long superstructure amidships. He thought she had probably been an ocean liner before the war. One of those giving "strength through joy" cruises to the Nazi Party members favoured by Hitler? But now she was less than a hundred yards away and men ran about her decks like disturbed ants as one of *Cassandra*'s light anti-aircraft guns fired a rapid burst over her.

He looked aft and saw the soldiers were on deck, a platoon of thirty men in the waist. They were grouped behind Chivers and the two dozen seamen armed with rifles who were his boarding-party. The soldiers would give him some extra hands to hold the ship. Smith turned back to the bridge. Kelso waited by the loudhailer, watching

Smith for orders, who gave them now: "You know what to tell 'em. There's a party coming aboard and if there's any resistance I'll open fire. Lay it on hard."

Kelso nodded and turned towards the troopship. He inflated his barrel chest, lifted the loudhailer and his voice boomed menacingly metallic: "*Achtung!* . . ."

As he went on with the rest of the warning, Harry Vincent, the navigator, straightened up from the compass and murmured, "Do they *really* say that?"

But there was no firing as *Cassandra* ground alongside the transport. Chivers and his seamen poured over the cruiser's side to board the *Wilhelmina* and passed lines to hold the two ships briefly together. Then the soldiers followed more clumsily.

Smith turned and saw *Ailsa Grange* anchoring astern of *Cassandra*. Her boats were swung out and being lowered. There were figures that would be khaki-clad but were black in the night, crowding her deck. Ellis was taking a chance bringing up his men so soon after firing from the shore. Or possibly he was demonstrating his trust in Smith, who breathed more easily as he saw that trust was not misplaced. *Cassandra*'s machine-guns were sweeping the shore and so were her light anti-aircraft guns, hurling the little 20 mm. shells into the square and the buildings. There was no answering fire now.

But beyond the little town, scarcely a village, the hillside was prickled with the darting flames of muzzle-flashes. That was the company of Ellis's soldiers that had been landed at the inlet and guided there by Corporal Lugg.

Smith faced forward and told Galloway, "Now bring up the marines." Then he snapped at Kelso, "Give me that!"

Kelso handed over the loudhailer and Smith demanded, voice crackling harsh and urgent between the two ships, "What's going on, Mr Chivers?"

Chivers appeared at the front of *Wilhelmina*'s bridge, lit by a searchlight's beam, as the echoes of the loudhailer died away. He answered using a hand megaphone, squawking, "She's ours, sir! Crew under guard and I've got her skipper and his officers here on the bridge. The skipper's surrendered the ship!"

Smith called, "Very good!" Chivers raised a hand in acknowledgment and Smith passed the instrument back to Kelso then turned on Appleby. "Bring your party!" Men were afraid in action. They would be bloody fools if they were not. Smith had to do something about this young officer – and see what Appleby could do for himself.

The midshipman looked thinner and paler under the big steel helmet he wore and in the flickering light from the guns. His voice followed squeakily as Smith slid down the ladders to the deck: "Aye, aye, sir!"

Merrick and his marines were gathered in the waist, going down into Per Kosskull's boat and one of *Cassandra*'s two launches. The rest of the soldiers still aboard would go in those launches. Muzzle-flashes and the darting beams of searchlights alternately dazzled the eyes or lit up the scene. Smith saw the sole launch carried by the *Ailsa Grange* was in the water and filling up with men. Ellis would be in it, but most of his soldiers would have to go ashore in the lifeboats from the *Ailsa Grange*, her seamen pulling at the oars.

When Smith reached the waist Appleby was at his heels and trailed by the two men Smith had asked for earlier. The signal yeoman had provided Sammy Williams, tubby, wide-eyed at the prospect of this landing under fire but a good signalman. The runner was Dobson. Jackman had detached him for this party because Dobson could run errands and Jackman intended to keep all his trained and experienced men. He had looked Dobson in the eye, seen the apprehension there and told him, "Just keep your head down, son, and do as you're told."

Dobson had replied with false bravado, "I'll be all right." And swallowed his nervousness.

Jackman could not answer that but cursed himself for the decision forced on him; he could not send anyone else.

Now Smith sent them down into Kosskull's boat, followed them and found Buckley waiting at the helm. At Smith's order the big leading hand eased the boat away from *Cassandra*'s side and turned it towards the shore. Smith, looking up and back, caught a glimpse of Galloway on the bridge and knew the Executive Officer was mentally shaking his head over Smith venturing ashore on this escapade. When Smith had briefed his officers Galloway had said, "You're going in with the landing party, sir?" Ostensibly a question but in fact a criticism. He had gone on, "Surely Major Ellis – "

But Smith had cut him off there, with the sparse explanation, "No. I am in command." And he would be there at the front, where he could see for himself if – when – things went wrong. Amphibious operations were complex. If Ellis had been experienced in carrying them out it would have been different. Or *might* have been. Smith grinned, being honest with himself, admitting he would probably have been in this boat anyway.

Appleby saw that grin and stared in disbelief. All of them in the long line of boats now heading towards the shore were crouching, automatically but uselessly, as the covering fire from *Cassandra* whined and howled overhead. And now there was firing again from the shore, the defenders there braving the steel flail that scourged the buildings in which they sheltered. Appleby heard a shriek of pain from forward in the boat, then saw another man collapse, to hang over the side of the launch some thirty yards to port. Hands reached out from the launch to drag him inboard. All this Appleby saw in the flickering, shifting light from the guns and the searchlights' beams. He felt Dobson shudder, pressed close against him in the sternsheets of the boat. Or was that the vibration from the engine?

Smith watched the boats and the shore. The launches from *Cassandra* and that from the *Ailsa Grange* were keeping in line with his boat but the pulling boats from the transport were falling further and further astern. He could have had them towed by the launches but that would have slowed the whole landing. Instead he was gambling that the initial landing by Merrick's marines and the hundred-odd soldiers in the three launches would distract the attention of the defenders from the slower boats. He would soon find out if he was wrong, prayed that he was right.

The stone wall of the quayside, glistening bottle-green with weed, was close now. The top of it stood six feet above the water of the little harbour but two flights of steps led up and Buckley was steering for one of them. To Smith's left lay the square. Ellis had to deal with that. But it was bare now, stripped of the vehicles that had crowded it earlier in the day. On the right was the forest that clothed most of the side of the fjord but here, close to the village, an area had been cleared. The narrow road coming along the side of the fjord ran out of the forest, through the clearing and into the town. There was only the small, squat hut in the clearing at the side of the snow-covered road. There was no sentry now and no firing from the hut. Had he run into the forest for cover?

Buckley laid the boat neatly at the foot of the steps and Merrick's launch bumped alongside. Smith sprang out onto the steps, skidded on weed then recovered and ran up them two at a time. He was aware of Merrick at the head of his marines just a running pace behind him. There was only firing from the houses in the square now, the barrage from *Cassandra* having ceased as the landing party charged ashore. Voices came only faintly through the scattered, echoing reports.

Appleby had frozen like stone under that flailing bombardment but now he was squeezed from his seat by the pressure of bodies, seamen and marines, forcing themselves out of the boat. Buckley's hand thrust into his back did the rest and he was out on the steps, taking Dobson with him.

Smith ran out onto the quay. He did not halt there in

that empty expanse devoid of cover but held on towards the road. In a few strides he was passed by Merrick, long-legged and young enough to be Smith's son. The marines, rifles held across their chests at the high port, raced after him. They fanned out as they came to the road, crossing it, then the clearing, and finding cover in the fringes of the forest.

The hut by the track was wooden but substantial, built of tarred timbers like railway sleepers, half a foot thick. Smith shoved at the door and entered as it swung open. He saw tools, axes and two-handed saws, stacked against one wall – used for clearing the timber outside? And he made out a table and a chair under the single window that looked out onto the road and the forest, then that grey square of the window was shattered by a bullet and he crouched below the table. Figures banged in through the swinging door one after the other: Appleby, Dobson, Sammy Williams clutching his signal lamp – and Buckley.

Smith glared at him. He had told Buckley to stay in the boat, given him a direct order but here he was. Buckley met the glare with a blank stare. Smith took a breath then let it out, promised himself he would deal with this later and instead snapped at Williams, "Send . . ." Orders to Galloway on board *Cassandra* to bring down fire higher in the forest. There were muzzle flashes up there and they would be from some of the German garrison. They had been taken by surprise and thrown out of the town by his two-pronged assault but they were still disciplined, still a threat. One of them had smashed the window. They had to be silenced and driven out of their positions.

He and Williams crawled past the others and out of the hut, round to the side away from the forest. Buckley followed them. Williams could use his lamp there and the signal blinked out. Smith bawled across to Merrick, "Sandy will be shooting-up the hill above you in a minute! Keep your men down till he finishes!" Then he looked past the clearing to the square and saw Ellis's soldiers crossing it at the double. There was no sign of firing from any of the buildings around the square now. The shelling had started fires in two of the buildings. They looked to be wooden and the flames were leaping high. He saw Ellis in the red light from the fire, pistol in one hand, the other arm outstretched and pointing as he shouted orders.

Appleby had watched Buckley leave the womb-like safety of the hut to follow Smith. Now there were only the two of them left in the deeper darkness in there and he felt rather than saw Dobson watching him. Appleby crawled out of the hut and with a shuddering breath stood up beside Smith. He found Dobson was behind him.

Smith turned and found them huddled close against him like . . . But the comparison would not be brought to mind. He warned, "Don't crowd together. You make too big a target." He glanced at Buckley, hunkered down behind a tree ten yards away and watching Smith, who nodded reluctant approval and muttered, "You bloody well ought to know." Then more mildly he told the other two, "Next time, spread out a bit but keep an eye on me for my orders."

The fire came in from *Cassandra* then and they all crouched. The shells shrieked overhead, showering them with broken branches and twigs from the overhanging trees before hammering into the forest. But now Appleby and Dobson, eyes on Smith, did not shake. When the guns fell silent again they heard Merrick's whistle and he and his marines climbed higher into the forested slopes. There was no more firing from up there.

Smith led his little party back into Bergsund and in the fire-lit square he met Ellis, who reported, "All secure. I've made contact with my company coming in from behind the town; in the form of your Corporal Lugg, in fact. Jerry has been squeezed out and he's now up in the forest." Ellis showed his teeth, white in a dirty face, a relieved grin. "He's probably wondering what the hell hit him. And it looks like you were right; he was only here in something like company strength." He waved his hand to encompass the empty square, "The vehicles and guns have gone, too."

Woodman, the interpreter, had appeared and now said, "I think I might be able to shed a little light there, sir." He had two men with him, one in his mid-twenties and in a khaki uniform, the other stout and twice his age, wearing a long overcoat and a fur hat. Woodman indicated the latter, "This is the mayor, for want of a better word. Anyway, he seems to be a local spokesman. He says the Germans are commanded by an *Oberst* Klaus Grundmann. He thinks there are about two thousand of them. They spent most of today unloading trucks, guns and supplies. Then later in the afternoon most of them set off to march inland. Just a couple of hours ago Grundmann loaded the rest into trucks and led them inland himself. He left one company to hold this place."

Smith looked at his watch and saw it was half an hour to midnight. And only one company left to hold Bergsund meant that the German commander – Grundmann – had not expected an assault by the British and was ignorant of *Cassandra*'s presence.

He asked, "Did this holding company have a wireless set?"

Woodman asked the mayor, who shook his head, but the tall young man in khaki spoke rapidly. Woodman listened and said, "He's sure they didn't have a set here."

Smith nodded. So Grundmann had relied on the telephone for his company holding Bergsund to keep in touch with him. That might be good news, because Corporal Lugg had cut the telephone lines, but the news of *Cassandra*'s arrival could be carried to Grundmann in other ways.

His gaze shifted to the young soldier with the mayor and he asked, "Who is this?"

Woodman answered, "This is Lieutenant Pettersen, Norwegian Army. The Jerries had him locked up as a

160

prisoner of war. I asked him where his unit was but he clammed up. Just says he came up from Oslo. He got here from Heimen by boat last night and Jerry grabbed him as he stepped ashore. But he wants to speak to you – the officer in command – sir."

The tall young man in khaki saluted. From Oslo? Smith nodded, "And I want to talk to him. Tell him I came here to embark a special cargo consigned by His Norwegian Majesty's government – eleven tons of it. Ask him if he knows anything about it."

Woodman put the question and translated the answer, sentence by sentence, the leaping light from the burning buildings casting shadowed hollows in the haggard face of the young Norwegian soldier as he poured out his story. "Well, sir, he says he and ten men of his platoon were detailed to escort this cargo up to Bergsund . . ."

Smith listened. They had boarded a train in Oslo before dawn on the 8th, nearly seventy-two hours ago. It was bound for the north and consisted of only one locked wagon holding the cargo and a coach to carry the ten soldiers and their two officers, Pettersen and a Major Edvard Vigeland, who had command. When they arrived at the railway terminus at Mosjöen the cargo was transferred to four trucks and continued north by road, heading for a secret hideaway. But when Vigeland reported to Oslo by telephone on the afternoon of the 9th he learned of the invasion and was told his orders were changed. He was to take the cargo to Bergsund instead, where it would be embarked on a British warship. Bergsund was chosen, presumably, because it was little more than a village and thought unlikely to be the objective of an invading force.

Just the same, when they arrived at Heimen after dark Vigeland decided not to go on to Bergsund. The road was bad for vehicles and once there he would have no room to manoeuvre. Instead he kept the four trucks and their cargo at Heimen under guard and ready to move north or south if need be. He sent Pettersen down to Bergsund by boat with orders to report to him by telephone as soon as the British ship arrived to embark the cargo. But when Pettersen stepped onto the quay at Bergsund he found he was looking down the barrel of a German rifle.

He was taken to the commander of the German force, *Oberst* Klaus Grundmann, who talked to him with sympathy but questioned him shrewdly. As time went on the sympathy was discarded and the questioning became harder. Pettersen gathered that Grundmann had taken Bergsund only a few hours before, one party of his soldiers coming in overland and cutting the telephone line before his ships entered the fjord.

Smith broke in sharply here, "Did he say ships? More than one?"

Woodman put the question and translated the answer: "He says there was a warship besides the *Wilhelmina*. He saw them both lying out in the fjord."

Smith wondered if that had been *Brandenburg*? If she had been here his landing would have been impossible. And cutting the telephone line? Smith grinned to himself. Tit for tat. Corporal Lugg had done that on Smith's order before *Cassandra* entered the fjord. "Go on."

Pettersen had tried refusing to answer Grundmann's questions, standing on the Geneva Convention and giving only his name and rank. But Grundmann jammed a pistol against his head and asked why a Norwegian officer had come to Bergsund. Pettersen was not sure whether he was bluffing and told him he had orders to report any German landing. Grundmann had then sat him down at the telephone and told him to report to Vigeland that all was well at Bergsund. But he was to say that the owner of the boat that brought him had gone down with an attack of dysentery so he would not be returning to Heimen until the man had recovered. Grundmann had listened in. Pettersen had talked with a noose around his throat ready to be snapped tight if he tried to convey a warning. Major Vigeland had ticked him off for not reporting sooner and

162

asked if a Royal Navy ship had arrived. Pettersen said it had not.

The same procedure was followed when he reported again, just before Grundmann left a few hours ago.

Smith said, "So the cargo is at Heimen?"

Pettersen confirmed through Woodman, "It is, sir, so far as he knows."

And Grundmann had gone inland. To Heimen, inevitably, because the only road out of Bergsund led there. Had he found the cargo? It would be a miracle if he had not. Was he still there?

Smith kept his face expressionless as he asked, "Is there an Englishwoman at Heimen?"

Woodman blinked but fed the question to Pettersen, who shook his head and replied tersely. Woodman said, "He doesn't know anything about Heimen. Says he was only there for a few minutes, just long enough to rout out the owner of the boat that brought him here."

Smith nodded, still wooden-faced, and told the interpreter, "Thank the Lieutenant and bring him along. Tell him we're going to look for his Major Vigeland and the cargo." He swung on Ellis, "Leave one company here to hold the place. Embark the other three companies in *Cassandra*." Leaving only one company was risky, as the commander of the sole German company left in Bergsund had found out, but Smith was going to need every man he could get. He sent Dobson running to tell Merrick to return to the ship with his marines as soon as the perimeter defences of the town were taken over by the holding company left by Ellis. Then he strode rapidly down to his boat where it lay by the quayside.

As Buckley laid the boat alongside *Cassandra* Smith ordered Appleby, "Get hold of Dobson when he comes back to the ship and keep your party aboard this boat." Then he was climbing the ladder to the cruiser's deck and on up to her bridge. There he brought Galloway up to date with the situation ashore then dictated to

163

the Yeoman a signal to Admiralty that he had taken Bergsund, submitted that the port would be a useful base for further operations, but warned that he could not hope to hold it without reinforcement and particularly air support.

Galloway was bawling orders down to the deck below where the soldiers coming off from the shore were swarming aboard: ". . . And get 'em *below*!" He turned and asked, doubting, "D'you think there's a threat from the air, sir?"

Smith said grimly, "I saw what the *Luftwaffe* did in Spain and I know what they did in Poland. They will be in business in Norway and without air cover we'll be sitting ducks." But he saw Galloway still did not believe him.

He asked, "Chivers?"

"Back on board, sir, with his boarding-party and the soldiers he had with him. Miller has the *Wilhelmina*."

Smith nodded, "Very good." Miller and those other survivors from *Hornet* who were fit for duty now formed the prize crew of the captured troopship.

He called Ellis and his company commanders to the bridge and briefed them and his own officers again as the last of the troops came aboard and the swirling snow thickened around them. Galloway, startled and worried, asked, "You're taking the ship up there, sir?" He did not believe this, either.

Smith grinned at him but mirthlessly, "I am." Then he went down into Per Kosskull's boat where Buckley waited at the helm. He took with him the grey-haired Olsen, young Lieutenant Pettersen and Woodman to join Appleby's party. There were also a dozen marines and two seamen with a leadline.

Up on the bridge Harry Vincent peered down through the snow at Smith in the boat and muttered to Galloway, "This man is worrying me again. Where the hell are we going?"

164

Galloway said drily, "You're the navigator."

"Oh, bloody funny." Harry flapped at the snow with a gloved hand, "But you can't see a yard forrard of the bridge in this muck. And what the hell is waiting for us at Heimen? We know there's a battalion and more gone up there *and* artillery. If we go aground then God help us. They'll use us like bottles stuck up on a wall and shoot us into very small pieces."

Galloway was of the same opinion but held his tongue. He had voiced his worries when Smith briefed his officers, and was worried still. As were all of them at the briefing. Only Smith had been confident. Galloway thought, He'd better be right, but –

He said, "I thought you'd changed your mind about him."

"I thought everybody had – even Ben Kelso. But now he leads us on a stunt like this!" Harry shook his head despairingly.

*Cassandra* sailed at midnight, with soldiers still milling on her deck and being herded below, boats from the *Ailsa Grange* being taken in tow. With Smith in Per Kosskull's boat leading the way she pushed into the blizzard that was raging now, sliding past the *Wilhelmina*. Miller, nursing his injured arm on the bridge of the captured transport, saw the cruiser as a grey ghost in a white world and said softly, "Good luck. You're going to need it."

Smith was still seeing the look of incredulity on Galloway's face as he said, "You're taking the ship up there, sir?" Smith had to. If he was to take Heimen in the teeth of Grundmann and his force then he would need *Cassandra*'s guns. But what if her gunners were blinded by the snow?

He was taking a calculated risk, backing his judgement of how Grundmann would act. He had to capture Heimen and the cargo of machine tools there, deny it to the enemy. That was his duty – though he had his suspicions about those "machine tools".

165

Then there was Sarah but he dared not dwell on thoughts of his daughter.

And, a constant spectre in his thoughts now, where was *Brandenburg*?

# 11

Sarah woke and jerked upright in the narrow, lumpy bed as the door of her room was kicked open. She had locked it before going to bed, as always, but now the lock was ripped from its seating and the door crashed back against the wall. The light blazed down from overhead as Fritsch flicked the switch. He stood framed in the doorway. All the time they had been in Norway, after leaving the *Altmark*, he had worn civilian clothes. But now he was dressed in grey-green service breeches and shirt, boots that glittered in the light.

He shouted at her, "Get dressed and packed! You have five minutes!"

The girl pushed at her blonde hair with one hand, still dazed after the sudden awakening, blinked sleepily at him and asked, "Now? Why?" Then more strongly as her thoughts came together, "You can't order me about like – "

But by then he had switched off the light and now grabbed a handful of the blonde hair. He dragged her out of bed and across to the window, snatched the curtains aside and thrust her face against the cold glass. He ordered, "Look!"

She saw the figures running in apparent confusion about the street, the sound of their boots muffled on the trodden snow. The first flakes of another fall drifted about them. Then she heard the hoarse, guttural shouting and realised these were soldiers responding to orders. Presumably they were the Norwegian troops who had arrived in four trucks

167

the day before and were quartered in a house at the other end of the village . . .

No.

She stared, at first shocked and bewildered. Then she felt sick as she accepted the awful fact. These were German soldiers.

Fritsch said, "They're here sooner than I thought. This place is now under German rule and so are you!" He threw her back towards the bed and barked, "Five minutes!" He drew the curtain, switched on the light again and strutted out of the room. He did not close the door. He had never had to.

Sarah closed it and sat on the bed as her knees gave under her. When she had met Fritsch again aboard the *Altmark* he had reminded her in that interview of her friend Frau Rösing and told her the young woman was in the concentration camp of *Sachsenhausen*. "She is guilty of crimes against the State." Fritsch had smiled at Sarah, "But those charges could be set aside if you co-operated."

Sarah did not trust him, but asked, "What do you mean by 'co-operate'?"

"I will see to it that Frau Rösing and her child are freed and allowed to go to a neutral country. All you will have to do in return is to make some broadcasts for us. You will be introduced as the daughter of an officer in the Royal Navy and you will name him: Captain David Smith. Then you will testify to the justice, humanity and benevolence of our National Socialist State and our Führer. And you will give some interviews to foreign journalists, for example from the United States, repeating the same – "

Sarah broke in, "Lies!"

Fritsch still smiled and finished, "– sentiments. And you will deny that you have been coerced; you will say you are acting of your own free will."

Sarah had agreed but privately resolved to renege on that agreement as soon as Mai Rösing and her baby were safe. She was sure Fritsch knew that but he had smilingly agreed and she knew why: He could not touch her while she was aboard *Altmark* but once ashore in Germany and in the Gestapo headquarters in the *Prinz Albrecht Strasse* she would be in his hands. She would honour the agreement then or take the consequences. She shrank from speculating on how much of the pain of those consequences she would be able to stand before she gave in and made the broadcasts.

And she had known all the time that he wanted more than the broadcasts, though he had not said so.

Now she dressed quickly with fumbling fingers, threw open her suitcase and began to pack. She had salvaged it from the *Altmark* the day after her boarding in the Jössingfjord. On the night of that boarding Fritsch had dragged her off the grounded ship and onto the ice as *Cossack*'s men freed the other prisoners in *Altmark*'s holds. He had told her, sneering, "That's a British destroyer but you're not going with them if you want Frau Rösing and her baby out of that camp."

So she had gone with him, climbing up the hillside from the fjord, and when she heard her father calling her name below she had obeyed Fritsch's orders for Mai Rösing's sake and shouted, "I'm staying with them! Leave me! I want to stay with them!"

But later when *Altmark*'s crew refloated her and sailed her back to Germany, Kurt Larsen going with them, Sarah had defied Fritsch: "I'm not leaving Norway until I see that girl and her baby!" To her surprise, Fritsch agreed, but she had to tell the British Embassy in Oslo that she did not want repatriation to England, wanted instead to stay in Norway with Fritsch. She also made that clear to the Norwegians. She and Fritsch stayed, but he insisted they leave Oslo and so they came to Heimen. He had driven her there in the Mercedes 170V given to him by the German Embassy in Oslo. In Heimen she had waited for news of Mai Rösing and Fritsch had waited for – what? She had wondered, not trusting him to release

169

Mai and her child, suspicious of his smug patience. Now she knew.

Yesterday the people of Heimen had heard on the radio that Hitler's forces had invaded Norway. They had told Fritsch that he was under house arrest. When the Norwegian Major Vigeland arrived with his soldiers he posted a sentry on the house to enforce that arrest.

That made no difference to Sarah. Norway had been neutral but was now an ally of her country. Despite that Fritsch still had his hold on her. If she did not obey him then Mai Rösing and her child would remain – and die – in *Sachsenhausen*.

Fritsch had told her, smiling, "You'll stay with me. And we'll wait."

Sarah fastened the suitcase, switched off the light and twitched back the curtains to peer out into the night. She saw the Norwegian sentry had gone from the front door, of course. There were the soldiers' voices still but they were German voices, cheerful and interspersed with hoarse laughter. The men did not run but walked and their rifles were slung on their shoulders. Any fighting was over but she had not heard a shot.

The *Wehrmacht* controlled Heimen and Fritsch's patience was explained: he had known the invasion of Norway was imminent. Now she could not turn to the Norwegians for help, was completely in his power.

And Sarah knew he did not want her just for the propaganda broadcasts. In that first interview aboard *Altmark*, Fritsch had said the member of the Berlin underground organisation captured by the Gestapo had told them a great deal. Sarah knew he was lying. The man had worked only on the fringe of the organisation, had known only her and the Rösings. And Mai Rösing could have told Fritsch little or nothing because her dead husband had been her only connection with the underground.

But Sarah had been an active member and knew a lot more. She could give names, point to faces and hideouts –

if she broke under questioning. And Fritsch would try any means to break her.

As if reading her thoughts he threw open the door and said softly, "Now you're in my hands. You will play the game by my rules. And in Berlin we will have a gathering of old friends."

She followed him out into the snow.

# 12

On *Brandenburg*'s bridge Gustav Moehle grumbled, "This snow is a curse as well as a blessing!" He sat leaning forward in his captain's chair to peer out into the blizzard. He was taking his ship into Narvik fjord to join the destroyers there. It was a long way past midnight and in the day just ended a British destroyer flotilla commanded by Captain Warburton-Lee had swept through the fjord, sunk two of the ten German destroyers in there and killed Bonte, the officer in overall command. *Kommodore* Bey now commanded the surviving destroyers.

Moehle said sombrely, "It's a sad business losing Bonte. And a lot of other good men have died. Bey should get out of there as quick as he can or the *Tommis* will be at his throat."

Kurt Larsen stood close by with Paul Brunner, the Executive Officer, both of them silent. They all knew a British naval force was cruising off Narvik fjord and strained their eyes now, looking for it. The snow was a blessing because it hid them, a curse because it also hid the enemy. Any sighting, any action, would be at point-blank range. The nerves of all of them on the bridge were strung taut by the tension.


Per Kosskull's fishing boat shoved chugging into an endless curtain of white on a surface of dull, rippled silver that was the ice-cold water of the fjord. Pettersen with Appleby and Dobson were in the little cabin out of the way but all those in the well were coated in snow. Buckley stood at the wheel with Olsen and Woodman alongside him, Smith just behind. Most of the marines were in the well, rifles slung over their shoulders, with one of the seamen waiting to take his turn with the lead. The other stood in the bow, casting the lead and calling out the depth, steadily, monotonously: "By the mark seven . . . By the deep eight . . ." Two of the marines crouched beside him, a Bren gun resting on its bipod legs between them.

*Cassandra*'s dark bulk loomed close astern of the boat, following the light in the boat's stern, seen from the cruiser's bridge as no more than a red spark burning in the night. The tubby Williams sat in the sternsheets, clutching the signal lamp on his knees and ready to send any orders from Smith to *Cassandra*. Olsen pointed out the buoys marking the deep water channel, continually wiped snow from his eyes to peer ahead, and muttered hoarse instructions to Buckley at the wheel. They were translated by Woodman standing hunched against the bitter cold. In between giving steering orders Olsen hummed softly, some tune that Smith did not recognise, and seemed elated by this adventure.

Smith grinned sourly and reflected that Olsen was in a position to be be relatively cheerful. But suppose he were responsible for the cruiser and all aboard her . . . That would be a different matter. If *Cassandra* ran aground or was crippled and sunk in this fjord by the enemy then Smith would face a court martial. And the lives lost would lie on his conscience. If he survived.

The night wore on as *Cassandra* crept up the fjord and Smith squinted at his watch again and again by the light of a torch. Time was slipping away and God alone knew what the sunrise would bring in terms of support for the enemy – or himself? But he dared not trust to the latter, had to assume he was, and would be, alone. And the light of day? None of them would see the sun in this filthy weather . . .

Until Olsen chattered eagerly at Smith, then Woodman,

frozen-faced and the snow caked on him, translated, "The village is around the next bend, sir."

Smith heaved a sigh of relief that they were there, then his breath quickened, though he did not realise it, at the thought of the action that was imminent. He was gambling and if he lost then these men, *Cassandra*'s crew and Ellis's soldiers, would pay for it in blood. The snow had eased, not much, but the circle of visibility had widened just enough for him to see the turning ahead, the line of the marker buoys curving to disappear between the steep walls of the fjord. Was that good news or bad? He said, "Thank Mr Olsen for his help." Then to Williams crouched in the stern with his signal lamp, "Order the ship to stop."

When the signal was brought to *Brandenburg*'s bridge it only heightened the tension. Moehle took the flimsy and read it silently then paraphrased aloud, "It's from Grundmann's holding force at Heimen: A British warship and transport have landed troops and retaken the port. Our troops have retired to consolidate their positions. In other words they've had to run like hell and they're screaming for help." He passed the signal to Brunner and ordered, "Tell the navigating officer I want a course for Bergsund."

Paul Brunner turned to pass on the order but called Kurt Larsen, "Do you want to bet which 'warship' that might be? I'll lay odds it's that damned cruiser we keep running into!" Then he finished triumphantly, "But if we can catch her in Bergsund fjord then we've got her!"

*Brandenburg* turned and headed out to sea.

*Cassandra* slowed and came to rest in response to the blinking of Williams' lamp while the boat circled with Buckley's hands on the helm, to slide in against the cruiser's starboard side. Smith climbed the ladder to her

174

deck and thence to her bridge then gave his orders. The boats being towed were hauled in to cluster along the starboard side with Per Kosskull's boat still holding Buckley and the others. The soldiers and marines from *Cassandra* went down into the boats and now the launches took them in tow.

The cruiser got under way and edged forward at a walking pace, turning slowly to round the bend in the fjord. Smith and Galloway had their glasses trained to port where lay the village, as yet unseen. There also lay the enemy. The boats, towed by the launches, bobbed along at *Cassandra*'s starboard side, protected by her from the fire of that enemy. The fjord opened ahead of them, a hillside lifting to starboard, grey and dimly seen through the falling snow, at the limit of their vision. And there to port was Heimen, also masked by the snow so the houses and other buildings showed only as furred black squares and rectangles against the soft-falling, drifting white, and surrounded by the ragged-edged silhouette of the forest.

They saw – and were seen. Flames spurted in the dark tunnels under the trees, shells howled over the ship and there was a *crash!* from forward. Galloway cursed and Smith said, "They're expecting us so the company Grundmann left at Bergsund must somehow have got a warning through to here." And whoever commanded here – Grundmann? Smith thought not, hoped not – but whoever commanded here, knowing there was no motor transport at Bergsund, had sited his guns to repel an attack from the fjord. But had he expected only boats and was *Cassandra* a horrible surprise?

Either way, this would not be easy. Smith opened his mouth again to order *Cassandra*'s guns to open fire then shut it again as the snow swept in thickly on the wind once more, and the village was blotted out of his sight. Instead he told Galloway, "Tell Sandy to be ready to return fire instantly when the enemy can be seen." Sandy Faulknor, the Gunnery Officer up in the director control tower, would be as blind as the rest of them at this moment. "When we're ashore I'll send orders by Williams." Then he went down to the fishing boat again.

This time he ordered the boats to stay together, the launches continuing to tow the others. The enemy could not see them. So as Buckley steered Per Kosskull's boat shorewards through the snow the three launches, one of them from the *Ailsa Grange* and the others from *Cassandra*, were lined out abreast on the port side. The pulling boats from the cruiser and the transport, soldiers hunched on their thwarts, were towed astern of the launches. Smith knew Merrick was in the launch next alongside, Ellis in one of the others.

Briefly, for just minutes, they moved in a near-silent, white-enclosed world with the only sound the throb of the engines of the launches and Kosskull's boat. Then the snow thinned ahead of them, the shore showed dark and shadowy at first but a second later hardened into sharp images. There was a stone quay and beyond it houses and buildings, scattered or grouped but few in number. The quay was lined with stacks of sawn timber awaiting a ship. The tide, nearly at the full, now lapped barely three feet below the quay.

The silence was shattered as the enemy guns hammered furiously. There were two of them, hauled in under the shelter of the trees at the forest's edge. They were quick-firing anti-aircraft pieces but the boats were too close to shore now. The guns could not depress far enough to lay on them and the 40mm. shells whined uselessly overhead. Small arms fire cracked and rattled from riflemen and machine-gunners hidden in houses and buildings. The Bren guns mounted in the bows of the launches and Smith's boat fired in return but only for seconds. Then the boats slid in under the cover of the quay and the firing died away.

The two marines in the bow were first out of the boat, jumping up onto the quay. Carrying the Bren and the spare ammunition, they raced for cover among the stacks of timber. But Smith was next and close behind them as the firing burst out again. It struck sparks from the stonework of the quay and bit splinters out of the timber as he threw himself panting into its shelter.

Appleby saw him go and found he was following, breath sobbing as he scrambled onto the quay, crouching almost double as he ran to join Smith. As he left the boat he called for Dobson and Williams: "Come on!" The squeak was lost in the din of firing but they went shudderingly after him anyway.

Smith saw them arrive, then Pettersen with Woodman and finally Buckley. When he saw Smith peering out over the top of the timber he puffed worriedly, "Keep your head down, sir!"

"Shut up! You sound like a bloody old woman!" Smith snapped, on edge, feeling a huge, fragile target. But he had to know what was going on. He had already seen Merrick dash across the quay only a score of yards away to the left with a crowd of his marines after him. And beyond him and further left still by another twenty or thirty yards, Ellis had charged ashore at the head of his men. All of them had taken cover among the stacks of timber and they were opening fire. But now Smith had to see what terrors lay ahead of them all so his head was lifted cautiously above the timber.

Like Bergsund, the village had been built in a clearing cut out of the forest that now stood back some two hundred yards from the quay. The two guns under the trees were still silent, this time because they were under a hail of fire from the marines and soldiers among the stacks of timber. The guns' crews were either dead or gone into cover. In front of the trees ran a belt of open ground, snow-covered and dotted with clumps of low scrub. Then, closer, were the houses and buildings of the village and firing still came from these. They were themselves torn by the fusillades from the quayside.

177

Between the stacked timber and the houses lay the road. The snow covering its surface was flattened, rutted and dirtied where the wheels of trucks had churned it up. Smith thought, Grundmann's trucks? The road disappeared into the forest on either hand, to Smith's left to meander along the side of the fjord back to Bergsund, to his right to join the main road inland running north and south. There was no motor transport parked among the houses or on the quay.

Smith gulped down a breath of relief. Grundmann had shown himself to be an energetic commander, had not been content to sit at Bergsund but had driven on to Heimen. Smith had judged he would not rest there, either, and was now proved right. He had gambled that the village would only be comparatively lightly held, that he would not have to attempt a landing in the face of Grundmann's entire force of more than a thousand men and their artillery. If he had been wrong the landing would still have succeeded in the end, *Cassandra*'s guns would have seen to that, but the bloodshed . . . He shied away from the thought.

Pettersen was tugging at his sleeve and pointing. Smith looked in that direction and saw, to the right of the straggling row of houses, one that was bigger but only single-storeyed, that stood on its own. Pettersen shouted above the din of firing and Woodman bellowed, "He says his trucks were parked there! They've gone! And that house was empty so Major Vigeland requisitioned it for quarters for him and his men! The soldiers were in there!"

And where was the cargo of machine tools? Smith shouted, "Mr Merrick!" He saw the marine's face turn towards him and in his turn pointed to the house standing alone. Merrick lifted a hand in acknowledgment then turned to Sergeant Phillips beside him, giving rapid orders, finger jabbing in his turn as he told Phillips what he wanted done. Smith's gaze lifted to the soldiers further along the quay as their firing built up so that it battered at the ears. At that same instant he saw a group of them break from the shelter of the timber piled at that far end of the quay. Under the cover of the firing they ran across the road and disappeared among the farthest houses. Then he heard the *thump!* of exploding grenades.

Merrick seized on that moment and charged out into the open, half of his marines with him. The dozen sheltering with Smith had already seen Merrick's hand-signal to them and now ran around the end of the stacked timber to join him. Phillips and the rest were left to continue the main attack.

Smith went with Merrick and his marines, crouching and swerving, floundering and skidding through the snow as they did. He saw from the corners of his eyes that Buckley was at his right shoulder, Appleby at his left and the rest streaming behind them. Again they reminded him of – what? But again he could not remember.

The stabbing flames of muzzle-flashes licked out from the windows of the house and he heard the *clap!* as a rifle round cracked past his head. But then Merrick and his marines were swarming around the house, lobbing grenades through the front windows and kicking at the door. The grenades exploded in succession, with the rapid regularity of a ticking clock. There was shouting from inside the house but no more firing. A hand showed at one window, waving what looked to be a blanket. Was that meant to signal a surrender? Now rifles were thrown out of the windows to fall into the snow.

Smith leant beside the front door, catching his breath. Buckley, Appleby and the rest fetched up close to him. Now, at last, he remembered: they reminded him of children clustered around their mother's skirts. He grinned at them, then turned his attention to the house again.

The front door had swung open under the battering from the boots of the marines. Now Merrick led them in – cautiously. Smith followed, peering into the gloom

179

of the house and fumbling for the torch in his pocket. The beam of another lanced out and danced around the narrow hallway then swept on to the rooms opening out on either side. Smith made out Merrick's tall, ramrod figure against the glow of it. The marine was holding the torch out left-handed and at arm's length from his side, away from his body. That was in case some enemy fired at the torch. He held his pistol in his right hand, its muzzle twitching to follow the beam of the torch.

There were *Wehrmacht* soldiers in both those front rooms, half a dozen in each of them backed against the wall with their hands held high. One lay on the floor, moaning. Another, that had taken the full blast of an exploding grenade, sprawled still and horribly dead. Blankets and packs littered the floor around them. A table in one corner held mess-tins, bread and sausage. The soldiers had obviously been quartered there – as had Major Vigeland and his men.

Smith remembered Pettersen at his back but Merrick was calling orders to his marines: "Look after that wounded man! Get the others outside!" Then he ventured deeper into the house and Smith went with him.

There were two more rooms, the doors of both of them locked. The marines kicked in one of them and they saw the room beyond it crowded with Norwegian soldiers. Their leader stood at the head of them, facing the door. He was a tall, heavy man, his hair cropped short and his eyes narrowed against the glare of the torchlight. Pettersen went to him, shoving past Smith, and the pair clasped hands.

Smith thought: Major Vigeland. He swept the beam of his torch around the room, the cone of light flitting over the pale faces that were nervous, blank or relieved. There were about a dozen of them and their blankets also still lay on the floor. They marked where the men had slept, slotted into the room like sardines into a tin. He saw that the room had been made into a rough prison. Planks had

180

been nailed over the outside of the only window and then crisscrossed by barbed wire.

He turned back to Vigeland and Pettersen and said shortly, "I command. Where is the cargo to be embarked?"

Vigeland answered in accented English, "It was in the four trucks outside, under guard."

Smith said, "There are no trucks outside."

Vigeland winced as if struck and then ground out through clenched teeth, "Then the thieves have stolen the – cargo."

Smith noted that hesitation and he did not believe the statement. Grundmann had taken the trucks to carry some of his men and so increase the mobility of his force. He would not burden his motor transport with eleven tons of – machine tools? He still thought the question mark – or of any other loot.

But Vigeland was going on, "They came out of the trees in the night and caught my sentries not ready. Two were guarding the trucks and one was outside the house of the German officer. They were caught before they could use their weapons or raise the alarm. Grundmann's men must have been watching from the trees for a time, seeing where the sentries were posted and marking this house where the rest of us were sleeping." He finished bitterly, angrily, "They took this place without firing a shot."

Smith read between the lines: Grundmann's men, those sent ahead from Bergsund on foot and the others following in trucks, had met short of Heimen. Then they had waited, watched and picked their time to strike. But . . .

He asked, "What German officer is this? What is he doing here?"

Vigeland shrugged. "I do not know. I found him here. I understand he came here with a woman about a month ago. They are in a house at the other end of the village."

Smith took that in with a breath of hope. He was aware that there was still firing outside, though distantly now. The trampling of the marines' boots filled the house and

181

from close behind him came the sound of hammering and splintering woodwork. Then he saw Vigeland watching him, curious, and Smith said forcefully, "No blame attaches to you. On the information you had, there wasn't an enemy within a hundred miles of you, let alone at Bergsund. And any defence you might have attempted would have been a waste of your men's lives. I shall say so in my report." Against odds of a hundred to one *and* artillery, it would have been suicidal for Vigeland to resist.

Merrick called from the hallway, "I think you should see this, sir."

Smith went to him and found the sound of splintering woodwork explained. The marines had forced the locked door of the last room and it was shoved wide and hung crookedly on its hinges. The beam of Merrick's torch shone into the room beyond and lit a stack of small wooden boxes. The stack was the size of a large table. *Machine tools*?

He ordered Merrick, "Leave a corporal and one man on guard here. Nobody enters but me. Make that clear."

"Sir." Merrick looked puzzled, as well he might.

Smith turned and found himself face to face with Vigeland, told him, "I think we've found your cargo."

The tall Norwegian nodded, "Yes. Yes!" He beamed with relief at seeing his charge restored – and because Smith had promised to absolve him of any blame for its loss and that of Heimen?

The house at the end of the village . . . But first: Smith pointed a finger at Dobson, "Find Major Ellis and tell him I would like his report as soon as possible. Tell him I will be working my way through the village."

Dobson swallowed unhappily, Adam's apple bobbing. "Aye, aye, sir!" He turned, hesitated, then plunged out into the open ground again, heading back to the stacks of timber lined along the quay.

Vigeland was trying to edge past Smith into the room

182

where the cargo was held. Smith stepped in front of him and said, "I would like you to wait here for me. My marines have orders not to admit anyone. I will return as soon as I can and then we will conclude our business."

Vigeland was ready to argue but then saw something in Smith's face that stopped him. He reluctantly agreed and Smith went on his hurried way.

He strode through the village, his little party trailing him. Dobson rejoined, breathless from running through the clogging snow but managing to grin now the firing had ceased. Ellis was with him, smoke-grimed and filthy as all of them were from the action, come to report: "The place is ours, sir."

He said his soldiers had got in among the houses at the far end of the village and rolled up the defences from there. The marines under Sergeant Phillips had started from the other end and in a matter of minutes the defenders had filtered away into the forest. They had retreated deeper into it as they were pursued. The guns were abandoned. Bodies lay as if tossed carelessly aside in the clearing between houses and forest, some in grey-green, some in khaki. In the night all of them looked like splashes of dried blood scattered on the trampled snow.

Now there was silence except for the occasional *crack*! of a shot in the middle distance, flat and muffled by the trees and snow.

Smith told Ellis, "We've got your cargo."

Now the major looked relieved, partly because of that cargo, but also because of the success of the landing and the few casualties. Some of his men were digging graves for the dead and carrying wounded down to the boats but there were mercifully few of either. Smith thought one was too many.

He went through the buildings, stores and houses, all with shattered windows and bullet-splintered timbers. One house had caught fire and a bucket-chain of Ellis's soldiers were trying but failing to douse the flames. The chain stretched up from the fjord and there were only five buckets. Buckley growled, "Might as well piss on it."

Smith apologised to the people he found and they told him through Woodman: "It seems Grundmann got here about three hours ago, sir. He just walked in. Then he left one company here, took some of his men and guns northward in trucks, and the rest marched south. All was quiet after that until about ten minutes before we arrived. One soldier staggered out of the forest on the road from Bergsund, yelling to wake the dead. Then all the soldiers here turned out and trained the guns round to bear on the fjord."

Then, listening to one glowering man: "This chap, sir, says Jerry had a wireless set up in his house. They turfed him out of the front room to put it in there. He's still bloody annoyed about it."

Smith nodded. So the company left at Bergsund had not held a wireless set or been able to tap the telephone wire to Heimen further up the road after Lugg had cut it. They had sent a runner and he had done well to get here before *Cassandra*, ploughing his way along a snow-covered road. But the wireless here would have passed on the news to Grundmann that *Cassandra* was at Heimen. He would be on his way back now.

Smith was a tangle of emotions now: grief for the dead, rage at the stupidity of this campaign because Hitler had out-manoeuvred the Allies – and anxiety warring with hope. At every encounter with a villager he had asked the same question. Woodman had shown his surprise when he first put it, but caught Smith's eye and translated it without expression. All those asked said a young woman was staying with a German officer in the big house at the end of the village, though none of them had been able to speak to her. The officer had forbidden it. But several thought she was British.

Smith kept to a steady pace though he wanted to run. When at last they came to the house Woodman put the

184

same question to the couple who lived there and translated their answer: "They say the girl spoke English to them but only the odd word or two, like 'Good morning'. It seems this German officer they all keep talking about was with her. They didn't like him. He came as a civilian but they knew what he really was. He was pleasant enough at first, wanting to board with them and he was paying well. But then he became arrogant. He did most of the talking and gave the orders. He wouldn't let the girl talk to them or them to her. He told them it wasn't allowed. When the people around here heard that Jerry had invaded they confined him to the house, but the girl stayed with him . . ."

Woodman listened again as the man spoke and the woman at his side nodded and put in a word here and there. When they were silent again Woodman said, "They say when the German soldiers came the officer dressed in his uniform. Then he took her away in his car. That was about an hour before midnight. They don't know where he's taken her."

# 13

Smith had no time to grieve or rage. Grundmann would be racing back to Heimen with his motorized transport now, as fast as he could on the snow-covered roads. He could arrive at any minute.

So Smith hastened back to the house that held the cargo. The air in the village stank of cordite fumes and the smoke that rolled across it from the blazing timbers of the house that still burned. *Cassandra* lay out in the fjord, a furred grey silhouette seen intermittently between flurries of snow. The wind moaned in up the fjord from the sea and the men's voices came through it thinly as they worked. They sounded cheerful, still excited by this action. Water rose in a darkly glittering column higher than the quay as the second of the German guns was shoved over to sink in the fjord and join the first. That was by Smith's orders.

At the house he found the two marines guarding the door leading to the cargo, their rifles held across their chests at the high port. Ellis, the Norwegian Major Vigeland and his men crowded around it. Smith pushed through them and the sentries stepped aside. He passed into the room and Vigeland tried to follow but the marines barred his way.

Smith said, "All right, let those officers in." And to Vigeland, "Major Ellis was sent with me to embark this cargo."

The marines edged aside again and Vigeland and Ellis joined Smith, who now used his torch. Its beam lit the dusty interior and the stack of small boxes filling the centre of the floor. The boxes were wooden, their lids screwed down and bound round with wire that was fastened with a lead seal. Smith measured them with his eye and estimated each was about fifteen inches long by six inches wide and six deep. The stack was four feet high, four feet wide and about nine feet long. He counted: 440 boxes. He lifted one an inch or two then set it back in its place. He guessed its weight at half a hundredweight, a heavy half-hundredweight.

He turned on Vigeland and asked him, voice dry but lowered so only Ellis and Vigeland could hear, "Machine tools?"

Vigeland shook his head and murmured, "Gold. There are two ingots in each box, sir. Eleven tons altogether, making about three million pounds in sterling."

Ellis breathed, "*Three million . . .!*" And stopped there, eyes starting out of his head as he stared at the stack of boxes.

Smith nodded his acknowledgment at Vigeland, "Thank you." So that was it. The Norwegian government was shipping its gold reserves out of the country before the *Wehrmacht* could seize them. This consignment was just a part of those reserves, evacuated early from Oslo.

Eight hundred and eighty ingots. Three million pounds. He worked out some rough sums in his head: One box would buy a dozen comfortable houses or fifty brand new motor cars. It would pay the wages of the two marine sentries at the present rate for the next fifty years. The whole pile of boxes would have bought for Hitler ten destroyers or U-boats, or two cruisers like *Brandenburg*.

But not now.

And it was clear why he had been ordered to risk his ship and his men, Ellis his soldiers. How many lives might ten U-boats have taken? One had sunk the battleship *Royal Oak* in Scapa Flow with the loss of a

187

thousand men only a few months ago. U-boats had sunk so much shipping in 1917 that Britain was almost starved into submission.

He took a breath and remembered: *Brandenburg* – where was she?

Smith turned his back on the bullion and told Ellis, "Transfer it to the ship. Put every man on it you can spare and every box is to be guarded every inch of the way." He shoved through the Norwegian soldiers still packed shoulder to shoulder in the hallway and so out of the house, Vigeland following him. There he ordered Sammy Williams to send a signal by his flickering lamp to Galloway, to expect the "cargo" of 440 boxes that was to be locked away below and kept under guard. Then he faced Vigeland. "I'll give you a receipt. What are you going to do? I can find room for you and your men and see you are landed in a British port eventually."

The Major shook his head. "We lost our battle but the war goes on. We will go into the forest and find other units of our army, then carry on the fight."

Woodman translated the terms of the receipt for Smith who signed for 440 sealed boxes. He thought of the oddity of the setting for this business transaction involving a fortune in gold. The receipt was signed by torchlight and was soiled and crumpled already from the grubby fingers that had handled it. The bucket-chain had abandoned its hopeless attempt to fight the fire, and the leaping flames from the burning house lit the scene, painted it in shifting, lurid colours.

A hundred or more soldiers obeying the shouted orders of Ellis were carrying the bullion down to the boats for transfer to *Cassandra*, leaning back under the weight of the boxes held in their arms. They piled the boxes in whichever of the three launches lay alongside the quay – they were running a shuttle service out to *Cassandra* – then ran back to the house for more. Sniper fire crackled on the outskirts of the village and there were bodies and blood on the snow. Little Appleby's thin face was smeared with dirt, black against the pallor of his skin, his eyes large. Dobson's skinny figure hovered close behind him. Smith thought, Sticking to him like glue. And both of them sticking to Smith. Buckley's big figure loomed at his back.

They followed him as he strode quickly down to the quay. He halted there and from that position supervised the withdrawal of the landing force. Williams used his lamp again and again as signals winked between ship and shore. Ellis and his soldiers went back to *Cassandra*, leaving only Merrick's marines in a thin screen holding positions around the outskirts of the village. Smith's head was cocked on one side now, listening. He saw Appleby watching him and asked, "Hear anything?"

Appleby nodded, "Yes, sir. It sounds like engines."

"And getting louder, closer. I think we're going to have company soon." And to Merrick, "All right, bring out your men now."

Merrick's whistle shrilled and the marines came floundering and sliding through the snow. They dropped down into the boats one by one, Merrick counting them, with the stocky Sergeant Phillips bouncing down last of all. The rumble of the labouring engines of the trucks was loud now as Merrick reported, "That's the lot, sir!"

The three launches chugged out into the fjord and now only Smith and his little party of Appleby, Dobson and Sammy Williams, the signalman, stood on the quay. The snow had thickened again and hid *Cassandra* so they seemed to be on their own. Dobson and Sammy exchanged uneasy glances and Appleby watched Smith. The first truck came swaying out of the forest a quarter-mile away. It ground to a halt and men spilt out of the back of it. They scattered to form a skirmishing line, dropped down into the snow and a rifle cracked, spurted flame. Smith did not hear the passage of the bullet, guessed that it had been fired hurriedly and high but he ordered, "Into the boat!"

Appleby and the others needed no urging as more bullets whined overhead or ricochetted droning from the stone surface of the quay. They jumped down into Per Kosskull's boat and Smith followed them. He stood, looking back as the boat surged away from the quay, balancing against the heel and pitch of it. He saw other trucks come out of the forest, lurching and sliding on the rutted, frozen road. They pulled up alongside the first and disgorged more soldiers. The trucks and the men would have made a fine target for Sandy Faulknor's guns but the snow hid one from the other.

A solitary tall figure stalked to the centre of the line of prone riflemen and halted there, staring after the boat. Smith thought that would be Grundmann and that he would be asking questions as to how Heimen had been taken and his captured bullion snatched from him. But not for long.

Smith wondered if Vigeland and his men had succeeded in slipping away into the forest, or had they been captured again? But now the rifle-fire ceased as the shore astern was hidden by the snow driving thickly on the wind and instead *Cassandra* loomed ahead. He saw that her boats had been hoisted inboard and those from the *Ailsa Grange* taken in tow astern. Only his boat was left. It ran in alongside and Smith jumped for the ladder dangling and bumping against the steel side as the cruiser rolled gently under the pressure of the wind. He climbed it and thence to the bridge where he found Galloway, obviously relieved at sight of him.

Galloway reported, poker-faced, "The – cargo – is locked away below and under guard, sir."

"Very good." Smith thought wrily that now they were just keeping up appearances. Galloway, like every other man aboard, would have a very good idea of the nature of that cargo in the small boxes that weighed so heavily.

He asked, "What about that shell that hit us?"

"Pretty small stuff, sir. 40 millimetre, I think. It made a dent in the shield of 'A' gun but that's all."

Smith swung up into his chair. "We'll get under way." Grundmann would not wait in Heimen for a long inquest into its capture by Smith, nor for the rest of his force to come up on foot. He would call out those troops that had retreated into the forest and cram into his trucks as many men as they would hold. Then he would start down the road to Bergsund. He would find it a long haul because that snow-bound road would be worse now. A lot more snow had fallen since Grundmann had driven out of Bergsund five or six hours ago. But the sooner Smith and *Cassandra* were back at that port, the better.

Buckley came to the bridge, bringing coffee and sandwiches for him. Smith realised he was bitterly cold and his exertions had exhausted him. He reached for the food but first told Galloway, "I want everyone fed, but the ship's company first." The soldiers would have to wait. Now the fighting ashore was over they were just passengers again, but the men of *Cassandra* might be in action soon. Now he chewed hungrily and gulped down the coffee.


Below on the mess desk Jackman paused by Dobson where he sat at a crowded table. Both were red-eyed from lack of sleep, grimy and stank of smoke. Dobson had a plate of bacon and eggs in front of him. He looked up from it, found Jackman's cold eye on him and said defensively, "Just having me breakfast."

Jackman nodded and growled, "You've earned it. I've talked to that big bastard, Buckley. You did all right."

And Dobson saw he meant it. As Jackman strode away one of the other men crammed around the table asked, "What was that about?"

Dobson opened his mouth – now was the time to start rehearsing his speech for the pub when he got home – but then he said only, "Dunno. Pass the sauce."


Smith saw nothing of Grundmann's lorries, little of the shore as *Cassandra* crept back along the buoyed channel through the snow and darkness. Per Kosskull's boat led the way, with Olsen and Woodman aboard, Chivers in command. The dawn came sunless, the night sky turning dirty grey and pendulous clouds hanging over the fjord. *Cassandra* slid along a tunnel through that greyness that was floored with a dull-green glassy surface scattered with the blue-white plates of floating ice.

At Bergsund they heard the faint crackle of rifle-fire from the port and saw the red pin-pricks of the muzzle-flashes in the night. But the firing was intermittent and came from the holding company left by Ellis, and the Germans driven out of the port, shooting at each other. Grundmann had not yet arrived.

"Signals, sir."

Smith took the two flimsies and read the first, passed it to Galloway. No reinforcements could be sent to Bergsund nor could he receive any air support. The port was not to be held after all. Ellis and his battalion were to return home in the *Ailsa Grange*.

He thought that the High Command was having to recast its plans hurriedly now that Hitler had stolen a march on them by invading Norway.

The signal went on to order him to embark in the *Ailsa Grange* the cargo *Hornet* had been sent for – if he had got it. Then he was to rendezvous north of Bergsund with a destroyer returning from the force blockading the Vestfjord, outside of Narvik, to Scapa Flow. She would escort the transport home. *Cassandra* would then proceed to join that force off Narvik.

Galloway speculated, "To support operations up there?

A landing and then a campaign to drive Jerry out?"

Smith thought that sounded logical but he did not like it. "We've no air cover. If they've secured all the major airfields, as I suspect, we won't be able to support a campaign."

Galloway said sceptically, proud of *Cassandra's* gunners, "I wouldn't say we would be helpless if attacked from the air, sir."

Smith showed his teeth in a mirthless grin. "Not helpless, but without our own air cover, vulnerable." He passed the second signal to Galloway. "*Gurkha's* been sunk by air attack." She was a Tribal Class destroyer like *Cossack*.

Galloway was silent a moment, then took a breath and answered, "I see, sir. Point taken."

Smith ordered, "Send to those soldiers by lamp: 'Prepare to re-embark. I am sending boats.' And tell *Ailsa Grange* and *Wilhelmina*: 'Prepare to get under way.'"

The company Ellis had left ashore was not fighting off an attack but it would be when Grundmann arrived. It was better to get those men off now when it would be comparatively easy for them to disengage. And as it seemed the German commander at Heimen had radioed to Grundmann the news of the arrival of *Cassandra*, then it was possible he had also called for help from further afield. A German naval force might appear off Bergsund at any time now. *Cassandra* and her consorts must not be caught in there.

He spoke to Sandy Faulknor up in the director above the bridge. "Be ready to cover the soldiers pulling out of Bergsund. There may be an enemy force on the road."

Within the hour the last of the soldiers had come off hollow-eyed from the action in sodden, filthy khaki. The wooden boxes of bullion captured at Heimen had been transferred from *Cassandra* to the *Ailsa Grange* and were now locked in her hold and under guard. She was hoisting in her boats and the *Wilhelmina* was also

193

getting under way. Then a lookout reported, "Trucks on the road, sir!"

Smith saw them emerging from the forest, slipping and sliding on the snow. He ordered, "Open fire." His warning to Sandy Faulknor bore fruit and the guns, laid on the road and ready, fired only seconds later. The trucks skidded to a halt as the bursting shells threw up snow and dirt around them. They reversed, wheels spinning and spraying muddy slush, back into the shelter of the trees. All save one that was hit, stayed tilted where it had fetched up at the roadside and now began to burn.

Under the trees *Oberst* Klaus Grundmann climbed stiffly down from his *Kübelwagen* and snapped at the driver of the squat, jeep-like vehicle, "Wait!" He was narrow-eyed and weary after forty-eight hours of work and action with only a few minutes of snatched sleep. He was also angry. Two of his companies had been savaged at Bergsund and Heimen and the bullion that had fallen into his hands had been torn from his grasp. He showed none of this, however, was still the cool, professional officer as he forced his legs to carry him creakily but briskly back to the wireless truck halted further down the column of vehicles. He reached in over the tailboard, grabbed a signal pad and wrote on it then slapped it in the hand of the signaller seated at the wireless in the back of the truck. "Send that."

The signal came to Moehle on the bridge of *Brandenburg*. He scanned the sheet and passed it to Paul Brunner. "Grundmann says the *Tommis* have pulled out of Bergsund: a cruiser and two transports, one of them the *Wilhelmina*."

His Executive Officer swore and said bitterly, "I hoped we'd catch that damned cruiser inside."

Moehle grinned at him, "You still think it's the the same

194

cruiser that's haunted us for months? I hope you're right, because that's one ghost I'd like to lay and now, at last, we can do it. She's clear of the fjord but we're faster than she is and she won't run anyway. Her captain will stay and try to protect the transports and the soldiers. So all we have to do is sight her."

But Kurt Larsen wondered, Will it be that simple?


*Cassandra*, with all her guns manned and Smith in his high chair on the bridge, led out the little force from Bergsund. The *Ailsa Grange* followed her, then the *Wilhelmina* with Miller in command and his men from *Hornet* standing guard over the transport's crew battened down below. It was full day now as the three ships steamed out of the fjord but the sun was still hidden behind that low, black cloud cover and there was little light. Lookouts strained their eyes; visibility was barely five to six miles. A leaden swell faded through the grey of distance to merge with the sullen, pendulous dark blue sky.

Smith gave his orders, *Cassandra*'s searchlight flashing the signals, its shutter clattering as the signalman worked it. The ships turned north, settling on a course to take them to the rendezvous with the destroyer coming down from Narvik. They steamed in line abreast, the *Wilhelmina* taking the inshore station with *Cassandra* to seaward and the *Ailsa Grange* between them. He saw that done then closed his eyes and was asleep at once.

He dozed fitfully, uneasily, the tight hold on his mind now relaxed so that his dreams were of his daughter, some of them pictures of her laughing but others nightmares of her in the hands of the enemy. He groaned in his sleep and came half-awake time and time again, aware of the cold grey sea and figures on the bridge before his eyes shut again. Galloway and Harry Vincent heard those muffled cries of agony and exchanged worried glances.

He was finally dragged from his sleep by the voices

195

that bellowed, half a dozen sighting her at the same instant, "*Ship port bow!*" His eyes snapped open, focused and he set his glasses to them. He recognised the ship before Galloway got over his hesitation and said, "It's *Brandenburg*, sir!" She had just shoved out of the greyness some five to six miles ahead of *Cassandra* and to port and seaward.

Smith nodded, climbed down from the chair and stretched like a cat waking from sleep. He stalked across the bridge and back again. He was stiff and still tired, ready to sleep for a week, but his back was straight and he was alert, equally ready to fight. Galloway and Harry Vincent noted it and this time the glances they exchanged were relieved. Buckley, tucked away at the back of the bridge, grinned.

The alarm rattlers were sounding, filling the ship with their raucous din. Galloway left the bridge at a run, heading aft to his station in action. Kelso came to take his place, swearing at having his breakfast interrupted. The guns were already manned, as they had been since sailing from Bergsund. They swung on their mountings so the long barrels pointed at the target, obeying the orders from the director above the bridge where Sandy Faulknor and his gunnery team stared at the ship shoving out of the murk to the north. They recognised her as *Brandenburg*, and like the rest of *Cassandra*'s crew as the "buzz" ran through the ship from mouth to mouth, they knew they faced death. Sandy, like all of them, thought, No way out this time. And then, like all of them, he concentrated on his job.

Appleby had run up the ladder to the bridge before the alarm rattlers ceased their clangour. His eyes sought out Smith where he stood at the front of the bridge. This time Appleby did not hide.

Smith ordered, "Open fire!" Then: "Port ten! Full ahead!" And to the Signal Yeoman, "Make to *Ailsa Grange* and *Wilhelmina*: 'Take evasive action.'" He just got the last words out before the salvo from *Brandenburg* roared overhead like an express train and *Cassandra*'s guns slammed and recoiled, hurling back her reply. Her bow was swinging around and steadied now to point at *Brandenburg* as Smith ordered, "Midships . . . steer that!"

The orders cracked out without him barely pausing to catch his breath. He had been ready for this, among other, anticipated situations. It had been possible he would meet an enemy, and if he did it would be inevitable that he would have to fight her and tell the transports to run. "Starboard twenty!" Wrenching his ship towards the huge water-spouts thrown up by *Brandenburg*'s last salvo, banking on her shortening the range for the next one because that last had gone over.

So had that of *Cassandra*. Smith, glasses to his eyes, saw the plume of foam-topped, dirty water lift beyond *Brandenburg* as Kelso, also peering through binoculars, reported it: "Over!"

Smith also saw the three flames lick out as one from the guns in *Brandenburg*'s forward turret. He stooped over the voice-pipe and ordered, "Port twenty!" To haul *Cassandra* back onto her original course. She was firing rapidly now, *Brandenburg* marginally slower but her nine guns to *Cassandra*'s five were an awesome threat to Smith's thin-skinned light cruiser. As the two ships manoeuvred to avoid the shells from the enemy there were times when only the forward guns of either would bear, "A" gun in *Cassandra* or *Brandenburg*'s forward turret. But these occasions balanced each other out. *Brandenburg* had a huge advantage in fire-power.

"Port twenty . . . twenty of port wheel on, sir!" That was Taggart, the cox'n now at the wheel, acknowledging the order and then confirming he had complied with it. *Cassandra* had only just returned to an even keel after that last tight turn to starboard. Now Smith felt the deck tilt sharply under his feet as she swerved the other way, bow

197

swinging to point again at the enemy. She was working up to full speed now and the seas broke in over the bow to sweep aft and wash around "A" gun just below the bridge.

*Cassandra* was still heeled in that turn when *Brandenburg*'s salvo roared in and plunged into the sea close off the starboard bow. Spray from that upthrown water fell on the bridge as *Cassandra* steamed through it and Smith smelt the cordite stink of it. Then his ship straightened up out of the turn, ran level except for her pitching to the seas and the guns *slam-banged!* again, shaking the hull and the bridge under his feet. And he ordered, "Starboard twenty!"

Jinking again – and towards that last salvo again. *Cassandra* was outgunned and could not run because *Brandenburg* was faster by three or four knots. Besides, she had to fight to protect the transports and the thousand and more men aboard them. But not a straight fight because she would never survive it. Smith had to use cunning, outguessing the gunnery staff aboard the big enemy cruiser. So far he had been successful. On his success or failure in the next few minutes depended his ship, what was left of his career and probably his life. But he swung up into his chair again and settled himself comfortably as *Cassandra* heeled over in the turn.

He saw Appleby watching him, remembered the young midshipman stealing glances at him ever since the action started and recalled that the youth had done all that was asked of him at Bergsund and Heimen. It had been worth the risk of taking him along. Appleby had helped himself. Smith grinned at him, and after a moment while Appleby blinked in surprise, the grin was returned.

But *Cassandra* was still heeling, tilting the chair and Smith in it. He felt it, forgot Appleby, set glasses to his eyes and trained them on *Brandenburg*. She had also turned, a point or two away from *Cassandra*, so now all three of her turrets, all nine of her guns would bear.

198

Smith saw sparks of light run along her hull as she fired and this time they seemed brighter against the greyness from which she had come. That background was now darkening to purple.

*Cassandra*'s salvo fell and Kelso called excitedly, "That was close to her! A near-miss!"

"Yes." Smith had seen the shells burst alongside *Brandenburg*, the water-spouts briefly hiding her until she steamed clear of them. Hit her? Not likely. But possibly the salvo had done some damage to plates in her hull. He used his telephone to tell Sandy Faulknor in the gunnery director above the bridge: "Good shooting." It would do Sandy and his team good to have their efforts appreciated, and it was lonely and exposed up there.

*Cassandra* had straightened up out of the turn. He was about to order another when *Brandenburg*'s broadside howled in. The shells burst in the sea around his ship, one of them so close on the port side that he felt it as a hammer blow on the hull. It had him grabbing at the arms of the chair to hold on and sent the staff on the bridge staggering. In that same instant the shrapnel from the bursting shell lashed the ship's upperworks. This time it was not stinking spray alone that hissed across the bridge but steel splinters. They cut halyards and smashed through the thin armour of the bridge. A bo'sun's mate fell, and Nisbet, the signalman, there as a messenger. He was always grousing, but not now as Appleby knelt over him.

Smith, thrown sideways in the chair, pulled himself upright and as he did so saw a huge tear on the inside of the left sleeve of his bridge-coat. A sliver of steel like the blade of a knife had sliced through between sleeve and body and embedded itself in the back of the chair. An inch or two to the left and it would have severed his arm. Another inch or two to the right and he would have been a dead man. It stuck out now as if waiting to impale him. He got down from the chair, swearing, and beckoned Buckley then pointed to the splinter. "Get that damned thing out, please!" Then he bent to the voice-pipe and ordered, "Port twenty!"

He had not outguessed *Brandenburg*'s gunners that time. Her broadside had straddled *Cassandra*. The next salvo from them might score a direct hit – or more than one. In the minutes since the action started the range between the two ships had closed to a scant three miles. He swept the edge of visibility – it could hardly be called a horizon – with his glasses. He saw the transports were gone from sight, hidden in the greyness between *Cassandra* and the unseen shore. He lowered the glasses and waited, holding the ship in this turn until she was turned broadside to *Brandenburg* and only then did he order, "Midships."

"Midships . . . wheel's amidships, sir."

*Brandenburg* had not altered course, her captain presumably thinking *Cassandra* was still zigzagging. Now he knew differently. *Cassandra* could now fire all five of her 6-inch guns and her broadside thundered out. At that moment *Brandenburg* could only fire from her fore-turret – but now she, too, was turning so that all her main armament would bear. Smith had turned his ship away from *Brandenburg*'s last salvoes but now he thought, When she starts to fire her broadsides again . . .

Buckley said, "There y'are, sir." He had dug the steel splinter out of the back of the chair and now held it out to Smith.

Who told him testily, "I don't want the bloody thing! Get rid of it!"

Then he glanced around as he heard the voice: "No, sir! I'm OK. I can carry on. Just help me to get on me feet!" That was Nisbet, arguing and demanding as the bearers lifted him onto the stretcher.

And Appleby, pale and shocked, voice a tone higher than normal but still firm, "No. You're bleeding from two or three places." He stood back and told the bearers, "Take him below."

Smith nodded absent-minded approval, his thoughts on *Brandenburg*, and ordered, "Starboard ten!"

"Starboard ten, sir . . ."

Kelso yelled, "That was a hit!" A shell from *Cassandra*'s last broadside had burst in an orange flash on the stern of the distant cruiser. Smith did not share Kelso's jubilation, only grunted acknowledgment. On the heels of that orange flash had come the rash of yellow flames along *Brandenburg*'s hull that marked the firing of her broadside and she had fired all nine of her 6-inch guns. Whatever damage had been done by that hit of *Cassandra*'s had not lessened her striking power.

He had evidence of that barely seconds later when the shells of that broadside fell. *Cassandra* seemed to check in her rush through the big, green seas and shuddered before charging on. Smith twisted in his chair to peer back along the length of his ship and saw the twist of smoke rising. He heard Appleby at his elbow shout shrilly, "We've been hit aft, sir!" The barrel of the 6-inch gun in the waist farthest aft sagged drunkenly, pointing at the sea.

Smith ordered, "Port ten."

"Port ten, sir," acknowledged Taggart. "Ten of port wheel on, sir."

The damage report, telephoned to the bridge and bawled across at Smith by Kelso, confirmed that the gun had taken a direct hit and was out of action. The crew of the gun were dead and there was a small fire. Smith could see men flitting through the smoke, fighting the flames laid nearly flat along the deck by the wind of *Cassandra*'s passage. He thought he saw Galloway's tall figure among them.

He faced forward. That gun had hardly come into action but now it was smashed and useless while the men who had worked it . . . Galloway and his damage-control party would have a sickening mess to clear up there. Smith had seen it before, could picture it now and he shivered, his stomach heaved. He stared out at *Brandenburg*. The other

201

shells of that broadside had fallen to port of *Cassandra*. Only his change of course to starboard had saved her from far worse damage. But *Brandenburg* had handed down a death sentence.

When he had first sighted her steaming out of the grey haze only minutes ago he had thought there was an inevitability about her appearance, that sooner or later the two ships were doomed to meet in one final, fatal confrontation.

He saw her guns fire again but could barely see *Brandenburg* herself. That darkening of the greyness around her that had turned to purple was now black. It was wrapping itself around her like a cloak. Then he heard the mounting roar as the shells of that last broadside plummeted down towards *Cassandra*.

# 14

The shells burst close but in the sea, one near enough again to shake the ship and send shell splinters scything across her deck in the waist. That last change of course had hauled *Cassandra* clear once more. She was out of the turn and running straight now. Smith swallowed a sigh of relief, his eyes on *Brandenburg*, or rather where she had been. That blackness covered her now and he could see it sweeping in over the sea towards *Cassandra*.

Ben Kelso blew out a huge sigh of relief and Smith grinned at him, "Now we see her, now we don't." Then he ordered, "Port ten."

The cox'n's voice acknowledged, flatly imperturbable, "Port ten . . . Ten of port wheel on, sir."

On the bridge they waited for him to order the wheel amidships, the deck canted under their feet, waited in an eerie silence now. The guns had ceased firing because Sandy Faulknor up in the director tower had reported that he could no longer see the target. And his opposite number in *Brandenburg* would not see *Cassandra* either. Smith waited until she had turned right around and only then ordered, "Midships."

"Midships . . . Wheel's amidships, sir." Now *Cassandra* was headed back up her wake.

The cloak that had loomed black in the distance as it blocked out the light had turned to the swirling white of snow as it closed on *Cassandra*. It swept over them and the circle of visibility shrank to a radius of less than a mile. On this course they would pass close to *Brandenburg* and if close enough for her to see *Cassandra* they would be under her guns at point-blank range. It was a desperate gamble - and her captain would know that.

Smith called to Harry Vincent, "Pilot! I think *Wilhelmina* and *Ailsa Grange* will be heading north and inshore of us but I want a course to the rendezvous again." Because the manoeuvring since the start of the action had taken them off course.

"Aye, aye, sir."

And the rendezvous because Smith had given its position to the transports and knew he could not hope to find them in this blizzard. He drew a deep breath and settled himself more comfortably in his chair. When the snow had driven between the two ships, stopping the fighting, both had been heading westward and out to sea. Instead of turning back in his tracks Smith could, more sensibly and logically, have kept *Cassandra* on that westward course or turned to port to run southward from *Brandenburg*, knowing that the transports were safe in the cover of the blizzard. He had been turning to port when *Brandenburg* had last seen him so it was a fair bet that she would be hunting him to the southward of that last sighting.

He would have to keep the men at action stations for some time yet because they might run into *Brandenburg* again, but – "Mr Kelso! I want every man to have a hot drink."

Kelso could give the orders to the cooks in the galley, and for every gun or department to send a man to the galley to draw the tea. And here was Buckley: "Coffee, sir."

Smith took the proffered mug, blew on the steam and sipped. "Thank you." Another bo'sun's mate and a messenger went on the bridge to replace the casualties. One of the hands was busy with bucket and mop, cleaning the blood from the bridge gratings.

Life went on, returning to normal, but men had died

204

and the crew of *Cassandra* were now heaving a collective sigh of relief. Galloway came briefly to the bridge to report the damage to the ship: the 6-inch gun in the waist was a total loss but the rest, the fire and the shrapnel, had done no harm that *Cassandra*'s crew could not repair or cover with a lick of paint. Apart from the loss of that one gun she was still an efficient fighting ship.

She had collected more scars to mar her faded elegance but in Smith's eyes she was still a lovely ship and he was relieved, could smile at Galloway. But when he spoke to the ship's company on the loudspeaker system, besides congratulations on their conduct he warned, "Keep a good lookout." *Brandenburg* would be looking for them.

Moehle was. He hungered for a sight of *Cassandra*. That last shell from her that had fallen aft had torn a huge hole in *Brandenburg*'s deck but she, too, was still fully efficient as a fighting ship. She could destroy the lighter enemy cruiser in a few minutes if only Moehle and his gunnery staff in *Brandenburg*'s director tower could *see* her. He craned forward in his chair, head turning as he tried to probe the insubstantial white wall, seeking her.

Kurt Larsen, like many others aboard *Brandenburg*, was narrow-eyed as he tried to penetrate the swirling snow as *Brandenburg* drove into it. Moehle had just reduced speed to a cautious ten knots, growling, "We don't want to run into her while we're going full ahead!" But he said it uneasily, because he was doubting the likelihood of that now.

Before the blizzard closed around them he had seen *Cassandra* hit, then turn away. He had considered the options open to her, scowling in thought: She doesn't have to worry about the transports now, knows we couldn't find them in this muck, and if she turns back she could wind up in our arms. So she's continued southward or run out to sea. She had been turning southward . . .

So Moehle had reached his logical conclusion and altered course accordingly – to run to the south. But that had been twenty minutes ago and *Brandenburg* should have overhauled her fleeing, ·but slower, enemy by now. Unless that cunning enemy had fooled them and had not turned southward. Moehle swore in frustration, but then he shrugged: that was pointless. He had lost the British cruiser and trying to conduct any kind of search in the present weather conditions would also be pointless.

Besides, there had been another signal from Grundmann at Bergsund: ". . . seriously wounded. Require assistance . . ." Grundmann had doctors to render immediate aid in the field but it had been intended that serious surgical cases would be taken to the *Wilhelmina* where there was an operating theatre and a surgical team. Grundmann could no longer do that because he had lost the transport. So Moehle dictated a signal to Grundmann: "Will render assistance your wounded." And told his navigating officer, "I want a course for Bergsund again."


Fritsch drove the Mercedes 170V hard through the night and northward. He wore a trench-coat to cover his uniform and a wide-brimmed trilby hat. Sarah was huddled beside him in the passenger seat but pressed up against the door, putting as much space as possible between them. Fritsch saw this but was in good humour and only amused by it. He taunted her, "You may be closer to me yet. We will be getting to know each other much better." He watched her face for some reaction but she managed to remain impassive, staring out through the windscreen at the road winding ahead.

He told her, "Bergsund and Heimen are small affairs.

206

Grundmann tells me he was only put in there to cut across north-south communications, cause disruption and panic and divert any Norwegian troops here in the north. But Narvik is a major port and he says Dietl's Mountain Division is there. So we're going to Narvik. If we have to talk to any Norwegians you tell them you're English and I'm Dutch. I'm an engineer with a job to do up there for the iron ore company and I'm giving you a lift. You've been staying with some relatives in Heimen but now you're going home. Understood?"

Sarah nodded. He had not asked for her agreement because he knew she had to give it. That last reference to "going home" had been a taunt. There were more to come.

There was no direct road to Narvik. Roads in that part of Norway were non-existent or bad but Fritsch had driven over this one several times before. He had always taken Sarah with him. He made good time despite the snow that swept around them every few minutes to cut visibility down to thirty yards or less. The beams of the bulbous headlights bounced back yellow from that whiteness that rushed at the screen. But the two-door saloon sat down on the snow-shrouded road and stuck to its slippery surface like glue, with only an occasional slither and drift as the tyres lost traction.

They only stopped when the road ended in another small town on the shore of another fjord. Fritsch drove down to the quayside and said, "That's luck. Hansen only puts in here once a week." He pointed at the little coaster tied up to the quay. Sarah had seen her here on some of those previous outings with Fritsch and had met Hansen, her captain.

She met him again now. Fritsch hustled her aboard the ship and then roused Hansen from his bunk. He came out blinking and only half-awake. He was pot-bellied, unshaven and bleary-eyed, dressed in a grubby singlet and pyjama trousers. Fritsch looked at him with disdain

207

but followed Hansen into his office to talk to him there while Sarah was left in the little saloon. They came out only minutes later and Fritsch was sliding his wallet back into his pocket. He sat by Sarah as the ship woke around them, the now hastily-dressed Hansen bawling at his crew. Fritsch said, "We'll soon be at sea. Our friend Hansen has a cargo aboard he has to take to Narvik anyway. He'd decided to postpone the trip now war has broken out up here and let the ship's owners take the loss, but I've persuaded him to go."

Sarah said, "You bought him."

Fritsch laughed. "Not exactly. He's a follower of Quisling and so are all his crew."

Sarah asked, puzzled, "Quisling?"

"A Norwegian who's a friend of the Führer. Yesterday he went on Oslo radio to say he is now Prime Minister of Norway. So you see, all I had to do was ease Hansen along a little. As you know, I've put myself out these last few weeks to get him on my side. You never can tell who will be useful." His mood became more triumphant, his gloating more suggestive. Sarah knew she was going to have to pay for Mai Rösing's life. She did not answer him, tried not to listen.

They sailed soon afterwards, the Mercedes lashed to the deck of the little steamer. She hugged the coast in the hope of avoiding British patrols and in the beginning the night also hid her. Then when the day came it was sunless and dark, one snow squall following another, all giving her cover. She made good her ten knots and in the early evening chugged into the harbour of Narvik where it lay below the surrounding mountains.

There were nine German destroyers in the harbour but of these two had been sunk, only their upperworks showing above the water. Three more were badly damaged, one of them tied up to the Post pier. Fritsch gaped at the destruction and did not laugh now. He was nervous and bad-tempered, shouted at the seamen as they used the ship's derricks to swing the Mercedes onto the quay, then he shoved Sarah into the passenger seat.

There was a reception committee on the quay, men of Dietl's Mountain Division in white smocks and overtrousers. They passed him through and gave him directions. He drove along the side of the harbour then turned to wind through the streets, swinging left when he came to the town square. He crossed a bridge over the railway that brought the iron ore from Sweden then held on until they came to the outskirts of the town. There he turned in through an open gate in a high wooden fence. The building it enclosed stood in a yard, was substantial and many-windowed. Sarah thought it looked like a school. Fritsch steered the Mercedes across the yard, pulled up before the front door and took Sarah by the arm to hustle her inside. He had discarded the trench-coat now and wore his SS cap with the death's head badge. The sentry at the door saluted the uniform and let them through.

Inside was a long corridor and a room opening on the right. It held a half-dozen lounging, white-clad soldiers and an *Unterfeldwebel* sitting behind a desk. He jumped to his feet when he saw Fritsch's rank and bawled at the others to come to attention. Fritsch flipped him, a casual salute and they talked. At one point the *Unterfeldwebel* glanced at the watch on his wrist and gave an order that sent most of the soldiers out of the room, shrugging their rifles onto their shoulders by the slings and eying Sarah as they passed. She stared straight ahead, ignoring them. Soon afterwards there was a rumble of voices in the corridor outside and the trampling of feet.

But then Fritsch turned to her and said curtly. "They have room for you here. I'm sure you will be comfortable. Your host will see to that." He nodded at the *Unterfeldwebel*. "He tells me that Dietl has his headquarters in the Grand Hotel and I will find a room there. I will look in on you every day. Now . . ." He pulled on his gloves. "I will leave you to it. I understand this is the evening exercise period. One of your escorts will go with you but that is just a formality, of course." Because Mai Rösing bound Sarah to him. But the escort was there in case she lost her nerve and tried to escape. Sarah knew this.

She followed him out of the room, two of the soldiers going with her. One of them took her case from the car and carried it into the school. The other pointed to the yard and she walked where he directed her.

Fritsch was still in the black mood that had descended on him when he saw the destroyers in the harbour. He climbed into the Mercedes and did not spare a glance for her as he drove away. The gate was closed now and the sentry who had been on duty on the door was now stationed there. He opened the gate to let the Mercedes out, then shut it again.

Sarah walked back and forth at one end of the yard, hands deep in the pockets of her coat, her head up and blonde mane flying in the wind. It was good to be out in the air and away from Fritsch. She obeyed the orders of the escort but did not speak a word in reply, though she spoke German as well as he. She looked through him or over his head.

A group of men strolled in a loose circle at the other end of the yard, figures vague in the gathering dusk and some fifty yards away. She concluded they were more prisoners, like herself, because soldiers stood around them. And that, she decided, was why the gate of the yard was closed – so that no prisoner would be tempted to make a dash for liberty. But the fence, surely that could be scaled. It stood some six feet high and an active man could haul himself over it in a second. But for a slightly built girl with an escort treading at her heels . . .? No.

Both the prisoners and the soldiers kept turning their heads to stare in her direction. She looked away, embarrassed.

She had only been walking for a few minutes when the men started shouting. She turned and saw a tall young man lash out at one of the soldiers and suddenly the yard was a mass of surging, shouting men, flying fists and rifle-butts. Her escort bawled something and ran her towards the door. Before she reached it she heard the *crack!* of a rifle being fired and saw the crowd stilled. It had been a shot fired into the air, no one had fallen. But then she was inside the corridor, being hustled along it and thrust into a small room at the end of it. The door slammed behind her and a key turned.

The only furniture in the room was a table and an upright chair. Two blankets had been thrown onto the table and her case lay on the floor. There was one window, narrow and set high near the ceiling. She climbed onto the table and peered out, only to see another yard at the back of the building and another sentry pacing there. She tested the window but found the metal frame had been welded into place to make the room a prison cell. She got down from the table, sat on the chair and stared up at the window helplessly, trying not to remember Fritsch's barely veiled threats and gloating.


Smith went below to the sickbay before noon. He talked to the burly Kilmartin, the young surgeon, and then to those wounded who could hear and understand him. Kilmartin told him, "Most of them should be all right, but young Williams . . ." He shook his head in anger and bitterness. "I've done all I can for him."

Sammy Williams, the young signalman who had been at Smith's side at Bergsund and Heimen, lay unconscious. He had lost both legs, was chalk-white and scarcely breathing. Smith took his hand gently and spoke to him but got no reply.

The other wounded were still in shock or with mouths

clamped shut against the pain of their torn bodies. Smith thought that this was only a part of the price to be paid for stopping Hitler. The politicians could have done that more cheaply years ago but instead had chosen peace at any price. This was it.

He talked to them, awkward words of thanks and encouragement, and they managed to grin and joke. Then he left them, climbed to the deck and took his Prayer Book from the waiting Buckley. He read the service for the burial of the dead and watched as the canvas-wrapped bodies were committed to the deep. They buried young Sammy Williams later that day.

An hour into the afternoon watch *Cassandra* made her rendezvous with the transports and the destroyer. The blizzard lay astern of her as a black bar along the horizon, but here the snow had ceased and a pale sun peeped intermittently through gaps in the low cloud. For a minute or two *Cassandra* ran alongside the destroyer, close enough for the two captains to talk by loudhailer.

Smith listened to the voice, metallic but clear and high. It came across the narrow strip of sea, that was churned into foam between the hulls: "Forbes and the Home Fleet have joined up with Whitworth in *Renown* and they're patrolling off Narvik." That was good news. Admiral Forbes was Commander-in-Chief of the Home Fleet and that was a powerful concentration.

"Whitworth chased *Scharnhorst* and *Gneisenau* the day before yesterday but they got away from him. Combination of speed and bad weather." Smith scowled. "Jerry is in Narvik and has landed troops and occupied the town!" That was as Smith had expected after Trondheim, but more bad news nonetheless.

Now the destroyer's captain came up with better news but with a sting in the tail: "Warburton-Lee took his flotilla into the fjord yesterday morning. He lost two of his ships but sank two of theirs and shot the hell out of the others he found in there. Then he sank an ammunition ship on the way out. But Warburton-Lee was killed." And that last was the worst news of all.

The destroyer set out for home, escorting the two transports. The men from *Hornet* lined the rails of the *Wilhelmina* to cheer and Miller, their captain, waved his cap from her bridge. Ellis saluted from the bridge of the *Ailsa Grange* while his soldiers cheered from her deck and Woodman held up both arms, thumbs up.

Before Ellis and Woodman had gone back to the *Ailsa Grange* the major had spoken privately with Smith in a corner of *Cassandra*'s bridge. "I may have been impatient and short-tempered this last day or two. If so, I apologise." Smith thought, May? And grinned at him.

Ellis took that as forgiveness and went on with relief, "To tell you the truth, this job was very important to me. I'd been twice passed over for promotion. It was bad luck on the colonel, breaking his leg but it gave me a chance. At the same time, I was afraid I'd make a muck of it. As it is, we've pulled it off. Due to you, really, but some of the glory will rub off on me as the senior soldier." It was his turn to grin at Smith. "We both know how it is. So thank you." He held out his hand and Smith shook it.

Then a minute or two later Woodman came to the bridge and said impulsively, "I wish I was going with you, sir."

Smith, startled, said drily, "You might well have regretted it. And your orders attach you to Major Ellis. He may need you yet. But thank you for your efforts. You did a good job." Then as the young man went down into the boat to take him to the *Ailsa Grange*, Smith thought, Thank you for the vote of confidence.

Now Ben Kelso said glumly, "We should have kept that lad."

Galloway agreed, "He's a first-class interpreter."

Smith, standing at the salute at the front of the bridge in acknowledgment of the cheers, said straight-faced, "Yes, but he's a little too conventional. He lacks Ben's dash and

213

ability to improvise. I'm looking forward to hearing him again."

That brought laughter from the bridge behind him and Ben Kelso muttered into his beard, "Buggered if I am."

Smith took *Cassandra* north. The reaction that always seized him when the fighting was done had come soon after *Brandenburg* had been left somewhere astern. It had wracked him but had gone some two hours before, so now his gloved hands rested on the arms of his chair and were not rammed into the pockets of his bridge-coat to hide their shaking. But he knew there was more action to come. Instinct warned him and logic confirmed that instinct; enemy destroyers could not be left undisturbed in Narvik.

Midnight had come and gone. *Cassandra* had made her second rendezvous, this time with Admiral Forbes' Fleet blockading Narvik, and now she was on patrol in the Vestfjord that led to the port and was ten miles wide at this point. In the afternoon and evening watches Smith had snatched a few hours of precious sleep in his sea cabin at the back of the bridge. Now he was back in his chair. There were only occasional flurries of snow now but the night was pitch black under an overcast sky.

"Ship Green Four-Oh!" That was the starboard look-out's hoarse call.

Smith lifted his glasses and stared out over the starboard bow, thought he saw a blurred shadow in the night but then lost it. "Anybody else see it?" And when no one answered: "Lookout! D'you still see her? Course? Speed?"

"Don't see her now, sir. Couldn't say about her course and speed. Maybe about the same as ours. Looked like a cruiser, but I only saw her for a couple o' seconds . . ."

He paused, hesitating, and Smith prompted, "Go on."

"Might have been imagination, sir, but I thought she had the look of *Brandenburg*."

Smith thought it might well have been imagination, a result of stretched nerves and recent actions and sightings, *Brandenburg* seeming to haunt them, but . . . He ordered, "Starboard ten." Because he, too, had thought the ship was *Brandenburg*. He picked up the telephone as *Cassandra*'s head came around. Her crew were already at action stations but now he spoke to Sandy Faulknor in the director tower above the bridge, "We may be on the trail of *Brandenburg*."

*Brandenburg*'s port side lookout had reported to the bridge, "Ship port quarter!"

Moehle looked for the vessel but did not see it. "Anyone?"

Kurt Larsen answered, "No, sir." And the lookout had lost sight of the ship now.

Moehle had been prepared to meet British ships in these waters but he did not want a fight now. He held to his course. He had embarked Grundmann's five wounded men at Bergsund. They were below in the sickbay and *Brandenburg*'s surgeon believed all of them would recover. Moehle was now headed for Narvik because his orders were to join the destroyers in Narvik fjord. He did not like those orders because he believed he could be taking *Brandenburg* into a trap. He knew the destroyers in there needed any help he could give them but in his opinion they should have been pulled out forty-eight hours ago, before the British destroyers led by Warburton-Lee had struck. They had not and had been badly mauled as a consequence. It might be too late for any of them now.

*      *      *

215

Smith and all the other searching eyes aboard *Cassandra* did not see *Brandenburg* again that night but there was another sighting. This one proved to be no more than an open boat with a mast and a lug sail. It appeared suddenly out of the darkness, and close. The sail was bellied out by the wind that drove the boat seaward like a train, with the outflow from the fjord helping it on. Harry Vincent, who had the watch, yelled, "Just look at her! Making better'n ten knots!"

Seconds after they sighted her the boat swung into the wind and hung there, sail shivering, as *Cassandra* rushed down on it. Then Smith stopped her to windward to make a lee and let her drift down to the boat. He thought, They're ready to turn and run.

There were two men in the boat. Onc, wrapped in a tarpaulin, was huddled in the stern. He was tending the tiller and the sheet, using both now to keep the boat's head to wind. The other man was bailing wearily but stopped when *Cassandra* hung above him. He cupped his hands to make a funnel and bawled through them, "Is that the Navy?"

Harry grumbled, "What the hell does he think we are? The Isle of Wight ferry?" But then he answered, booming through the loudhailer, "Yes! Are you British?" Because all of them on the bridge had expected the men in the boat to be Norwegian.

But then the reply came from the man in the stern of the boat, a thick Yorkshire accent, "Aye! And bloody glad to see ye!"

They had to be lifted from the boat, seamen from *Cassandra* climbing down a scrambling net hung over her side to put a line around each of the two men. They staggered and weaved when they stood on the ship's deck. Smith talked to them in his sea cabin with Galloway listening in. The faces of both were drawn and stubbled, their eyes slitted with exhaustion. As *Cassandra* got under way again Smith asked, "Who are you? Where did you come from?"

216

The one who had bailed wore a bedraggled overcoat, a scarf knotted at his throat and a chequered tweed cap pulled down tight on his head so it would not blow away on the wind. He peered out at Smith from under its peak but it was the Yorkshireman from the sternsheets, still wearing the tarpaulin like a cloak, who answered, "Ted Smethurst, seaman in the old *John Hopkins*." He jerked his thumb at the other, "Wilf Collins here, he was the cook."

He paused as a steward entered and thrust steaming mugs at them. They muttered their thanks, cuddled the mugs in clasped hands and sucked greedily at the thick brown cocoa. Then Ted Smethurst licked his lips and went on, "Our ship was lying in Narvik, loading iron ore, when Jerry came in. That was the day afore yesterday, first thing in the morning. They took us all ashore and locked us up in a school, officers in one classroom, the rest of us crammed in the others. The windows were welded shut and there were sentries outside but they let us out for exercise first thing in t'morning and then late on. They marched the whole crew of us out into the yard last neet, just as it were gettin' dark. One o' the Jerries used his rifle to shove a big Scotch lad – "

Wilf grumbled, "He had no bloody call to do that!" His voice had a nasal Cockney twang.

Ted nodded, "That's right. The lad wasn't doing owt. Anyway, Jock shouted at him and hit him wi' a right-hander. Then a lot more started barracking and pushing and shoving all round the yard. That's when me an' Wilf managed to slip away. We nipped over the fence into the street, got down to the harbour and saw that boat tied up at the quay. There were a Norwegian feller working on it. We got him to see who we were and what we were up to and he sent us away in it. We've been at it ever since, me steering and Wilf bailing."

Wilf shivered. "Freezing bloody cold it was. We didn't have any grub and there was nothing in the boat except a bottle o' water. We hadn't planned anything, d'ye see?

217

And we didn't dare hang about on the quay 'cos there was Jerries swarming all over the place. We reckoned the Navy would be out here somewhere, but when we saw you we thought you might be a Jerry and we were ready to run for it again. If we hadn't come up with you by morning we were thinking of heading for the shore and seeing if the Norwegians could help us."

Smith asked, "How many British seamen are held prisoner in Narvik?"

Ted and the cook looked at each other and Ted said, "Well, there were two other ships besides ours. There'd be about ten or a dozen officers and sixty out o' the fo'c'sle aboard them?"

He looked the question at Wilf and the cook nodded in confirmation, "That's abaht it."

Ted went on, "But I don't know where they've got the rest of the fellers locked up. There was just our crew in the school – thirty-two of us altogether."

Smith asked, "Where is this school?"

Wilf Collins said, "You ain't thinking of trying to get 'em out, are you, sir? Because you haven't a bleedin' earthly chance. That school's on the far side o' the town, about three-quarters of a mile from the harbour. There's half a dozen destroyers in the harbour and the town's full o' them mountain troops. You've got to go right through the town to get to the school. Me and Ted, being just two of us and in civvies, and me knowing the town a bit, that made it easier, see? But we was still lucky. You and your lads wouldn't get any further than the harbour."

Smith was silent for a minute. If the prisoners had been held in a ship and he knew which ship . . . But even if they had, a cutting-out expedition would be doomed to failure because of the destroyers in the harbour. It seemed that thirty-two British seamen were condemned to spend years in a prisoner-of-war camp. The Navy had rescued the three hundred seamen from the *Altmark*, saved them from that fate. But now the Navy – and

218

at this moment he was its representative – appeared helpless here.

He saw Galloway scowling in frustration but watching him. Hoping?

Smith asked, "Can you draw me a map? Show me where the school is in relation to the harbour? Mark in the German positions?"

Ted blinked bloodshot eyes. "Aye. I'm not an artist but I can sketch a bit. If you can get me some paper and a pencil, I'll draw you a map. I expect Wilf can fill in what I don't know or can't remember. And he knows the town better'n I do."

Smith stared at them. They drooped, shivered in the cold and their exhaustion. He hungered for the information they could give him but they hungered for food. And they had done enough – for now. He said gently, "Thank you, but that can wait. Now you'll be given a meal and then you can draw my map and answer some questions. After that you'll be able to sleep for an hour or two."

Galloway took them away and Smith returned to the bridge. He strode back and forth, face impassive but brain churning. He paused once to stare out over the bow in the direction of the distant, unseen shore. *Brandenburg* was out there, somewhere, he was sure. And Sarah?

He went back to his restless pacing. They had to start soon after dawn. He had the germ of an idea but whether it flowered would depend on the map and the seamen's answers to the questions he would put to them. It would have to stand up to the cold light of reason. He would not recklessly risk men's lives. But if he could save those thirty-odd men . . .

# 15

Smith said, just loud enough to be heard above the chatter of the little engine, "Stop her." The big Colt .45 pistol dug into his side and he shifted the holster, easing the pressure. He stood in the well of Per Kosskull's boat, leaning on the roof of the cabin and looking out over the bow. The snow had stopped, for a while at least, but the night was pitchy.

He had spoken to Leading Seaman Donnelly, the man standing alongside him at the wheel. The engine died and the boat slid on through the slight swell tilting the surface of the water even this far inside the fjord, bow nodding. The way came off her and she was still but for that gentle lift and fall.

Smith used his torch to flash the three shorts of an "S" in a signal to the two launches following astern. Their engines cut out and silence settled over the three boats. There was only the whisper of the water cut by the launches' bows as they ran down on the fishing boat. They changed from mere humps in the night to distinguishable craft and lay rocking a score of yards astern.

They did not look what they were. A hasty attempt had been made to disguise them as fishing boats like Per Kosskull's. They were painted black, names and numbers lettered on their bows and sterns. Smith thought the disguise would have worked but it had not been needed.

The three boats had left *Cassandra* in the Vestfjord at noon. A night approach was not possible; Smith wanted the night for the actual operation and escape afterwards.

They dared not leave later than noon because the outflow from the fjord that had helped the two escaped seamen would be dead foul for the three motor boats butting into it. But they had traversed the Vestfjord and then the long dog-leg of the Ofotfjord without being seen by the enemy. Or seeing him. The visibility was bad when it was not snowing and when the snow squalls swept over them every few minutes it was reduced to a scant hundred yards or so. But they had picked up their landmarks one by one and finally, an hour after nightfall, they saw the headland of Framnesodden at the mouth of Narvik Harbour. The Framnesodden light, like all the navigation lights, had been put out, but the rash of yellow pin-pricks in the darkness showed where the town of Narvik lay.

They had passed it and gone on along the coast but out of sight of it. Now they had closed it again. Mountains surrounded the fjord. Narvik was built on a round tongue of comparatively flat land sticking out from the southern shore of the Ofotfjord. The root of the tongue, its eastern side, was set in the mountains. The southern edge ringed the harbour while the northern and western sides were washed by the Ofotfjord. The railway that brought the iron ore from Sweden ran down to the harbour and the town had been built up from there. Now it half-filled the tongue, stretching back from the harbour but the northern and western half of the tongue was still empty, hilly and wooded. Smith was steering for that north-western corner. He was going in at the back door.

Now he asked, "Do you see anything you recognise?"

Wilf Collins stood beside him, elbows propped on the roof of the cabin. He peered into the darkness at the lift of the shore ahead of them and shook his head, "No. See, I only saw it from the other side a couple o' times. And I'm a cook, remember, not a navigator."

And shouldn't be there. Like Buckley, who was sitting in the sternsheets. Smith, turning, saw him hiding a grin now at Wilf's remark. Smith had detailed a cox'n, Donnelly, for

Per Kosskull's boat when giving his orders, but when he had gone down into the boat, last of all by tradition, he had found Buckley already there. And he had drawn a rifle. It had been too late to order him out of it then. Smith had glowered at him and growled, "I'll talk to you later."

Ted Smethurst had produced his roughly pencilled map in Smith's sea cabin but Wilf Collins had provided most of the information, explaining: "This school where we were – " finger tapping the map "– was up by the hospital – here." His finger moved then tapped again. "I know just where it is because last year – afore Ted signed on wi' us – me and some other fellers took Billy Finnegan up there. He'd got crushed trying to nip atween two railway wagons. That was after we'd been ashore for a few drinks and we was on our way back to the ship."

Wilf was silent a moment, remembering, and Smith waited for him. Then the cook went on: "His own bloody fault mind, he was a daft bugger, but still, he didn't deserve that. The doctors did all they could for him up there but he only hung on a few days and never come to. They had him shot full o' stuff to ease the pain. We used to walk up through the town to the hospital to see him."

Smith had asked him, "What about the country on the other side of the town?"

A shrug. "That? It's just woods and hills. A forest o' bloody Christmas trees but we knew Billy wouldn't see another Christmas. I used to walk out along the road after looking in on him until I got to the sea. Then I'd look in again on the way back to the ship. But he was always just lying there."

Smith had said, "Tell me about the road."

And later he said, "We need a guide. The map isn't enough." Moving across strange country at night using a compass and a makeshift map would be a time-taking and dangerous business.

For a moment that didn't register with the cook but

Smith stared at him and waited again. Then Wilf said, "You want me to go back there?"

Smith nodded.

Wilf said, "I'm a civilian. You can't order me."

"I'm not ordering anybody. I'll be taking only volunteers." If there were any.

Wilf brooded, then said slowly, "If this war turns out anything like the last lot, then I've just as much chance of copping it in the Merchant Service as I would in the Navy."

Smith remembered 1917, when the U-boats were sinking ships so fast that Britain was in danger of being starved into submission. "That's true."

That conversation had taken place in the light and the relative comfort of Smith's sea cabin. Now they were in the bitterly cold darkness off an enemy shore. Smith said, "As you only saw it from the other side, we'll take a look at it from there." He told Donnelly, "Slow ahead."

The engine stuttered into life again but was swiftly throttled back to a mutter and the boat stole in towards the shore. The launches lay immobile and waited for the next signal from Smith's torch. He said quietly, "There's a headland showing to port."

Wilf nodded, non-committal: "I can see it."

Now a lookout, one of the two seamen stationed in the bow, called softly, "House over to starboard!"

It stood back from the shore some fifty yards or so – it was hard to judge distance in the night – a black box.

Wilf leaned forward, as if the extra inches would enable him to see better. "I think mebbe . . . ." Then he pointed with a stubby finger, "S'right! That should be the little hillock I told you about." Beyond the white frill of surf that marked the shore stood a fringe of fir trees. Among them and just above them rose a low, bald hilltop.

Smith ordered again, "Stop her."

The boat slid on silently, just the ripple under her bow, and all of them listened, breath held. Were there enemy patrols? Or a section of troops watching them from the house?

There had been volunteers in plenty – Galloway had said wrily that the entire ship's company had put their names forward, and he was one of them. Smith wondered at that, why they wanted to go with him on this risky adventure. But it enabled him to pick his men. Galloway had been rejected and argued but Smith was adamant: the Executive Officer had to stay in command of *Cassandra* while Smith was away. Buckley had not volunteered, had decided already that he was going with Smith anyway.

Kelso, Sergeant Phillips and Buckley shared the well with Smith. Four marines sat in the little cabin. Another dozen were shared between the two launches and Merrick commanded them. It was a small force but Dietl, who commanded the *Wehrmacht* in Narvik, had two thousand mountain troops. Smith could not fight him. This task would have to be brought off by cunning and surprise. He had brought with him the bare minimum to do the job. And the space in the three boats would be needed later on – if his plan worked.

They heard nothing. The bow of the boat grated on shingle and the seamen in the bow jumped into the shallows and hauled it up. Phillips walked along the narrow strip of deck at the side of the cabin and knocked on its roof. The marines spilled out into the well and followed his stocky figure as he jumped off the bow onto the shingle. Smith told Wilf Collins, "Wait here till you see my signal to the boats." He then set off after Phillips.

His boots crunched on shingle as he ran across it, then he caught up with the marines at the edge of the trees. They were down on one knee and very still, watching and listening. Phillips turned and whispered, "There's a road, sir. Is this the place?"

"Looks like it." Smith turned, saw without surprise that Buckley stood behind him, and used his torch to flash the short and long of an "A" to the launches hidden in the darkness offshore. Then he moved on up to the road, though he found it was little more than a track running along the shore. He told Phillips, "See who is in that house. Take Kelso with you."

Kelso trotted up then with Wilf Collins, who looked about him and now nodded confidently, "This is the spot. Sometimes I'd sit up on the hill, sometimes I'd come down hereabouts."

Ben Kelso panted, "Right on the nose, by God!" And eyed Smith with respect. It had been an impressive feat of navigation.

Wilf's overcoat and cap had gone. Instead he wore the uniform of a seaman and a duffel coat issued to him on Smith's orders. He had told him, "If this operation goes wrong that uniform will save you from being shot as a spy." The cook had answered, "Thank you very much."

Kelso hurried off along the road with Phillips and two of the marines. Now the launches were coming in. They ran ashore either side of the fishing boat and marines spilled out of them. They ran across the shingle and into the trees, spread out along the line of the road and Merrick came to Smith. Who told him, "We're waiting for Kelso and Phillips."

But it was only a minute or two later that Phillips returned. Kelso, puffing behind him, reported, "Just a man and wife and their kids in there. I got it through to them to keep their heads down tonight."

That was good advice. Now Smith turned and used his torch again to flash a signal out to the boats and he saw all three haul off from the shore, turn around and chug off into the night. They would wait out there, out of sight from the shore, until recalled. Now Smith and his landing party were committed.

He said, "The hill."

Merrick called, "Corporal."

Lugg was there at his shoulder. As Merrick led out

across the road and set off into the trees Lugg went with him, a pace or two behind and to his right. Another marine moved into position on Merrick's left. Smith followed Merrick, trailing him by five or six yards. Then came Buckley, Collins and Ben Kelso, one behind the other and spaced at the same distance. Marines kept pace with them on both flanks and Phillips brought up the rear.

They flitted through the deeper darkness under the trees until they came to the foot of the little hill. The main body halted there while Lugg and two of the marines went on. The minutes dragged but then he returned to report to Merrick, "Nobody up there, sir, but somebody's been digging. Looks as if they might be going to put a guard-post there."

So tomorrow might have been too late to attempt this rescue. They were only just in time. Or were they? Smith told himself not to count chickens.

They went on to the top of the hill. It only stood some sixty feet above the shore where they had landed but it commanded another road which ended on this hilltop and down which they had to go. This led down from the hill and wound away into the trees, towards the town less than a half-mile away. There were lights in plenty outlining the spread of it.

Smith saw where the digging of weapon pits had been started but as yet they were only a foot deep. It would be hard work using an entrenching tool in that frozen earth. He left Sergeant Phillips and four marines with two Bren guns to hold the hill. Then Merrick led the column on down the road into the trees again. All of them now marched at the side of the road. The snow crunched and squeaked softly under their booted feet. Their breath steamed in the cold air and the lights of the town crept nearer with every stride.

They had marched a quarter-mile from the hill when the marines ahead of Smith halted and the whole column

226

followed suit. A minute later Merrick came back and reported, "They've got a road-block up ahead. There's a hut by the side of the road and a sentry on duty. There'll be some more of them in the hut."

Smith glanced around him then waved a hand to indicate the forest hemming them in. "Can't we get around it through this?"

"Should think so, sir."

"All right. Single file and I'll come with you. I want to see this place."

So they went on in a long straggling line, Merrick leading and Smith now only a pace or two behind. They moved through the trees making a wide arc and once Merrick paused, turned to Smith and pointed to their right where lay the road. Smith could see between the firs to a stretch of it. There stood the black square of the hut with a strip of light showing at one poorly curtained window. The sentry, a pale figure in his white snow-smock and trousers, trudged up and down at the side of the road with his rifle slung on one shoulder. He was trying to keep warm.

Even as Smith watched the door of the hut opened, letting out a band of yellow light like a torch's beam. It sprang out across the road into the forest and spilled over Smith and Merrick. They froze.

Two men came out of the hut and the door closed behind them. The murmur of voices came faintly on the cold air as the three men, now outside the hut, talked. Then the original sentry went back to the hut with one of the two newcomers, leaving the other to take his place on the road. The door opened and closed, the band of light splashing across the road and wiped out again. Smith and Merrick had witnessed the changing of the guard by an NCO.

They moved on. Smith turned his head on his shoulder and saw that the marine marching a dozen yards in his rear was following again. The whole column was in motion.

227

Then they rounded a bend in the road and now anyone on it would no longer be in sight of the sentry. Merrick led on to the road again and trod once more at its edge. Smith waited there, waved the next marine – Corporal Lugg – on and when he had passed saw Wilf Collins, Buckley and Kelso coming up. Smith beckoned them and then strode off after Lugg.

Now they were back on the road again the long file shook out into its original formation. So when they approached the side road on their left all four of them were trailing Merrick and Lugg. The cook said in a hoarse whisper, "That's the road up to the hospital." They were still fifty yards away and saw a car pull out of the side road. They froze again but it turned away from them, swung around the next corner and disappeared. They went on again and passed the road leading to the hospital. There were streets of houses now to their right and ahead where the road they were on widened. And here it forked, one branch going on, the other swinging to the left. Wilf Collins nodded towards the latter, "That's it. The school's down there – 'bout a coupla hundred yards."

Merrick turned and asked Smith, "Close up, sir?"

"Yes."

Now they were entering on the period of greatest risk. The road leading down to the school was empty. Smith could see the building behind its fence at the end of it. There was a light showing in the school and others in the houses to the right, but no streetlights. The left side of the road was shadowed by the trees that overhung it – growing in the hospital grounds? The shadows offered some cover as the column moved forward again, all on that left side of the road and with only a few feet between each man and the next.

Smith halted when only the width of the road separated him from the gates of the school. These were closed but they were made of slatted timber and he could see through to the yard beyond. A sentry stood inside the gate. The main door set in the face of the building was closed and a car stood in front of it. He whispered to Wilf Collins, "I can't see any other sentries?"

The cook breathed in his ear, "T'other one's round the back. That door at the front – there's a passage inside it that runs right through to another door at the rear. Sentry wanders up and down behind the house. We could see him at it from our window. Couldn't open the bastard anyway, though. They'd welded it shut."

And inside that front door, on the right, was the guardroom. Collins had told Smith earlier that he thought there were about eight or ten soldiers altogether, with an NCO. Smith's little group outnumbered them, but first they had to get inside. He said, "They've strung barbed wire along the top of the fence."

The fence itself was barely six feet high and slatted timber, like the gates, no obstacle for an agile marine. But now the wire, running on metal supports, added a further two feet of height and a crucial hazard.

Collins whispered, "That weren't there before. They've just done that since we got out."

And because he and Ted Smethurst had escaped. Before it would have been comparatively easy for Lugg or Phillips to have quietly rolled over the fence and stolen up on the sentry inside the gate. Not now. Smith swore under his breath. He was conscious of Merrick close behind him, waiting for orders. And the others, doubtless uneasy now at this delay. They were exposed here. If he sent Lugg or Phillips to try to scale the fence and the man was caught on the wire . . . An attempt to break in by main force might succeed but there would be shooting, men killed and wounded. They would then be faced with a fighting retreat for half a mile, carrying the wounded, before they reached the doubtful safety of the boats. He would not risk men's lives in that way.

Should he abandon the enterprise after having come this far?

Sarah sat in the only chair and Kurt Larsen stood under the high window. *Hauptsturmführer* Gerhard Fritsch waited by the door, restlessly shifting from one foot to the other. He had driven the Mercedes there with Kurt in the passenger seat beside him. They had gone first to the hospital, where Kurt had visited the wounded transferred from *Brandenburg*. He had gone to make sure they were being well treated, because their ship was about to sail. He had also wanted to go with Fritsch on this trip on account of the girl. Fritsch had talked as he swung the car through the streets of the little town because he was nervous. Kurt had answered in monosyllables or not at all. He knew more about Fritsch now and did not want to betray his feelings.

But now it was he who said, "We're taking you out of this hole." He looked around with distaste at the bare little room, little more than a cupboard.

Fritsch put in, "I told you it might not be for long." He inspected the room in his turn and went on, "But anyway, it is good enough. There are worse places. You must ask Mai Rösing to tell you about them."

Sarah ignored him and answered Kurt, "Thank you."

Kurt's anger that had simmered for weeks, born of his outrage at what he had learned of Fritsch, boiled over. He forgot Fritsch was an officer in another service with the power of life and death. He rapped out the knowledge that enraged him: "About that lady – Frau Rösing. Before we sailed on this operation I had a week's leave. I made some enquiries." He had had to be discreet; asking questions about concentration camp prisoners could lead to the questioner being arrested for 'interrogation'. "Frau Rösing and her child died on Christmas Day. The child of malnutrition and pneumonia. The mother took her own life."

Sarah stared at him, a part of her mind rejecting what

he had told her as too horrible to be true. But she knew it was. And Fritsch had lied to her from the beginning, from that first interview aboard *Altmark*. He had known then that Mai Rösing was dead.

Kurt said, "So you don't have to give in to blackmail on that score."

"Shut your mouth! You've said enough!" Now Fritsch was angry, his fears forgotten for a moment. His narrowed eyes shifted to Sarah and he threatened her, "You'll still do as you're told if you know what's good for you. We know a few tricks to make the stubborn ones co-operate and you will. And if the Rösing bitch and her whelp have gone I can soon find a replacement. You have other friends," and he shot a malevolent glance at Kurt, "whose loyalty to the State may be found to be suspect."

Kurt recognised that threat to himself and knew it was real. He had said too much, should have waited until he could tell the girl on her own. While he was on his ship and under Moehle's protection he was safe, but once back in Germany Fritsch would have the power of the Gestapo behind him. But that realisation only fanned the flame of Kurt's anger.

Fritsch threw open the door, "Let's get out of here." He reached out and gripped Sarah's arm, dragged her out into the passage. Then Kurt's fist smashed onto his forearm and he grunted with pain and let the girl go. She fell back against the wall and Kurt held her overcoat, helped her into it, then picked up her case.

He took her arm, but gently, and said, "Come." They started along the passage.

Sarah walked with her head up, shaken and furious, hating Fritsch. Mai and her baby . . . She asked stiffly, "Where are you taking me?"

Fritsch answered from behind her, rubbing the muscle that Kurt had numbed, "To Berlin." There was triumph in his voice.

231

Kurt said, "You're going aboard my ship, *Brandenburg*. He won't touch you there." But afterwards?

They passed the guardroom, Fritsch waving a hand at the *Unterfeldwebel* inside, and then were out in the cold night air. Fritsch said, "We sail within the hour." He had come to Narvik confident that the *Wehrmacht* would overrun Norway, but now he had seen two of Bonte's destroyers sunk in Narvik harbour and three more so badly damaged they were unfit to fight an action. Bonte himself was dead and what was left of his flotilla was now commanded by *Kommodore* Bey. And outside the mouth of Narvik fjord cruised a fleet of the Royal Navy.

Suddenly it seemed the invasion might fail. Fritsch had learned that *Brandenburg* had received orders to return to Kiel. He had gone to her captain and showed him a letter of authority signed by Himmler and given to him before he left Germany. He had demanded passage for himself and his prisoner as business of the State. Moehle had reluctantly agreed.

Fritsch slid in behind the wheel of the Mercedes, started the engine and sat with fingers tapping impatiently on the wheel as Kurt opened the rear door. He helped Sarah in and passed her the suitcase before taking the front passenger seat. As Kurt closed the door Fritsch let in the clutch and the Mercedes shot forward, turned tightly then headed for the gate. Sarah held on to the seat in front of her as the car rocked under the acceleration. She saw the sentry swinging the gate wide and then they were through and still accelerating as Fritsch gunned the car up the road.

He was running in fear for his life and Sarah was going with him.

# 16

Smith saw the three figures emerge from the school and go to the car. He spoke rapidly to Merrick and Corporal Lugg standing close behind him, his head half turned on his shoulder to throw the low-voiced orders at them but eyes still on the school. Then the sentry started to open the gate and Smith reached back a hand to tap Lugg on the shoulder, "Go!"

The tall, heavy-shouldered Corporal crossed the road, running lightly and keeping the right-hand gatepost between him and the sentry. He stopped in the slender cover of that gatepost – the gate was hinged on the other post – and stayed pressed up against it. The car swerved out of the gateway and turned to race away up the road towards the town. The sentry pulled the gate around to close it and was almost at the post when Lugg slipped around it. He took the sentry by the throat with one hand while the other jabbed a bayonet's point under the man's chin, forcing back his head.

Smith was already running, Merrick and the rest chasing him. They shoved through the gate and ran past Lugg who was walking his man backwards to the door of the school. Smith was first through that door, seeing the empty passage stretching away before him, kicking open the door of the guardroom on the right and going in with the big Colt .45 pointed. He stopped with the muzzle of it only a foot from the face of the *Unterfeldwebel*. Then the room was filling with marines, backing the startled soldiers against the wall while their NCO sat very still with hands splayed on his desk in front of him. He stared down the muzzle of the pistol and swallowed again and again.

Smith left him to the marines. He turned and Buckley, standing close behind him, moved quickly out of the way to let him pass. In the passage he met two marines bringing in the sentry from the rear of the building. He looked as dazed as his counterpart from the front gate, now being pushed into the guardroom by Lugg. Smith asked, "Any trouble?"

One of the marines shook his head, "No, sir! We opened the back door nice and quiet and there he was, only a few yards away and with his back to us, stamping his feet to keep warm. So he never heard us till we were right on top of him."

"Very good. Put him with the others."

Now Merrick emerged, with men coming out of doors along the passage behind him. The doors had been smashed open by the boots or rifle-butts of the marines. The men crowding out into the passage were dressed in a mixture of overcoats, well-worn serge suits, overalls – whatever they had been wearing or able to grab when they were captured.

Merrick said, "I told 'em to keep quiet, sir. No cheering or bloody nonsense of that sort."

Collins, at Smith's shoulder, said, "What abaht the bit o' stuff?"

Smith turned to look at him, "You mean a woman? A prisoner here? British?"

The cook shrugged. "She was a prisoner, but she had a room of her own somewhere. We never got to talk to her – only saw her at the other end o' the yard when we was let out to stretch our legs t'other night – but we thought she was English. She *looked* like one of our gals, but I suppose she might ha' been Norwegian."

Smith's eyes searched the crowd and he asked, "Did you find the young woman that Mr Collins says was here?"

Merrick answered, "No, sir."

234

Wilf Collins muttered at Smith's shoulder, "That's our skipper."

He stood at the front of the men, a man in his fifties, burly and greying, red-faced. He introduced himself, "Harry Bentall, Master. I heard what you said about the lass. I don't know her nationality. She was blonde, twenty or maybe a bit older, good-looking girl."

Collins nodded emphatic agreement, "A cracker. Not tall, mebbe five-two or three. But she stands very straight, looked down her nose at them guards."

Now he and Bentall were both nodding. The skipper said, "I think they've moved her. Only a few minutes ago I heard her voice out in the passage and then the front door opening. She was with somebody, one man or two, and they were talking German – the lass as well, I mean. We thought she might be British, but now I don't know."

Could that be Sarah? But –

Ben Kelso came from the guardroom. "I've talked to the sergeant or whatever he is in there. He says the woman has gone. I asked who she was but he says he didn't know." He finished apologetically, "That's all I can manage, sir."

Smith said, "Thank you." If the woman was his daughter then he had watched her driven away. Sarah had passed within a score of yards of where he stood in the shadows.

He looked around him, then lifted his voice, "Wrap up the guards and we'll be on our way." He strode to the front door while Merrick and his marines set to work. They herded the former guards into one of the rooms from which the prisoners had come and locked the door. Then they hauled desks and chairs out of other rooms and piled them in the passage, blocking that door.

Meanwhile Smith had opened the front door a crack and was peering out at the gate across the yard. It was shut – the last man in had done that. As the seconds ticked by and the crashing of furniture lessened then ceased he saw

235

no one in the road outside. Then Merrick said at his back, "Ready, sir."

Smith turned and spoke to the merchant seamen filling the passage. They were whispering excitedly among themselves and shuffling their feet, eager to be gone from this prison. But his voice cracked harsh and urgent, silencing them: "You've been told to keep quiet. When we leave here you do exactly as you're told and quickly. We can't wait for stragglers." They looked into the ice-blue eyes in the thin face and were still, breath held. Then he said, "Come on!" He threw the door wide, ran across the yard and they surged after him.

Already the marines had shaken out into a loose screen surrounding the escaped prisoners. Merrick and a pair of marines were only a pace behind Smith. With them came Buckley and Kelso, Wilf Collins puffing between them. They checked for a moment as Merrick swung back the gate, then Smith was out in the road. When he saw the car he shouted, "March!"

It was a black saloon and had turned into the road, coming from the town, and was running down towards the school. It braked when the driver saw the hurrying crowd of men crossing ahead of him, armed soldiers escorting them. The car skidded on the snow and stopped broadside across the road. A window wound down on the passenger's side and a man leaned out his head, an arm and a shoulder. He wore the soft-topped cap with a small peak and silver eagle of the mountain infantry.

Smith thought, An officer. Come to inspect the guard and make sure they're alert? He kept up the bluff and bellowed, "*Achtung*!" Then he saluted, looking the officer full in the face. He was still aware from the corner of his eye that Merrick and the marines were marching as he had ordered, rifles shouldered and arms swinging. He could hear Ben Kelso cursing softly.

The officer stared at them, uncertain for a long few seconds, only a score of yards away but too far for Lugg to attack with his bayonet, too close for the officer to be fooled. Smith did not want shooting but now he saw the blank face under the cap take on outraged life. The arm was withdrawn into the car and the shoulder shrugged furiously. Smith knew he was wrestling a pistol from its holster. Meanwhile the car reversed, starting to turn to go back the way it had come. The hand came out of the window holding the pistol and Smith lifted the Colt .45 and fired three times.

The shots cracked loudly but flat, without echo, muffled by the snow and the cold air. A tyre collapsed on the car and it skidded again. Smith did not know where the other two shots went but the hand holding the pistol jerked back into the car, the head with it. The engine was revving and the wheels spinning on the snow, then they found traction and the car fled back along the road, rear end sliding sideways as it took the corner at speed and then was lost to sight.

Smith said, "Blast! That'll wake 'em up." He broke into a run again.

Merrick said beside him, "You couldn't do anything else, sir. He'd have hit somebody for sure. He couldn't miss a crowd like this and we don't want to have to cope with casualties."

Smith knew that was true, had known it when he opened fire; as he knew now that they would be hunted.

He glanced behind him and slowed to a trot. He could not run all the way back to the boats, nor could the prisoners he had rescued, several of them men older than himself. Wilf Collins was ten years younger but already he was dragging his feet and rocking in his stride. They passed the side road leading to the hospital, saw no one and trotted on. They did not take to the forest until Merrick prompted, "Coming to that block in a minute, sir."

Smith was aware of it but raised a hand in acknowledgment, saving his breath. He turned off the road into the trees, slowed to a walk and motioned to Merrick to take the lead. Merrick took it, had been fretting for it and muttered to himself under his breath, "I should have been here as soon as we broke out. You've got more guts than sense sometimes – sir."

Smith glanced over his shoulder and saw the ragged column of rescuers and rescued winding through the trees behind him and Buckley close on his heels. In place of the soft drumming of boots on the snow-packed road there was the crunch as they compressed untrodden snow and the low crackle of dead wood underfoot. Could that be heard on the road where the guard stood? It had not sounded so loud when he had led his little group in. But now there were three times as many feet and instead of picking their way cautiously, they were hurrying.

He faced forward again as Merrick held up his hand. Smith did the same and heard the rustle of the column die away as it halted, but he went on to stand by Merrick. The lieutenant pointed. There was the guard hut but now there were four soldiers on the road outside it, all peering into the forest. Smith thought he could see others at the windows, thrown open – there was no reflection from glass. The men on the road seemed to stare straight at Smith.

Merrick whispered, "I don't know if they've seen anything or maybe heard us, sir. We're making a hell of a row." The tall figure of Lugg showed on his right now, another marine on his other side.

Smith answered, "The shots will have brought them out. We can't help making a noise now. We haven't the time to go quietly." They were in a race, and if they lost it they would be dead or prisoners again.

There came a yell from the road, a challenge or a warning but unintelligible. Then a shot cracked out and Smith heard the bullet rip through the branches close overhead. He told Lugg, "Fire!" The rifle blasted close by his ear, one-two-three quick shots as the corporal worked the bolt. One of the guards on the road fell and the others ran back into the hut for cover, dragging him by his arms.

Smith shouted at Merrick, "Get 'em moving! At the double! Tell 'em to keep as low as they can but to run like hell!" Because there was no time to wriggle cautiously around the guard-post making use of cover. They would have to rely on the trees and the darkness. And that darkness would be total now for the guards; every time one fired the muzzle-flash from his Mauser carbine would destroy the night vision of all of them for minutes on end.

That worked two ways. Smith found himself groping from tree to tree as he followed Lugg, just a tall blur in the night as he ran forward again. But every dozen strides he would halt and throw a rapid shot at the guard hut. When Smith turned his head he saw the flashes where other marines were doing the same. That served to keep the guards' heads down. There was little firing coming from the hut in that first minute or two. After that it intensified but by then Smith had left the guard post behind him, the trees thinned ahead and suddenly he and Lugg were out on the road again. They had passed the post and a curve in the road hid them from the guards in the hut.

Buckley and Kelso came out of the trees then, followed by two marines and the first of the merchant seamen. Smith waved them on and told Lugg, "Keep going! Quick march!" And to Kelso, "Take the lead with Lugg! All the way to the shore and call in the boats!"

"Sir!" Kelso panted away after Lugg, now striding rapidly up the road. He was obeying Smith's order to "Quick march", given because few of the seamen would be able to run at the double for long.

He called to them as they trotted past, "Did anyone fall? Look at the people with you – is anyone missing?" No one answered but some shook their heads and Wilf Collins was one of them. He was with the last of the crew to come out of the forest, trotting along beside his skipper, Harry

Bentall. He had looked to be one of the oldest men and now he slowed his shuffling trot to a walk to match the others ahead of him, wheezing and gasping.

Merrick came last of all with four marines. Smith told him, "Kelso has the lead, taking them down to the boats. We'll bring up the rear. Did you see any stragglers or wounded?"

The lean Merrick, sweating despite the cold, answered, "No, sir." Then they started after the tail-end of the strung-out column, darkness hiding the head of it. That was when Smith found Buckley had hung back and was trotting along with him. There was still scattered firing behind them as the guards in the hut fired at fancied targets. And there was another sound from the direction of the town behind them, that of engines being gunned.

Merrick glanced at Smith, "Sounds like trucks coming up the road after us, sir."

Smith nodded and pointed at the next curve in the grey ribbon of the road, "We'll wait there." And at that curve they took cover in the trees, the marines throwing themselves down in the snow, rifles pointing back the way they had come. They did not have long to wait.

The first truck swayed around the last bend in the road, just over a hundred yards away, and Smith ordered, "Fire!" The six rifles fired as one and at that range they could not miss. The leading truck snaked on the slippery surface as the driver braked. Then it slid, or was driven, off the road and into the forest with a crackling of snapped branches and a flurry of snow shaken down. The second truck was only a few yards behind the first, followed its wild career but finished in the trees on the other side of the road.

Both of them now had some cover in the forest. Men could be glimpsed jumping from them but made poor targets. The marines fired at them but Smith did not see any fall. Then the return fire came at them, snarling past or kicking bark from the trees, cutting twigs to fall on

240

them. Smith was prone as the others now. He did not fire the Colt because at that range he knew he would be lucky to hit a truck, let alone any of the men hidden in the forest and only marked by the prickling flames of their carbines. And not only carbines. There were several sub-machine-guns chattering in short bursts. His little holding party here was heavily outnumbered and outgunned, could not hope to survive for more than a minute or two.

Head turning, he watched those orange tongues. So when Merrick looked over at Smith he was ready and anticipated the lieutenant. "Yes, they're outflanking us. Take two men and pull back to the next bend." He waited as Merrick and his two men wriggled away into the trees. Once well into their cover they rose and went on in a crouching run then merged into the darkness. Buckley and the two marines still with him fired rapidly and steadily while continuously shifting their positions so that the enemy could not fix exactly where they were, nor how many faced him.

Smith counted to ten then shouted, "Fall back!" He started back through the trees, wriggling on his belly, but making sure that Buckley and the two marines were with him. Then they were up and going at a blundering, crouching, swerving trot through the darkness between the tall trunks as the bullets from the carbines clipped twigs from the branches over their heads.

In a hundred yards they came up with Merrick and his men, passed through the staggered line of their prone figures, dark against the snow, and ran on. The little hill lifted ahead and then they were climbing its gentle slope. A voice challenged out of the darkness of the crest, "Who goes there?"

Smith panted the password, "*Cassandra.*" The ground levelled off under his feet and he slowed to a walk, halted when he saw Sergeant Phillips rising out of that darkness almost at his feet.

Phillips reported, "Mr Kelso and the rest have gone down to the beach, sir. The boats are in."

"Very good. Hold here until you get the signal from Mr Merrick or myself, then get down to the boats as quick as you can. Understood?"

He saw Phillips' teeth show white in a grin as he answered, "You bet, sir!"

Smith went on across the top of the hill, Buckley and the two marines still at his back. He heard Phillips challenge again, and the answer, "*Cassandra!*" That was Merrick and his men, forced to pull back already. That meant they had been in danger of being outflanked and their pursuers were moving very fast. And how many? There had been two trucks and he guessed at thirty men. He had tried to count the muzzle flashes back there in the forest and he'd made it about thirty. And some of them were armed with sub-machine-guns, that cancelled out the fire-power of the two Brens with Sergeant Phillips. Smith broke into a run down the far side of the little hill. He had to get his men and the rescued prisoners into the boats and away. Quickly.

He heard the Brens come into action then, stuttering away behind him. The firing had built on itself and now was incessant, the racket seeming to echo all around him as he ran through the deeper darkness under the scattered trees. He stubbed his toe, staggered and fell. His head cracked on a root or rock and for a second the trees danced and circled him, then they were still.

Buckley's hand clamped on his arm but Smith slapped it away and he pushed himself up. He snarled, "I'm all right, damn you!". He ran on, legs shaky now and he had to wipe blood from one eye. It ran down from his head and it felt like the wound he had taken at the boarding of *Altmark* had been torn open again.

But the trees were thinning and then he was out on the road that ran along the shore, crossing it. Marines were sprawled on the far side behind their rifles, watching the forest, and Ben Kelso was on the beach beyond. Smith saw Per Kosskull's boat with its bow drawn up on the shingle at the water's edge, but not the two launches. But as he came up to Kelso, Ben told him, "I've got all the prisoners aboard the two launches and sent 'em away. They're lying off and waiting for us." He stopped, leaned forward to stare at Smith's bloody forehead and face and then started to ask, "Are you wounded – "

Smith cut him off, "No! Just bumped my head! Now get aboard!" He fumbled in his pocket, found the whistle and set it to his lips. He blew three shrill blasts, paused and blew three more. He heard the signal repeated from in the forest and knew that was Merrick. A minute later he trotted out of the forest with his two marines and came to Smith. He cast his eye, head turning, over the men lying by the road and then those with him, counting. Then he reported, "All present, sir. Except Phillips and his gang, of course." He cocked his head on one side, listening. The Brens had ceased their stuttering. He said, "Sounds like he's on his way now."

Smith said, "Kelso's aboard. Send your men down to the boat." They filed past him down to the water's edge, until only he and Merrick – and Buckley – were left on the beach by the road. Smith watched the trees in front of him. The firing had eased, become sporadic. But the firefly sparks of flame were either side of him now. That firing out on the flanks had to come from the mountain troops, shooting at shadows but closing in. *Where was Phillips?*

The marines came out of the trees in a shuffling group. Two of them carried the Brens while Phillips and the third carried the fourth between them, holding his arms across their shoulders, his head down on his chest and his legs dragging. As they crossed the road Phillips gasped, "He went arse over tip as we came down the hill – breathing all right but he's out."

Smith said drily, "He's not the only one to have done that."

Phillips glanced over his shoulder. "They seem to be all around us, sir."

"Take him aboard! Give them a hand!" Smith shoved at Merrick and Buckley and they grabbed at the man's legs and lifted them. Then with the four of them now sharing the weight they broke into a trot as they carried him down to the boat. Smith swept one last look around from right to left and as he did so saw three figures flitting pale between the trees on that left flank. He realised they were white-clad mountain troops even as one of them fired and he saw the lick of flame and heard the rip of the bullet past his ear.

They would use the men going down to the boat as targets, pick them off at will. He had brought his little force and the rescued prisoners this far without loss. Now they were threatened at this last by a handful of the enemy. Who held his daughter. He had hoped to find her this night and that hope had been dashed.

He ran at them, raging, lifting the big Colt .45 and squeezing at the trigger. They were firing at him and he heard again the ripping of air close by his head. He felt a tearing burn along the side of his jaw as if a steel-knuckled fist had swiped him. He was almost at the first of the trees when he saw one of them fall, then another. The third was right in front of him, working the bolt of his carbine frantically, lifting it. Then Smith was on him as the foot-long flame leapt from the barrel. He felt that sear his neck like the friction burn from a rope snatched tight. He pulled the trigger of the Colt but nothing happened. He had fired off the magazine and it was empty. So he used the two-and-a-half-pound steel weight of the pistol like a club to strike back and forth at the head within a yard of his own. He saw blood fly and the man fall away but he hit him again as he went down.

He stood over the three of them, taking gulping breaths, peering around him into the trees but seeing no one. He became conscious of voices yelling, turned and saw Buckley pounding towards him through the shingle, Merrick and Phillips coming after him. All of them were shouting to him to come back to the boat. He could only make out a word here and there because the Brens were firing from the boat, hosing the top of the hill with tracer. But he knew they were shouting at him to go back. It made sense.

He went with them, all silent now and hurrying. He climbed in over the bow last of all, stepped between the two marines prostrate behind the Bren guns on the roof of the cabin and jumped down into the well. Per Kosskull's boat went astern and the Brens hammered again, now sweeping the trees at the back of the shore as the Mauser carbines opened up from there, and silencing them again. Donnelly spun the wheel, the boat turned and surged away. The shore receded, then was lost to sight.

Smith took the empty magazine out of the Colt and shoved in another taken from his pocket. He holstered the pistol and then had nothing to do with his hands to hide their shaking. He jammed them in his pockets.

*Brandenburg*'s launch slid in to the foot of the accommodation ladder hanging against her side. Kurt Larsen helped Sarah onto the ladder and preceded her as they climbed. A seaman carrying her suitcase brought up the rear and Fritsch was left to make his own way. As they all reached the deck Kurt pointed him towards the officer and party on duty at the head of the ladder. "They're expecting you. They'll find you a berth." But Fritsch had to step aside and wait because the officer and his men were busy. The accommodation ladder was being hoisted inboard, the launch being hooked on preparatory to following it. He stood watching the work and scowling.

As Kurt led Sarah away he said with grim satisfaction, "He's not exactly a welcome guest." He took her to a cabin and set her suitcase down by the narrow bunk. One corner of his mouth lifted in what was half grin, half humorous grimace. "It's not palatial but I think you'll find it more comfortable than the hole you were in."

"Thank you." Sarah glanced around the little box of a cabin. "I had one like this when I was last aboard, before you transferred me to *Altmark*." And before Fritsch had recognised her and taken her for his own prisoner. She found a smile for Kurt and still stood very straight.

He said, "I apologise for Fritsch. He is without honour."

Sarah said flatly, "He is a monster. And he threatened you."

Kurt said contemptuously, "He's full of wind. He can't touch me." He hoped that was true but doubted it. His temper and his fondness for this girl had led him to set his career and maybe his life at risk by defying Fritsch.

But Sarah believed him and said with relief, "I'm glad. I wouldn't want you to come to harm because of me." They had been happy together in the days of peace and she had been fond of him, though no more than that.

They felt the deck rock gently beneath their feet. *Brandenburg*'s engines were turning over. She asked, "Are we sailing already?"

Kurt nodded, "We're getting under way." He hesitated a moment because she was an enemy alien, a prisoner, but then he decided there was no harm in her knowing. He said, "Our captain is moving the ship down the fjord, an hour's steaming nearer the sea. It's too late to try to slip through the British blockade tonight. Tomorrow night we'll sail as soon as it gets dark and have all the hours of darkness to cover our passage. We may be glad of that extra hour before we're through."

Sarah challenged him, "You may not get through."

"It's possible we may be seen and exchange fire," he conceded, "but we won't be stopped. The ships that are big enough to fight us are too slow and the ones that can

246

catch us we can deal with. But the night will be our ally and will hide us as we slip away."

"I wouldn't be too sure if I were you."

Kurt grinned at that, "I'm not over-confident." He thought that there was one particular cruiser that had bedevilled *Brandenburg* for months now, and said seriously, "You can always get a nasty surprise at sea."

He stepped back to the doorway and indicated the curtain hanging there. "As when you were aboard before, there's no door but I'll close this and it will give you privacy. But don't try to wander; there's a sentry outside. Goodnight."

Sarah answered, "Goodnight." As the curtain was drawn across she sat down on the edge of the bunk. *Brandenburg*'s engines were beating more rapidly now, the rocking motion more pronounced as she worked up speed. And Sarah knew that every turn of the screws was taking her nearer Germany. Once there she would do as Fritsch said or . . .

They were out in the Ofotfjord and Per Kosskull's boat had the lead now, the two launches following in line astern. Smith stood beside Donnelly at the wheel, his arms resting on the roof of the cabin, peering ahead. The two Bren gunners were now in the well behind him but their places on the cabin roof had been taken by the two seamen acting as lookouts. And Smith had told them crisply, "Keep a sharp lookout! We're not out of the wood yet!" Nor would they be for some hours.

That warning had been necessary because all of them were weary now and there was also a sense of anticlimax. There was little talking in the three boats. Despite the cold, men dozed crammed together in the little cabin or crowded shoulder to shoulder in the sternsheets. The snow squalls swept in again and again, blinding lookouts and helmsmen alike. Donnelly steered by the compass but each launch followed the darker shadow that was the boat ahead of it, seen only dimly through the white curtain.

When the snow had gone the night was still dark. In one of those clear periods a lookout called, "Ship starboard quarter!"

Smith turned quickly and saw the black mass of her coming up astern, a half-mile away or maybe less. In the night it was impossible to see what ship she was or to judge her size. She might have been a big destroyer or a cruiser. *Brandenburg*? But why should she be here? And then again, why not? If it was her, trying to slip out past the blockading squadron patrolling outside the Vestfjord, then she had chosen a good night for it – but left it too late. She should have started earlier, to have been past this point by nightfall and so have all the hours of darkness to cover her escape.

But had she seen the three boats? It was unlikely on a night like this and she was not slowing nor altering course. And here came the snow again, at first only a few big white flakes flying on the wind and then a thickening cloud that came between Smith and the distant, shadowy ship. Then she was blotted out.

The long, weary journey went on. They finally sighted *Cassandra* in the first grey light before the sun was up. She saw them, altered course a point and ran down to them. Every man aboard her whose duties did not require him to be elsewhere lined the rails. There was no cheering but a host of helping hands to haul them inboard and plenty of laughter and excited talk. Smith knew he was the subject of a lot of it, saw glances directed his way and that look on their faces again – respectful, awed, admiring? He heard Ben Kelso telling Sandy Faulknor and anyone else in earshot, "The Old Man was terrific! He charged at them like he had a regiment at his back!"

Smith knew what he was talking about but took no notice, walked away from them all and went up to his sea cabin. As he took off the holstered Colt, Buckley tapped

248

at the door and entered with a thick china mug filled with coffee. Smith remembered Kelso and the others shouting at him, calling him back from that wild charge. He could not recall any words, except those of Buckley: "You mad bastard – sir!" Now he decided it might be better if he did not recall those, either. And Buckley had virtually stowed away in Per Kosskull's boat to be part of this last expedition. Smith had threatened to talk to him later – but now seemed too late. It was all over.

Buckley was staring at him now. Smith asked, "What are you gawping at?"

"You look a bit of a mess, sir."

Smith looked in the mirror and saw one reason for the stares he had received. His eyes, sunk deep in dark circles, glowered out at him. His face was gaunt and bony, smeared with dried blood from the shallow wound re-opened on the side of his head and from a new ragged tear along the line of his jaw. A red weal marked the burn from the muzzle of the carbine.

Buckley said, "If you ask me, sir, I don't think you should take risks like – "

Smith said, "I'm not asking you. Thank you for the coffee. Now get away to your breakfast."

Buckley said resignedly, "Aye, aye, sir."

When he had gone Smith ran water into the basin and washed. Before he had done Kilmartin had rapped on the door and entered. Smith asked, "How's that marine – the one that fell down the hill? Stephenson?"

"That's right, sir. He's got a bit of a headache – concussion – that's all."

Then the surgeon examined Smith's injuries – Smith would not describe them as wounds: "The cut on the head came from tripping over my own feet. Any cook could have got burns like those on my chin and neck from falling against the galley stove in bad weather."

Kilmartin sniffed. "That's true as far as appearances go. But I never heard of a stove that fired a carbine in

249

your face, sir. From what I hear you are damned lucky to be alive."

"I am – with the kind of young quack we have practising in the Navy now."

But Kilmartin only grinned at that, applied dressings and went away.

Smith sat on the bunk and sipped at the coffee. He told himself he should be content. He had penetrated the enemy's lines, brought out the merchant seamen held prisoner and all without a single casualty except the one man who fell on the hill. When he wrote his report he could describe the operation as a success, though there was no euphoria now. He was simply very tired.

Had he missed Sarah by only minutes, let her be whisked away under his nose? Had it been her or some other young woman? Would those questions haunt him for the rest of his life?

Then Merrick came and told him, "We have orders, sir. The Fleet's going into Narvik fjord to sink or capture all the enemy ships still in there."

# 17

"Starboard ten!" Smith growled it, leaning over the voice-pipe, holding onto it as *Cassandra* pitched under his feet. The sea was still lively here in the Ofotfjord.

"Starboard ten . . . ten of starboard wheel on, sir." That was Taggart answering from the wheelhouse.

Then as *Cassandra*'s head came around, "Midships! Steer one-one-oh!"

"Steer one-one-oh, sir."

To start on a dog-leg across this narrow neck of sea.

Smith cursed, scowling, and the bridge staff, from Galloway to the lookouts on the wings, kept quiet and clear of his foul temper. It was past noon of a filthy day, bitterly cold with intermittent snow squalls driving in under a lowering sky. And *Cassandra* was not going to the party after all. Her crew were at action stations and she was ready to fight but not going to. Ben Kelso had grumbled, "All dressed up but nowhere to go." And Smith had snapped at him to keep his comments to himself. That was the mood they were in.

Only part of the Fleet had been ordered to go in to sink or capture the enemy destroyers at Narvik. A squadron under Whitworth had been given the job and *Cassandra* had followed him in through the Vestfjord but only as far as the mouth of the Ofotfjord. Then she had been ordered to patrol in the Narrows, there to watch for any enemy ship that might slip past Whitworth's ships in the foul weather. Like a terrier set to watch a rabbit hole after the ferrets had gone in. For a moment Smith could see the ferrets – just – three miles or so ahead, and they were big ones. There were nine destroyers and among them, like a swan among ducklings, cruised the thirty-thousand-ton battleship *Warspite* with her eight 15-inch guns. Whitworth had transferred his flag to her from *Renown*.

Then the snow swept in again on the wind and hid the ships from him. Smith swore again. As he had sworn, along with every man aboard *Cassandra*, when they received those orders. And at the weather. Now there was fog added to the snow. It misted his binoculars, clung damply to his bridge-coat and trickled coldly down his neck inside the towel wrapped around it.

He told himself he had chosen to be here, pleaded for a ship, when he might have kept his mouth shut and stayed in the sunshine of Montevideo. He could have been spending a siesta in bed with the long-legged Hannah Fitzsimmons now. That was a warming thought. Was there any real choice there? He burst out laughing then, just as a wave broke over *Cassandra*'s bow and spray flew back to slap him in the face. He saw Galloway and Kelso staring at him and said, "I just thought of something funny."

They smiled politely, waited for him to go on and tell them the joke but he only looked them over then turned away, grinning. Galloway thought they would never understand this man.

Smith had taken off his cap but his steel helmet still hung on the hook below the screen. The dressings put on by Kilmartin were now reduced to one strip of plaster along the line of his jaw. His eyes were still sunk in dark sockets and the face was thinner than Galloway remembered from their first stiffly formal meeting in Montevideo, but bare-headed he looked younger. Especially when he laughed. John Galloway thought, He's a hell of a good skipper.

He said, low-voiced so only Smith would hear, "The men are very tired, sir."

"They have reason to be. I'll rest them as soon as I can." Smith glanced at his Executive Officer. "How is morale?"

"I had a word with Taggart and he agreed with me: morale is sky-high. They all think this is a lucky ship, now." He hesitated, then added, diffidently because it smacked of flattery, but honestly: "I think that's down to you, sir."

Smith knew it was not. Well, possibly some of it. He shook his head. "They've been in almost constant action and they like it." That was a truth he had learned a generation ago.

Galloway went on, smiling now, "The only thing that worried them was *Brandenburg*. She was becoming a bit of a bogey, the way she kept turning up. It was as if she was hiding round every corner, waiting to get us. But she didn't."

Smith only answered, "No," to that. He recalled his own premonition that there would be a final confrontation with *Brandenburg*, but he had been wrong. Thank God. The last time they had met she had been headed south and would soon be berthed in Kiel. There had been those sightings of last night and the night before when he had thought he might have seen *Brandenburg*, but they *had* been at night. That was when the eyes played tricks and you saw what you expected, sometimes subconsciously expected, to see.

Galloway's words had cheered him. He thought that he was proud of his ship and her company. She was shabby and workmanlike but still graceful, an overworked, ageing beauty. Still proud. And the men. They had all come a long way since he had first stepped aboard in the harbour of Montevideo just three months ago. The applications for transfer had all been withdrawn. Galloway had been first, after they had left Bergsund, then Kelso, and the rest followed in a rush.

The island of Baroy lay astern and there was the coast off the starboard bow. The Ofotfjord was only two to three miles wide at most but you couldn't see half-way across it in this weather. Time for another leg of the dog.

"Port ten!" Crisp but not crotchety this time.

"Port ten . . . ten of port wheel on, sir."

And was that answering voice a little more human, Taggart at the wheel sensing his mercurial captain's change of mood now? And as *Cassandra* settled on the new course: "Coffee, sir."

Smith thought, The prize diviner of his captain's mood. He took the mug. "Thank you." Had Buckley waited these past ten minutes, gauging the moment, knowing that if he had come earlier Smith would have sworn at him? Probably.

He sipped at the coffee, hot and sweet, felt it warming him. They would continue this zigzag progress along the Ofotfjord until they opened the Breivika inlet, a side fjord really, on the port side. The Narrows ended soon after that, the limit of *Cassandra*'s patrol.

He cocked his head on one side as the deep rumble of gunfire, from big guns, came rolling down the fjord. All of them on the bridge had their heads up. Galloway said, "Sounds like *Warspite* is in action, sir."


*Brandenburg* was anchored in eight fathoms in the Breivika fjord. She had steam up ready to sail, although Gustav Moehle did not intend to leave the shelter of the anchorage until sunset. That intention was changed by the signal he received just after noon. Paul Brunner brought it, running, to where Moehle lay in his sea cabin. He was sleeping, having been up most of the night and expecting to be on the bridge all through the night to come.

He sat up in the bunk as the Executive Officer shook his shoulder and panted, "From *Künne* to Bey and also to us." The *Herrman Künne* was one of *Kommodore* Bey's destroyers.

Moehle read the crumpled slip of paper. *Künne* had sighted a British force of a battleship and nine destroyers advancing into the Ofotfjord. Moehle said, "God help Bey and his men now."

254

He swung his legs off the bunk, pulled on his seaboots and grabbed his bridge-coat. He was at the door, straddling the coaming, one leg still inside the cabin and the other out in the passage when he froze, listening. Brunner, a yard ahead of him in the passage, stopped with his head turned to stare back at Moehle. They both heard the distant thunder of the guns.

Brunner said, "It's started. That's a battleship firing."

Then they ran.


Sarah heard the alarms and the pandemonium of running men and shouted orders, guessed that *Brandenburg*'s crew were racing to their action stations. She pushed aside the curtain, put out her head and asked the sentry, "What's going on?" She asked in German but he would not answer her, only scowled and waved her back into the cabin. Frustrated, she called him a very rude word she had learnt in Berlin. That got a reaction. He flinched, shocked, as if struck, but still waved her back and drew the curtain again.

Sarah swore.


*Brandenburg* weighed anchor and got under way. On her bridge Moehle sat in his high chair and listened to the reports coming in rapid succession from all the ship's departments, that they were closed up for action. He told Brunner and Kurt Larsen, "I don't like leaving the destroyers." He thumped the bridge screen with his clenched fist. "But they should have been pulled out two or three days ago. We can't save them. If we tried it would be a useless sacrifice. We have no chance against a battleship. I have nine hundred men aboard and I'm not going to throw their lives away. Besides, I have my orders, to return to Kiel. I'll carry them out."

He paused then, the decision taken, but bitter. He knew

brother officers in the destroyers now trapped in Narvik fjord, knew they would fight and that many of them would die.

He went on, "The British force has passed us in here. I think the way may be open. We'll take the chance offered to us and go now."

Fritsch, standing unobtrusively at the back of the bridge, heard the decision with relief. He did not cheer or applaud, but it was just bad luck that Moehle turned in his chair and saw him then. *Brandenburg*'s captain asked coldly, "What are you doing here?"

Fritsch explained, "I just wanted to know what was going on." Moehle was well aware of the power of the *Gestapo* and that Fritsch claimed respect as its representative. But there and then Moehle commanded a warship and the lives of all aboard her were in his hands. Fritsch was no more than a passenger and Moehle disliked the man. He said savagely, "You don't come onto my bridge without my permission and you haven't got it. This ship may be in action shortly and I have no room here for useless spectators."

Fritsch blinked at him, "You said – "

Moehle cut him off: "I said the way *may* be clear but the British might have left a gatekeeper. Now I'll thank you to get off my bridge."

Fritsch left, quickly and readily, running awkwardly down the ladders. He did not want to be on that exposed bridge if *Brandenburg* was under fire.

Appleby saw her first, voice breaking high as he shouted, "Ship fine on the starboard bow!" Then a dozen pairs of binoculars were trained out to starboard, Smith's among them. He saw nothing but a horizon made hazy by mist, nor did any of the others.

Ben Kelso rumbled their doubt, "Are you sure, Mid?"

"Certain, sir." And Appleby was confident. He admitted,

"Can't see her now but she showed just for a second before that fog came down again. There's a ship in there."

So they were still studying that grey distance over the bow and saw her appear again. Appleby said triumphantly, "There she is!"

Nobody answered him for a moment. The wind had rolled away the fog to expose the distant ship hull-up on the horizon. Visibility had cleared, for this part of the Ofotfjord and for this time at least, so that they saw her at a distance of six or seven miles. That was Smith's estimate and now Sandy Faulknor's voice squawked on the loudspeaker from the director control tower, "Ship bearing Green Two Oh, range . . ." Smith converted the 13,400 yards into sea miles: six and three-quarters as near as dammit.

Sandy's voice again, "I think it's *Brandenburg* – or one of her class, sir!"

There was a moment of silence, disbelief, voiced by Ben Kelso complaining, "I thought she'd be back in Kiel by now." And then a mutter of agreement: "But that looks like her." It was echoed by Galloway and then he left the bridge on the run, headed aft to his post in action.

Smith said, "That just about makes it unanimous. It's her all right. Well spotted, Mid." He thought, There's a young man who's improved by leaps and bounds.

He let his glasses fall to hang from their strap against his chest, and put on his steel helmet while using the telephone to talk to Sandy Faulknor: "Fire when ready."

"Aye, aye, sir!"

Kelso said, "Signal, sir." He handed it to Smith.

He took it and read, grinned at Ben and passed the signal back to him. "We should get a drink out of that later on."

Ben laughed, "That we should, sir!"

Neither spoke the thought: If there is a "later on".

Smith turned back to *Brandenburg*. He recalled that gut-feeling, that *Cassandra* was fated to fight *Brandenburg*. Logic dictated there could only be one end to that.

*Brandenburg* was faster, bigger, outgunned *Cassandra* two to one and her crew were as good as their ship. They had shown that in the previous unfinished encounters.

And in his favour? Only that *Brandenburg*'s speed could be discounted here in these constricted waters of the Ofotfjord. She could not run rings around *Cassandra*, or ease away from her to leave her out-ranged. This would be a fight in a small ring and the ropes were the rocky shores of the fjord.

But he had to stop her, could not allow her to escape to raid again, sinking ships and taking lives. His duty was clear – and how to carry it out. He knew what he had to do, had already decided on his course.

The barrels of the guns were training round to point at the ship on the horizon. The three guns *Cassandra* still had aft of the bridge would not bear as yet, but – Smith worked out a little problem in triangulation, with the distance between the two ships now as the base of the triangle and using their estimated speeds and courses, came up with an answer. He ordered "Port twenty! Full ahead!"

*Cassandra*'s head came around, her deck tilting as she heeled over in the turn. Smith thought that Sandy would be cursing at this change of course when "A" gun forrard was almost on target. But: "Midships! Steer that!" *Cassandra* righted herself, settled on the new heading and now the guns aft of the bridge would bear – just. But while *Cassandra* had been changing course the enemy cruiser had not and her guns had flamed seconds ago. Now *Cassandra*'s four guns replied in one racketing blast of flame and smoke that whipped back over the bridge. And Smith shouted above the last echoes, "Hard astarboard!"

On *Brandenburg*'s bridge Paul Brunner had burst out, "By God! I don't believe it! It's that same cruiser, I'm certain of it!"

Gustav Moehle ordered, "Open fire!" He studied the

258

other cruiser and agreed reluctantly, "It looks like her. Might be another of the same class." But he did not think so. And he had hoped to have a straight run.

Kurt Larsen said quietly, "I think it's her, sir."

Gustav Moehle shrugged, "It doesn't matter, anyway." She was two thousand tons or more lighter than *Brandenburg*, smaller, nearly twenty years older and outgunned by her. *Brandenburg*'s guns fired now, all nine of them in a broadside that rocked her over onto her beam ends. And when their thunder had died away Moehle went on, "Because we aren't stopping to fight her. Maintain course and speed." They would brush her off and leave her astern. *Brandenburg* was faster, too.


Kelso voiced Smith's thought, "About thirty seconds." That was the time of flight of the shells fired by *Brandenburg*. He held up his watch, eyes on its dial and the second hand ticking around. "Now!"

They heard the cloth-tearing sound as the shells ripped through the air and then they came down, lifting huge water-spouts off the port quarter. Smith ordered, "Port twenty!" And held on as *Cassandra* leaned hard over in the turn, held her in that turn until he had brought her back to her previous course plus a little more adjustment to meet the answer to his triangulation problem. He would have to make more adjustments, forced on him by any change of course *Brandenburg* might make and those he certainly would. Because he had to avoid those broadsides from the bigger cruiser by always turning towards the last one to fall. Just one of those 9-gun broadsides bracketing *Cassandra* could cripple her, possibly sink her.

He barked out the orders for changes of course so that *Cassandra* swerved first to starboard then to port, only on an even keel for seconds at a time. Her own guns hammered again and again while the shells from *Brandenburg* fell to port and starboard and the range closed by the

259

combined speeds of the two ships, two hundred yards every ten seconds. Smith stood at the bridge-screen, binoculars lifted and lowered as he watched for the fall of *Cassandra*'s shot, looked for the fall of *Brandenburg*'s as he heard the rasping roar and the shells came in.

He found time to glance at the men sharing his bridge: Ben Kelso, young Appleby, the signal yeoman and signalman, a bridge messenger and Buckley hovering discreetly at the back. Smith grinned at them. He looked over his ship. Spray broke high over her knife-edged stem to be flung into his face, icy cold, as she raced towards the enemy. Her big battle ensign cracked on the wind and laid out on it flat as a board. He looked beyond her to the distant snow-capped mountains and the cruel coast. He saw the black shadow darkening the sky to port that marked yet another snow squall sweeping in. Then his eyes went back to the big cruiser looming bigger with every minute.

*Cassandra* was first hit right aft. The broadside swooped in and fell in the sea to port, except for one shell. Smith and all of them on the bridge felt the leap of the gratings beneath their feet as they were deafened by the shellburst. Kelso yelled, "Hit aft, sir! Looks like 'X' gun!"

Smith ordered, "Hard aport" And demanded, "Get a report!"

Kelso supplied that a minute later: "'X' gun took a direct hit, sir! Total loss! Two of the crew have been taken down to the wardroom but there's no hope for the others!"

After a direct hit any survivor of the gun crew could consider himself lucky to be alive. Or could he? Smith thought there were worse fates than dying. To live on, horribly mutilated . . . He shuddered.

Now *Cassandra* was reduced to only three of her 6-inch guns. She had lost one in the previous action, forty-eight hours ago. And the wounded had been taken to the wardroom because . . .

\* \* \*

260

The big and burly young Surgeon-Lieutenant Matthew Kilmartin was aft in the wardroom, his post when *Cassandra* was in action. His Sick Berth Attendants were manning a dressing station in the sickbay forward. His assistants in the wardroom were the messmen, cooks and stewards. They were already occupied with wounded from the exposed upper deck and the two from "X" gun.

They had shaken to the shock when "X" gun was hit. A minute or two later the two wounded had been brought down. As Kilmartin bent over them a shell burst in the cabin flat next door. The impact threw every man of them to the deck in a torrent of spilt instruments and dressings. Splinters sprayed through the wardroom and ricochetted off the bulkheads.

Kilmartin shoved to his feet cursing, an angry giant. Blood trickled down his face from a jagged tear in his scalp where a splinter had almost killed him. He shouted, "All right! Let's get on with it!" His assistants picked themselves up, lifted some of their mates who now lay senseless and tended to them.

Kilmartin stooped his big frame again over the two men from "X" gun. He had little hope for them and the men working with him knew it. But you tried, you couldn't give up.


That hit was also felt on the bridge and reported to Smith through Ben Kelso. He acknowledged it but his eyes were on the big cruiser off the starboard bow. The range was now down to four miles and closing rapidly. He told Ben, "Tell the TG we'll be engaging to starboard." The Torpedo Gunner was aft with the tubes, would swing them out on that order.

He took a turn across the bridge, strolling, then returned to lean on the screen again. He set his binoculars to his eyes and *Brandenburg* came up close, a hard, sharp image. She looked to be making twenty knots or more. She, too, had been hurt. Smith had seen the hits and she trailed smoke from a fire amidships now. She was taking avoiding action, swerving to avoid the fall of shot, but not turning away because there was nowhere for her to run in this narrow fjord – except to escape to sea. It was clear that was her intention and Smith had to stop her.

He saw the prickle of flame that marked the firing of her broadside and ordered, "Starboard ten!" The time of flight of the shells at this reduced range would be about – fifteen seconds? He counted them, lowering the glasses to hang from their strap, ordering, "Meet her . . . Steady . . . Steer that!"

He glanced out to port and saw the snow squall closing in, a pewter-coloured wall rushing towards the ship. He looked forward again, seeking *Brandenburg*, still counting: "Fourteen . . ." Then the world exploded in a white lightning flash and a wind that plucked him from his place behind the screen. He fell into the darkness.

Snow was chill on his skin, flying on the wind past his upturned face. He was lying at the back of the bridge. He started to move, rolling onto one elbow, and now Buckley's face appeared above him, Buckley's hands pressed on his shoulders. He was squatting on his heels beside Smith, face anxious. "Hold still, sir! We'll get you down to the doctor!"

What was he talking about? "Doctor be damned!" Smith batted the hands away and grabbed at Buckley's shoulder instead. "Give me a hand to get up." Buckley rocked back on his heels then stood, hauling Smith to his feet. He staggered and held on to Buckley for a moment as the deck swayed beneath him. *Cassandra* was tearing through a blizzard once again, the unending cloud of whirling white flakes seeming to part to fly past on either side of the bridge.

He looked around the bridge, taking in the carnage, then

262

pushed away from Buckley and weaved forward to the screen on shaky legs. Kelso and everyone else were down, except – young Appleby, white-faced and big-eyed, was getting to his knees, lifting his head to peer up at Smith.

He looked first of all for the enemy but *Brandenburg* was hidden somewhere out there in the blizzard. That was why *Cassandra*'s guns were silent; Sandy Faulknor up in the director tower couldn't see a target. But equally *Brandenburg* could not see them. There were no shells coming in.

He spoke into the voice-pipe, "All right down there, Cox'n?"

Taggart's voice came back, metallic and imperturbable as always, but this time with a hint of relief in it? "Yes, sir! Got shook up a bit but we're O.K."

There was no point in telling him about the shambles up on the bridge. Smith said, "Very good." Which it was not. He knew now how he had ended up at the back of the bridge, what had caused the damage here. "A" gun right forward of the bridge had taken a direct hit. The blast and splinters from that had beaten the bridge staff to the deck. Stretcher-bearers were at work behind and around him now.

Appleby told the two who came to him, "Leave me alone. I'm not hurt." At least, he didn't think he was badly hurt. He, too, had blacked out when the shell burst on "A" gun and had been tossed to the back of the bridge like a bundle of rags. Now his back and shoulders were one huge bruise and his legs felt weak. But he saw his captain on his feet at the bridge-screen and got his own legs under him.

Smith used the telephone to speak to Sandy Faulknor in the director tower: "'A' gun took a direct hit and we've had casualties on the bridge. How are you up there? Anything seen of the enemy?"

Sandy's voice squawked distantly in Smith's ear and he realised he had been deafened. "We saw the gun catch it, sir, and we collected some splinters up here but nobody was hurt. Can't see anything at the moment. This bloody snow – "

"You'll see something soon." These snow squalls only lasted a few minutes. "And I think you can look for her off the starboard bow. We've held our course and if she's held hers – "

"Clearing now, sir!" Sandy cut him off.

Smith could see it for himself now, the sky above him lightening, the white horizon retreating around him. When *Brandenburg* appeared there would not be much sea-room left between her and *Cassandra*.

Ben Kelso said beside him, "I'm here, sir."

Smith shot a glance at him, saw his beard bloodied, saw him wipe more of it from his nose with the back of his gloved hand. "So I see, Ben. Can you function?"

"Yes, sir."

Visibility was stretching out with every second and now Sandy's voice came over the loudspeaker on the bridge, "Enemy in sight bearing Green Four-Oh, range Four-Two-Double-Oh!"

Smith lifted his glasses to his eyes but for a moment saw only a distant grey haze. Sandy had a better viewpoint high in the director tower. But then the haze thinned and he saw her big and clear. She was still trailing smoke from her fire but if anything he thought her speed had increased. There was a big, white bow-wave thrown up as she raced for the open sea.

He snapped at Ben Kelso, "Torpedoes starboard side!" And bent to the voice-pipe as Ben lurched over to the torpedo sight. "Hard aport!"

"Hard aport, sir!"

*Cassandra*'s two remaining guns fired and then the deck tilted as Taggart put the helm hard over. Smith swung *Cassandra* around until she was almost broadside to *Brandenburg*. Ben Kelso's voice came, baritone lifted to tenor as he intoned, "Fire one! . . . Fire two! . . ." All four torpedoes leapt from their tubes in the waist and plunged into the foam kicked up by *Cassandra*'s bow wave.

Smith ordered, "Starboard twenty!" Bringing her round again onto that original course with *Brandenburg* off the bow. He thought, prayed, that one of the torpedoes might strike her, but without much hope. In an action like this you needed a wide spread of 'fish' to give a chance of hitting and four just wasn't enough. "Meet her . . . Steady . . . Steer that!"

"Torpedoes!" The lookout's call came high, almost a shriek. Moehle heard it, head turning, sweeping with his binoculars and finding the lines of phosphorescence marking the tracks of the torpedoes. He gave his helm orders calmly, watching his ship's head come around, steadying it when he saw she would "comb" the tracks of the "fish". They passed either side of her and then he brought *Brandenburg* back onto her original course.

The three guns in the turret just forward of the bridge fired and as the echoes died Kurt Larsen said, "The after guns won't bear now, sir. We're too close. It looks as though she will run across our bow!"

"And fire right into us with what guns she has left." Moehle nodded. He knew the enemy had been badly mauled, could see smoke from where she was burning, had noted that only two of her guns had been firing. But he knew he would be staring into the barrels of those guns in barely a minute. "That will be the last chance she'll have. After that we'll leave her astern." *Brandenburg* had also been hurt, suffered casualties and was on fire. Paul Brunner had reported the mounting toll of damage. But she was still intact as a fighting ship, had all her main armament and was working up to her full thirty knots. He would take her back to Kiel.

\* \* \*

265

*Cassandra* was back on an even keel and her two remaining guns fell silent. Sandy Faulknor stared out over her bow at the enemy cruiser and called to the bridge through the loudspeaker, "Range Two-Four-Double-Oh but guns won't bear!" Smith heard that, knew it already. Just as he knew that, as the two ships closed the gap between them, *Brandenburg*'s two after turrets would no longer bear and only that forward of her bridge could now fire on *Cassandra*. He saw the three guns in that forward turret flare now. He did not hear Sandy, off the speaker and shouting at his crew in the director top, "We're going to run across the bugger's bow! We'll be able to shoot right into her!" Then Sandy was thrown from his chair as *Brandenburg*'s salvo struck.

One shell fell just short, a near-miss, but the splinters driven inboard claimed a dozen casualties in the waist. A second shell destroyed the port side torpedo tubes. By a miracle not a soul was hurt but Per Kosskull's boat was reduced to splinters. Admiralty would have to compensate him. The third shell struck the foremast and brought it down and the director tower with it. The wreckage spilt forward across the bridge. Smith and the others there, thrown down on the gratings once more, had to fight to their feet through a tangle of smashed spars and rigging.

Smith had fallen near the voice-pipe and rose to wrap his arms around it now. He saw that *Cassandra* still held to her course, would pass across the bow of *Brandenburg*, and bent to call into the voice-pipe, "Hard astarboard!"

"Hard astarboard, sir!" Taggart acknowledged.

Smith saw Ben Kelso at his side and asked him, "Is the tannoy still working?"

"I'll check it, sir!" That was Appleby, clambering through the tangle to get to the back of the bridge and the loudspeaker system. Smith saw Buckley rising there, holding his head and glaring about him bad-temperedly, but alive. Smith sucked in a breath of relief. He stood with knees slightly bent as he balanced against the heel of the deck. But he stood very straight, hands resting lightly on the rim of the tube, eyes narrowed, judging distances, speeds and angles, working out the problem again in his head, updating it. He ordered, "Meet her . . ." *Cassandra*'s bow had swung far enough.

"Meet her, sir!" Now Taggart was spinning the wheel the other way, to check that swing.

Appleby shouted, "It's working, sir!"

Smith said into the tube, "Steady . . ." Kelso and Appleby were watching him now. He was not aware of it. He was intent on what he was doing but he showed no sign of tension. He seemed relaxed as he stood there, took off the steel helmet and ran his hand through the fair hair sweat-plastered to his skull, rumpling it. He replaced the hat and spoke into the tube, "Starboard a point."

*Cassandra*'s bow edged fractionally around. He saw that *Brandenburg* was now, too late, trying to turn away. That was all right; he had expected it and allowed for it. "Steer that, Cox'n. And hold on down there." He raised his head from the tube but Taggart would still hear him as he called, "Mid. All hands. Stand by to ram!" And he heard that passed, Appleby's voice high as he shouted into the tannoy.


Galloway, down in the cabin flat and filthy with smoke and grime from fighting fires and clearing away wreckage, heard it and muttered, "Jesus Christ!" He shouted to Jackman and his party, "Come on!" He climbed the ladder to the upper deck then started to run forward. He could see *Brandenburg* ahead through the smoke and spray, was already planning what he would need.

So was Jackman, pelting along behind him and producing an identical list: "Shores for a start, for a bloody certainty!" And to Dobson and the others forcing weary legs to try to keep up, "Don't hang about back there! Get up here!"

267

The ships were now less than a cable's length – little more than a hundred yards – apart. *Cassandra* was charging in at better than twenty knots while *Brandenburg* was trying to turn away, making close on her full speed of thirty knots. She was coming up to *Cassandra*'s bow, passing it, but that sharp stem was driving in. Not at ninety degrees to bury itself in the other ship's hull, but at an acute angle. Smith nodded his satisfaction and clamped his hands on the bridge-screen, set himself for the shock and shouted into the voice-pipe, "Stop engines!"

*Brandenburg*'s steel side rushed up at him and he glimpsed faces in her bridge looking down at him. Then *Cassandra* struck her just below the bridge and drove down her port side. *Brandenburg*'s seven thousand tons heeled over to starboard under that hammer blow. Smith had been given his precept when he saw *Glowworm* ram *Hipper*. But while *Brandenburg* was bigger than *Cassandra* she was not a heavy cruiser like *Hipper*, did not have her thickness of armour plate. And *Cassandra* was not a destroyer of thirteen hundred tons but a cruiser of four thousand.

She ran her bow down *Brandenburg*'s side like a tin opener. She opened her up along her length as the iceberg had opened up the *Titanic*. When *Cassandra* fell away a gap of sea opened up between the two ships. The guns were silent. Both of them were stopped. Both might have been sinking.

# 18

When *Cassandra* struck Galloway and his party were running forward on the starboard side. They could see through the drifting smoke and tendrils of mist to the bulk of *Brandenburg* looming right ahead like a steel cliff. Galloway shouted, "Hold on!" He threw himself down and clasped a bollard.

Jackman echoed his warning and added to himself, "Bloody *hell*!" He grabbed at a stanchion and clung to it. He was only feet away from a ragged hole in the deck that vomited smoke. The air above it quivered in the heat from the fire raging below. Then *Cassandra*, charging ahead at better than twenty knots, ran into that steel cliff. Jackman was jerked forward along with the rest of them but his stanchion had been weakened in the damage already wrought, now buckled and broke under his weight and he was hurled into the pit.

He saw the hell he had spoken of beneath him, reaching up its red arms to claim him. Its hot breath seared his face and scorched his eyebrows into ash. But there he hung, just a foot below the deck because somebody had grabbed his ankle as he fell into the hole and was holding him up. Then there were other hands stretching down to seize him and haul him up from the flames, out of the pit and back onto the deck.

He saw Dobson, sitting on the deck and gasping for breath, still gripping his ankle. Jackman asked, "You?"

Dobson nodded and Jackman reached forward and slapped his back.

But then Galloway was up and running again and they were all chasing after him. The deck listed to starboard beneath their feet and *Cassandra* was still grinding her way down the side of the big cruiser. One of *Brandenburg*'s guns fired, seemingly over their heads, deafening, the blast thrusting at them so they staggered. Then they were piling in through the screen door at the fo'c'sle break, finding the mess deck inches deep in water that had sluiced in through the deckhead, ruptured when "A" gun had taken the direct hit. It washed back and forth, a scum of rubbish on its surface, clothing, sandwiches, cigarette ends.

Then they were dropping down ladders again, to the lower deck and moving forward to another mess deck, gingerly opening watertight doors and hatches, fearful for the spurt of water that would mean the next compartment was flooded. Seeing the bulkheads weeping, feeling they were in a tomb and fearing that if the bulkheads gave . . .

When *Cassandra* struck Smith was thrown onto the voice-pipe. It drove the wind out of him and hurt like hell. He held on to the pipe, grimacing, as *Cassandra* cut her way down the side of *Brandenburg*, laying her open to the sea. As she rolled over to starboard so did *Cassandra*. He saw men on the deck of the enemy cruiser and her guns pointing at the sky as she was laid over on her side. One of them fired with a flash that hurt his eyes. It set his ears ringing and the blast threatened to tear him from his hold on the voice-pipe. Then *Cassandra* was easing away from the other ship and rocking back onto an even keel. She surged on with the way still on her, as did *Brandenburg*, a gap of churned sea opening between them.

Smith croaked into the pipe, "Starboard twenty!" And heard that acknowledged by Taggart, saw his ship's head start to come round. He let go of the pipe then and went to the starboard wing of the bridge to try to get a sight of *Brandenburg*.

Moehle shouted, "Stop engines!" They were still driving her forward but also driving the sea into that yawning wound running for fifty yards or more, a quarter of her length, down her port side. That was a mortal wound. Moehle did not know that yet, had no reports, but in his heart he was sure. He could feel it in the motion of her. Her engines stopped and now her engine room flooded, she slowed and then lay still. Moehle listened to the reports that came to him then and gave his orders, quickly, calmly but hopelessly. She lurched over to port with the weight of the water she'd already taken aboard. And more was flooding in every second.

*Cassandra* had pulled away in the opposite direction. The combined speeds of the two ships when they struck had totalled over fifty knots. After they parted that opened a gap between them before the way came off both vessels. *Cassandra* had her helm over to starboard, circling, so now she was a mile astern of *Brandenburg* and on the same course. Smith ordered, "Slow ahead." He dared not order any faster speed than that until he knew the extent of the damage inflicted on the bow.

Ben Kelso almost wailed, "My God! Will you look at it!" The bow had crumpled from the capstan forward, a length of twenty feet, and now pointed down at the sea. The wreckage of the foremast and director tower still lay on it. A party under Chivers was picking its way into that tangle to start to clear it – but cautiously because there were craters in the deck like hungry mouths with the red glow within them, and the tangle continuously shifted its huge weight, threatening to trap and crush the men working on it. That dead weight was pressing the bow still further into the sea so the fractured and gaping stem gulped in tons of sea water. Only the watertight bulkheads would stop the flood from washing right into the bowels of the ship and sinking her. Was one of them holding?

Smith shouted to Appleby, "Go below and get a report on the bow from Mr Galloway!" Then he ordered, "Port ten!" To steer away from *Brandenburg* and also allow the two 6-inch guns aft to bear. *Brandenburg* was still firing. Not her main armament because now those big guns pointed at the sea with the list on her. But some of her anti-aircraft guns still hammered away rapidly, as did *Cassandra*'s. Those shells would not seriously damage the fabric of the ship but could cause fearful casualties among the men working on the exposed decks.

The gun just abaft *Cassandra*'s bridge fired, then "Y" gun right aft, each of them laying and firing manually and independently now that the director was destroyed. They kept on firing, steadily, as *Cassandra* crept up on the listing cruiser ahead and to starboard, that gap to starboard gradually widening as *Cassandra* steered away.

Appleby returned, panting: "Mr Galloway says the mess deck bulkhead is holding. He's shoring it with mess tables and stools and some baulks of timber. He says he suggests that when he's finished we should be able to make ten knots."

Smith answered, "Very good." It was. He could rely on Galloway's judgment. Besides, grim but valid reasoning, Galloway was down in that steel tomb with only the bulkhead between him and oblivion. He would not recommend a speed of ten knots if he thought the bulkhead would not stand it.

*Cassandra*'s guns fired again, one cracking report running into the other, and he saw the shells burst on *Brandenburg*'s upperworks. Her list now seemed more pronounced, she had lurched even further to port. He wondered what it must be like in that ship now?

When *Cassandra* struck Gerhard Fritsch was sitting in the

272

cramped cabin they had given him below decks. Down there in the bowels of the ship he was insulated to some extent from the immediate horrors of the fighting. He saw no shell strike the ship nor any killed or wounded but he felt the shocks when shells burst inboard, shaking the fabric of the hull. He felt the different shudder and heard the thunder as *Brandenburg* fired her broadsides and the ship heeled over to them.

He told himself that he only had to wait. *Brandenburg* would force her way out of the fjord because the other cruiser did not have the strength to stop her, then she would use her superior speed to escape. He was on his way back to Germany with his prisoner and she would buy him his promotion – whatever he had to do. So he sat on the bunk and planned his campaign, trying to shut out the noise of the battle.

That worked until *Cassandra* struck. Then he was thrown across the bunk and onto the deck as the ship was forced over onto her beam ends. There was a din of screeching, rending, tearing metal that went on and on for several seconds while he lay on the deck, paralysed with terror. He did not know what was happening. Then the din stopped and *Brandenburg* sagged back, briefly, so the deck was level. He clawed at the side of the bunk to lift himself to his feet but she lurched and the deck tilted again. This time it was to port, so he half ran, half fell into the passage outside.

He could no longer stay in that claustrophobic cabin, had to get up into the light of day. But as he turned towards the companion leading upwards he saw instead the sea pouring into the passage where he stood. One second it swept in to wash across the deck and the next it filled the passage from the corticene underfoot to the deckhead.

It swallowed him and his screams.

*    *    *

273

When *Brandenburg* was hurled over onto her starboard side by the thrust of *Cassandra*, that sudden canting of the deck threw Sarah's sentry into the curtain covering the doorway to her cabin. Wrapped in it and blinded by it, he tripped over the coaming and fell at her feet where she sat on the edge of the bunk.

He scrambled up again, fighting free of the hampering folds of the curtain and clutching his rifle. Automatically she stooped and put out a hand to help him. Both of them stood, heads turned, listening to and deafened by the shipyard clamour as *Cassandra* drove down the side of *Brandenburg*. That noise had barely ceased after *Cassandra* had hauled away when *Brandenburg* rolled over to port and they were thrown the other way.

They ended out in the passage and then the sentry saved Sarah's life. He may have been driven by the instinct for self-preservation, but he gripped her arm and ran her along the passage to the foot of the ladder leading to the deck above. They were half-way up when the sea burst into the passage behind them. The sentry yelled something at Sarah then shoved her up through the hatch. He followed her and slammed the hatch-cover shut behind him as the sea foamed up the ladder to squirt out of the narrowing gap with the force of a high-pressure hose. Then he threw his weight on the cover to close it and twisted the clips around to lock it shut.

They started up the next ladder, Sarah leading the way, the sentry urging her on, pointing to the bulkhead at the end of the passage on this flat and yelling, "It's going!" She could see it, the steel incredibly bulging from the pressure of the water behind it. She scrambled up the ladder and was near the head of it when she heard the sentry shout wordlessly and heard a clatter behind her. She turned her head and saw he had fallen. He lay at the foot of the ladder and his head was bleeding. She started down again, feet fumbling for the rungs of the ladder, eyes on the straining bulkhead.

\*     \*     \*

274

Gustav Moehle faced the inevitable. His ship was sinking and nothing could save her. He stared out across the mile of sea churned into white foam by the fast manoeuvring of the two ships to where *Cassandra* was slowly limping up to come abreast of *Brandenburg*. He said, "She's followed us like an albatross." Paul Brunner, grimy and soaked to the skin from his duties with damage control, nodded weary agreement. Moehle took a breath and ordered, "Abandon ship."

Kurt Larsen went down to his station on the port side. Some of the boats and life rafts had been destroyed by gunfire. With the other officers he saw the remaining boats filled and lowered, the surviving life rafts launched. There was no panic; the crew maintained discipline. The wounded were brought up from below and sent away with the first of the boats. When all boats and rafts had gone the men that were left began to jump into the sea that was now almost lapping the deck on which they stood. Heads dotted the water as they swam away.

Smith watched *Brandenburg* as *Cassandra* slowly hauled up level with her but with a mile of sea between. He saw that none of her guns were firing now and she was launching her boats and rafts. He ordered, "Cease fire!" He heard that broadcast through the tannoy by Appleby and then told him, "They may not have heard that aft. Go back there and pass the word."

"Aye, aye, sir!" Appleby ran.

Ben Kelso said uneasily, "She hasn't surrendered, sir."

Smith accepted that *Brandenburg* was not flying a white flag nor had she hauled down her ensign. But she had ceased fighting, presented no threat to his own ship or crew and he saw no point in slaughtering men who were now only trying to save their lives from

275

the grasp of the sea. He said, "Prepare to pick up survivors, Ben."

"Aye, aye, sir."

Now, at last, his duty done, Kurt could look for the girl who had been in his mind since Moehle gave the order to abandon ship. He did not have to search far. Almost immediately he saw her coming up from below, stepping through a screen door onto the tilted deck and holding the arm of her sentry. He had lost his rifle, his face streamed blood and he seemed dazed. But he managed to stand to attention when Kurt spoke to them: "What happened?"

Sarah explained, "He fell on the last ladder." She said nothing of her scrambling descent of the ladder and then shoving the half-conscious and blundering man ahead of her up the ladder again. Or of finally slamming shut and clipping that last hatch herself. But Kurt Larsen guessed something of this.

He said, "Thank you. I'm grateful." And to the sentry, who wore a life-jacket. "You'll have to swim for it. Good luck to you." He saw the man away and then took off his own life-jacket and tried to fit it on the girl.

Sarah resisted and objected. "What about you?"

"I'm a very good swimmer." He put her hands aside and fastened it on her. "The sea will be cold, but you will soon be in one of your boats." He pointed and she saw the other cruiser had crept in close to *Brandenburg* and the sailors in the sea. Now she had stopped and was lowering boats. It occurred to her that this might be her father's ship but she was not sure. There were another dozen cruisers like her and this could be one of them.

Sarah looked up at Kurt. "Thank you." She knew that was inadequate. This young man had risked his life more than once by standing up to Fritsch and the Gestapo on her behalf. He was saving her life now. But they were the

276

only words she could find. Kurt gripped her shoulders. "For old times' sake."

*Brandenburg* settled lower in the water. There were internal rumblings as bulkheads gave way then the sea washed in over the port side and swirled around their knees. Kurt said, "It's time to go!" He spared a few seconds to tear off his shoes and outer clothing then he shoved Sarah and they fell forward into the sea. She gasped at the shock of it and struck out. Kurt kept pace with her and steered her to where he judged the rescue boats to be. Down in the troughs they could see little but the wave-tops in front of them with occasional glimpses of the cruiser's upperworks.

But he steered her aright and soon one of *Cassandra*'s boats lifted on the swell ahead. The rowers were resting on their oars as a pair of *Brandenburg*'s seamen were hauled in over the stern. Kurt pushed the girl towards it and shouted, "Boat ahoy!" Sarah gripped his hand for a moment, then struck out on her own. Kurt saw the rowers turn and look towards him, then wave. He watched, treading water, until he saw the girl clutching at the boat's stern. Then he turned and swam away.

He would not be taken prisoner. Somehow he would get to the shore and join General Dietl's mountain troops in Narvik. He swam for a long time, circling to pass around *Brandenburg*. She seemed, at the last, to be fighting for her life. Although her upper deck was awash she did not sink.

He had laboured around until he was between *Brandenburg* and the shore when he was picked up by one of her boats. Her crew dragged him into the sternsheets and the young *Leutnant-zur-See* at the helm stripped off the bridge-coat he wore and gave it to Kurt. He huddled, shivering, into its warmth and looked round as one of the men pulling at the oars muttered, "There she goes."

*Brandenburg* rolled still further to port as if trying to hide the wound *Cassandra* had inflicted, but then there was more, deeper rumbling that may have been her engines breaking loose and she slid slowly down beneath the waves.

Smith, standing on the wing of the bridge, saw her sink. He was sorry, as always, but there was also a sense of relief because he and *Cassandra* had won an unequal contest. He was lucky she was still afloat, lucky to be alive. He was very tired.

Buckley said, "Cup o' coffee, sir." His voice was raised and he set the mug down on the shelf under the screen with a bang that slopped some of its brown contents. Smith realised Buckley had brought another mug some time ago and it had gone cold on the shelf. He sipped at this one. "Thank you." Buckley was smoke-grimed as all of them were and there was blood on his face from some bump taken during the action. He grunted now and retired to the back of the bridge.

Ben Kelso said, "The boats are coming back, sir. There's no sign of any more swimmers."

Smith nodded. And below him, on the fo'c'sle, Chivers and his party had pulled Sandy Faulknor and his party out of the wreckage of the director tower and they were able to walk aft on their way to see the surgeon. Sandy lifted a hand and waved; Smith returned it.

Galloway came, the immaculate Executive Officer now filthier than any of them from his work below. "All secure, sir. She's good for ten knots. The bulkheads are shored and I've organised a watch on them."

"Very good. Ben – show that signal to John."

Kelso's teeth showed through his beard in a grin as he passed the open log to Galloway, who read that last signal received before *Cassandra* went into action. Then he

278

looked up at Smith blank-faced and said, "They're giving me a command, a destroyer."

"Congratulations." After Smith had left hospital he had urged, pleaded and demanded of Admiralty that they give Galloway a command: "He's a first-class officer, fitted to command, long overdue for it." They had been annoyed with him but he was used to that and persisted. It had worked and justice had been done – or maybe it would have been done anyway.

Galloway said, "Thank you, sir." And meant it. Then he went back to his duties.

Smith thought that if he sat in his chair he would fall asleep. He saw the boats had all been hoisted in and told Ben Kelso, "We'll get under way."

"Aye, aye, sir."

*Cassandra* moved ahead, slowly working up to her ten knots, heading seaward. He thought she was a bedraggled as well as an ageing beauty now with her crumpled bow, but still proud. As he was proud of her and the men in her.

He discarded his steel helmet and picked up his cap. "*Sir!*" That was Buckley bellowing his name. What the hell was wrong with him?

Smith turned and saw the big leading hand waving at him to go to the back of the bridge where he stood. Smith decided Buckley was presuming too much on their – friendship? He hesitated at the word but then admitted it was right. But weariness added to his irritation and while he was captain of this ship no one aboard her would address him like that. He would not have favourites. He stalked down on Buckley, now standing hurriedly to attention, and rasped, "What is it?" And whatever it was, he would get a dressing-down.

"On the deck below, sir. Among the prisoners." Buckley jerked his head, indicating the enemy seamen crowded down there where they had come aboard. Enemy? They were only survivors now, thirty or more of them. There were a lot more of *Cassandra*'s crew gathered there, come out of the boats, or handing out blankets, tending wounded. When they saw him up there, slight, thin-faced, hair ruffled by the breeze, they cheered him. Galloway was down there now, grinning up at him, mouth a pink hole in a black face as he waved his cap and led the cheering.

Then Smith's weariness fell away when he saw the small figure swathed in a blanket. Her blonde hair straggled in rat's tails but she smiled up at him.